IN

THE WOUNDED SKY

"Diane Duane has written AN EXCELLENT STAR TREK NOVEL. She's made the familiar folk of the *Enterprise* her own, and created fascinating alien characters as well. There are white-knuckle space battles as exciting as anything out of Lucas' films . . . totally believable and ALWAYS ENTERTAINING."

—Michael Reaves, author of *Dragonworld*

THE WOUNDED SKY

"IS A REMARKABLE NOVEL IN ANY CATEGORY AND BEYOND A DOUBT THE BEST STAR TREK NOVEL EVER WRITTEN."

—C. J. Cherryh, author of *Downbelow Station*

Look for *Star Trek* fiction from Pocket Books

#1 *Star Trek: The Motion Picture*
by Gene Roddenberry

#2 *The Entropy Effect*
by Vonda N. McIntyre

#3 *The Klingon Gambit*
by Robert E. Vardeman

#4 *The Covenant of the Crown*
by Howard Weinstein

#5 *The Prometheus Design*
by Sondra Marshak & Myrna Culbreath

#6 *The Abode of Life*
by Lee Correy

#7 *Star Trek II: The Wrath of Khan*
by Vonda N. McIntyre

#8 *Black Fire*
by Sonni Cooper

#9 *Triangle*
by Sondra Marshak & Myrna Culbreath

#10 *Web of the Romulans*
M. S. Murdock

#11 *Yesterday's Son*
A. C. Crispin

#12 *Mutiny on the* Enterprise
by Robert E. Vardeman

#13 *The Wounded Sky*
by Diane Duane

#14 *The Trellisane Confrontation*
by David Dvorkin

#15 *Corona*
by Greg Bear

#16 *The Final Reflection*
by John M. Ford

#17 *Star Trek III: The Search for Spock*
by Vonda N. McIntyre

#18 *My Enemy, My Ally*
by Diane Duane

#19 *The Tears of the Singers*
by Melinda Snodgrass

#20 *The Vulcan Academy Murders*
by Jean Lorrah

#21 *Uhura's Song*
by Janet Kagan

THE WOUNDED SKY

DIANE DUANE

A STAR TREK® NOVEL

PUBLISHED BY POCKET BOOKS NEW YORK

This novel is a work of fiction. Names, characters, places and incidents are either the product of the author's imagination or are used fictitiously. Any resemblance to actual events or locales or persons, living or dead, is entirely coincidental.

Another *Original* publication of POCKET BOOKS

POCKET BOOKS, a division of Simon & Schuster, Inc.
1230 Avenue of the Americas, New York, N.Y. 10020

This Book is Published by Pocket Books, a Division of Simon & Schuster, Inc. Under Exclusive License from Paramount Pictures Corporation, The Trademark Owner.

ISBN: 0-671-60061-3

First Pocket Books printing December, 1983

10 9 8 7 6 5 4 3

Printed in the U.S.A.

This book is for Tom Swale and Duane Poole—
stalwart instructors in screenwriting,
experts in the care and feeding of other people's
characters, and much-beloved friends;

and for the wonderful Linda Wright,
fellow handler of tribbles and other peculiar alien
creatures at Starfleet's Northridge Annex

Acknowledgments

These are the people who assisted me while I was writing this book—by good advice, technical or logistical support, or just reading it and letting me know what worked.

Dennis Ahrens ("His tail does *what??*"); Anna Brand ("What in the *world* are you talking about?"); C. J. Cherryh ("You certainly sound like you're having a good time!"); Jeff Carver ("Gonna write about ol' Mr. Spock, huh?"); Chris Claremont ("'Captain, if you beam down there, it's certain death!' 'It is? . . . Okay, let's go.'"); Arthur Byron Cover ("Well, I don't know about you, Diane. . . ."); Paul Dini ("You mean they *let* you write those?!"); Wilma Fisher ("My God, Dee, that's outrageous!"); the Spring 1981 San Fernando Valley GSLP ("You're writing a *what?*—Well, why not?"); Robbie London ("So what happens?"); Don Maass ("Well, let's see what you've got."); Lydia Morano (smile and silent headshake, with optional rolling of eyes); Arthur Nadel ("It must be nice to be independently wealthy."); Michael Reaves ("Lord, now *I* want to write one of these things."); William Rotsler ("His middle name is Edward. You want his serial number?"); J. Brynne Stephens ("That was really nice."); Pam Vincent ("You went through a whole box of correcting tape in *one day??*"); Ben Yalow ("Right."); Jane Yolen ("Is this contagious? Can I get shots?"); Marc Scott Zicree ("When will it be finished?").

Very special thanks are due in a few cases. This book could not have been turned in on time without the incredible generosity of Michael Reaves and Brynne Stephens, who lent me their Apple II and were heroically patient with me during the book's production. David Gerrold, as usual, was calm and matter-of-fact about the good parts of the work-in-progress, and cutting about the parts that were less than good—a technique I hate, and for which I thank him profoundly. And a very late dinner at Denny's with the incomparable Marty Clark Rich produced a glass spider that jumped into her plate, and then stalked away dragging a *Trek* novel behind it. You did it to me, Marty! Thanks and love. . . .

. . . Two great powers are on our side: the power of Love and the power of Arithmetic. These two are stronger than anything else in the world.

—E. Nesbit, *The Island of the Twelve Whirlpools*

One

The problem with waiting around in space to see a starship go by is that, when a ship is in warp drive, she's hardly there at all. The otherspace in which the warp field embeds her is just that—*other;* a neighboring alternate universe in which natural laws are different, and light moves many thousands of times faster than in the universe to which the six hundred eighty-three species of humanity are native. A starship in warp carries a shell of that otherspace with her, so that within it she moves at many multiples of lightspeed through the analogue universe, without really being in our universe at all, or running up against its intractably low speed of light. Within the ship, of course, sensors are calibrated to edit out the slight strangeness of the other-universal starlight, that all the humanities find so unsettling. Outside the ship, all there is to be seen of her passing is a tremor of starlight as space itself is shaken, wrinkles, and slowly smooths out again. At the heart of the shimmer, there might be the faintest, palest ghost of light, not even an image. An impression, a hint, maybe an illusion.

It is a long wait before the many-colored fires that are the stars begin to tremble in one small patch of the endless night. Far out there, behind the tremor, is a wake of light too faint for all but the keenest-eyed species to perceive unaided—disturbed radicals, fragments of elementary molecules floating free in space, excited to higher energy-states and glowing hot. The tremor-wrinkling gets closer, covers more area. Drifting lazily in its path is a cold comet, far out from its primary—a dirty, dormant snowball. The tremor runs at it, unconcerned. Sensors have confirmed that there's no traffic of any kind for parsecs around—which is as well, considering that a warp field and a physical object can meet and retain their mutual integrity only under carefully managed conditions. Those conditions are not met here. The ship in warp runs, in otherspace, right through the comet, unharmed, barely noticing.

In this universe, however, space writhes and wrenches, its fabric strained; the comet contained in it shatters into a cloud of stone splinters, ice fragments and twinkling water-vapor snow. Yet after a little while the troubled space quiets, the ripples flow away—and the remains of the comet, not having been hit by anything in this universe and thus taking no acceleration from the "impact," continue on along the same orbit through the long night.

Three hundred and a few years from now, two sentient peoples formed up for battle will be watching the skies for the comet which has since time immemorial been the gods' signal to them to begin killing one another. Instead of the comet-banner blazing across their sky, however, what they will get is a dazzling rain of stars. Tremendously relieved, they will rejoice at the long-prayed-for sign of an armistice in Heaven, go back to their homes, and beat their swords into plowshares.

Here and now, an unseen something fleets by so swiftly an observer would probably never perceive her at all. A flicker, a shimmer, a passing thought in the endless silent ruminations of the universe, the USS *Enterprise* cruises through on patrol.

No matter how many times they rebuild this ship, thought James T. Kirk, *they'll never put in enough room to pace properly . . .*

The *Enterprise*'s captain, multiply decorated for courage in the face of threatening circumstances, and commended for calm in the most nerve-frazzling situations, was pacing up and down in his inner office and scowling at everything. The holos of previous *Enterprises* on the walls; the small collection of native art of several planets, bright colors and raw rough shapes in wood and metal, boxed in inertrogen and veriglas; the impeccably neat shelves and tables and the immaculate desk—all of them brought scowls. The desk in itself was a particularly bad sign. Jim Kirk never cleared the clutter of cassettes and pads and report-chips off his desk unless he was at the end of his commandatorial rope about something. The word was out, of course; all over the ship, departments that had been letting things slide a little were shuddering hurriedly into optimum shape, and desks in them were not only being cleared off, they were being scrubbed.

None of this made Kirk feel any better, though he was pleased that his people respected him enough to handle their departments so that *he* didn't have to handle them. Right now he would cheerfully have traded all the holystoning going on in the downlevels for one particular piece of good news.

He scowled at the wall screen, which with its usual

mulishness was refusing to do what he wanted. *Try to get the damn thing to keep quiet,* he thought, *and it announces Klingon invasions, sector-level disasters, mysterious distress calls. Now look at it, sitting there like so much scrap.* His mouth quirked in annoyance, unrepressed for once since his crew couldn't see.

The screen stayed predictably silent. Finally Kirk grimaced at himself and resorted to the old cadet exercise of "making-it-worse"; he stood there and considered all the reasons he had to be mad, and concentrated on getting madder and madder. *Six months now, this business of the drive has been going on. Every time they're about to announce who gets it, they postpone the announcement because of the damned political infighting going on over who gets the credit, who gets the publicity-plum of having their sector's starship test it. No consideration of ship or crew merit—* and that was the part that was *very* easy to be mad about, for James T. Kirk knew that if merit were being considered, his ship would sail away with the drive, no contest. *Months of squabbling over destination of the first test mission, arguments over petty details—who gets to be on what committee determining who gets what parts-and-supply contract, who gets to pick who to do the paperwork, damn, damn, DAMN!!* He got mad, and madder. He ground his teeth. And as usual, the mad abruptly vanished, replaced by a sense of the profound silliness of the situation—a seasoned commander, standing here gritting and twitching over what couldn't be hurried, helped or fought.

He laughed out loud at himself and went to the wall for a uniform tunic—pulled out a gold-colored one, idly wondering how long this generation of uniforms would last. *They said the announcement would be today,* he thought with rueful humor, *and they've said that seven times before. Or is it eight? The hell with this; I'm going down to Rec to look at Lieutenant Tanzer's forest.*

And the wall screen whistled at him, startling Jim so badly that he spent a fraction of a second crouching toward an attack-or-defense stance before he realized what the sound was and straightened up again. "Screen on," he said, lowering his hands out of pickup so the white knuckles clenching on the tunic wouldn't show.

The screen came on, revealing the Communications board, and Uhura's beta-shift communicator-in-training, Lieutenant Mahásë—a craggy-featured hominid, gray-skinned and gray-haired and gray-eyed (even to the "whites"). "Your pardon for disturbing you, sir," he said in the usual mellow Eseriat drawl. "I have a squirt from Starfleet for you, with maximum-security scramble and Captain's Seal on it. Shall I transfer it to your terminal?"

"No need," Kirk said, and reached over to touch the combination of controls on his desk that would allow the main computers access to his personal command ciphers. "Implement, and read it."

Mahásë nodded, putting his transdator in his ear with one hand, touching various controls at his own console with the other. Jim listened to his heart hammering. Finally, "Nonstandard transmission, code groups 064-44-51852-30," Mahásë said. Kirk exhaled, and held the swearing in very tight—for there was the 064 group that was one-flag-officer-to-another code for very bad news. *Dammit, someone else got it, how could that have happened, we were the logical choice even by* their *standards! Even Spock said the odds were—*

"Begin message 'To: James T. Kirk, commanding NCC 1701, United Systems Starship *Enterprise,* in Coma B patrol corridor. From: Halloran, R.S., Vice Admiral, Starfleet Command, Sol III/Terra. Subject: T'pask-Sivek-B't'kr-K't'lk Elective Mass Inversion Apparatus. Body: You are directed to abort present patrol, which will be assumed by USS *Henrietta Leavitt.* When relieved you will proceed with all due haste to shipyards at Hamal/alpha Arietis Four/StarBase Eighteen for installation of prototype apparatus in *Enterprise,* maintaining class-four silence while in transit—' "

MY GOD! MY GOD! WE GOT IT—

" '—specialty personnel to be involved in mission have been notified. Roster rendezvous at StarBase Eighteen to be complete by stardate 9250.00—' "

Kirk let the straightness in his spine loosen up a touch. " 'Roster follows—,' and they add it, sir. It's in the computer for you." Mahásë paused. "There's an addendum after the seal and verification, Captain."

Jim nodded at the lieutenant. "It says, 'Jim: for me, it was bad news. I wanted it for *Raptor*. Happy hunting, you lucky bastard, and give the Galaxy next door my best. Regards, Rhonda.' "

"Thank you, Lieutenant Mahásë," the Captain said. "Please put the message in the department heads' network and flag it on Mr. Spock's and Mr. Scott's terminals." He kept himself looking like the picture of calm, with just a quirk of pleased smile added, as if doubt were entirely foreign to him. "And tell the Heads we'll be meeting later this afternoon. I want this ship ready to head out of the Galaxy in five days."

"Aye, sir," Mahásë said, as calmly as if he would be able to manage the whole business himself. "Bridge out."

"Screen off," Kirk said, and waited a long breath or two, to make sure the screen was dead. Then he glanced at the door to be sure it was sealed. He took another breath.

"YEEEEEEHHHHAAAAAAAAAAAA!!!!!"

On the Bridge, Mahásë winced, and smiled, and took the transdator out of his ear. "I think he'll be all right now," he said. No one paid him much attention. The Bridge people were busy with screaming of their own, pounding of backs and clapping and hugging, and in a few cases, settling of bets. In the helm, Sulu sat still as a statue of some bemused old-Oriental god, saying nothing, but wearing a small and delighted smile on his face—

Down in Engineering, Scotty glanced away from the barely-tamed lightning of the matter/antimatter plasma mix cylinder to see his computer-link pad flashing at him. He picked it up as gingerly as if it were alive, read it, and then began whooping with delight and ordering his people to dismantle the Hilbert field torus they had just spent two weeks assembling—

—on the observation deck, in meditation under that water-wavery, bizarrely-colored starlight that most of the humanities avoided so scrupulously, a still form in Science Department blue sensed meselectronic relays shifting states in his pad, and diverted enough attention to read the message that formed on its surface. A half second later, Spock turned his eyes back up to the unnerving blankness that trembled with its troubled fires above him. He seemed unmoved; but one who knew him well might have noticed that his dark eyes seemed to reflect a bit more than they had, as if the universe had suddenly gotten larger—

—all over the *Enterprise*, people of all the ninety-two kinds of humanity represented among her crew hollered, cheered, ritually grimaced, bowed to one another, shook hands, applauded, and broke out private stores of food and drink to celebrate with. Even for the *Enterprise*, a ship almost inured to wonders and terrors, this was an occasion worth celebrating.

They had been to the stars. Now they were headed beyond them.

"Coming up on alpha, Captain," Chekov said, watching the star's computer-corrected spectrogram shift into the blue on his board.

"Status, Uhura."

"Engineering's secure—"

"Crew departments report all secure—"

"Defense departments, aye—"

"Ship's secure, sir."

"Go sublight, Sulu."

"Aye aye." Sulu's hands moved with their usual quick care over the board, double-checking the intrinsic velocity and vector the *Enterprise* would be carrying when she dropped out of warp. Even computers developed bugs, after all, and Sulu had no desire to run a starship full tilt into a planet or a sun—at least, not while he was piloting it. He checked one last time, was satisfied, and touched the control that struck the warpfield—

—from outside, it seemed as if a great patch of star-pierced sky had gone mad. Stars veered and wobbled in it, changed colors wildly, bloomed and faded like burning flowers. And suddenly whiteness was there, with hard sharp edges, and the stars went sane again—the ones that could still be seen. Between the stars and the local traffic loomed a great graceful shape, braking down fast as she skimmed by—upper primary-hull disc, lower secondary-hull cylinder, the two slender nacelles on their outward-angled supports rising from the secondary hull. There she went, no ghost any more, now almost too real to bear: a silvery blaze, blindingly plated with the fiery orange-gold light of alpha Arietis, a class KO giant star. The only part of the ship that didn't shine was the black charactery on the upper and lower sides of her primary hull. The letters were thick and squared, Terran-Roman letters—for she was one of the twenty-two "heavy cruiser" starships of Terran registry, the flagship of Earth's fleet and the pride of the oxygen-breathers in that part of the Galaxy. Slowing down, easing her majestic bulk into a long lazy orbit around alpha until Base orbital control could give her a docking vector, *Enterprise* made starfall at Hamal/alpha Arietis in a yellow blaze of splendor.

And far out beyond any sensor's range, undetected in the cold dark wastes, something stretched, and strained intolerably—and slowly began to tear. . . .

Two

StarBase Eighteen, in orbit two hundred million kilometers from Hamal, could be seen from a long way off; and the sight was lovely. At distance, what one saw was a golden-tinged oblong, rounded at the ends like a cigar, and shimmering delicately as it end-over-ended through space. Closer, though, the size of it became apparent—other starships, light cruisers and cutters in for repair or scheduled maintenance, were nested among the innumerable spikes and struts and spires of its outer surface. The whole structure glittered in a thousand shades of blinding gold as StarBase Eighteen tumbled on around Hamal, ponderous and beautiful and a bit amusing.

"We have our vector, Captain."

"Good, Mr. Sulu. Take us in."

Kirk watched with satisfaction as Sulu's fingers flickered over his board. *Thank God, no more mail runs!* Jim thought. *No more boring Starfleet errands for a while! Something big, to stretch my people—to stretch* me, he added to himself after a breath. Lately the feeling had been creeping up on him that the Galaxy was getting ordinary, that the commonplace was settling into it—one planet, one new species, one crisis with the Romulans was beginning to feel like all the others before it. *Do I need a vacation? And where the hell do I go, when the fringes of the known universe are getting boring?*

—well, that's *getting handled—*

The screen changed views, and the flicker brought Kirk's attention back to it. Mr. Sulu had gone over to Base sensors and was picking up their image of the *Enterprise* coming in. Kirk smiled at her, loving the stately lady for the thousandth time—and then was surprised when she abruptly went mischievous, a thousand kilometers out from the Base. The world stayed right-side-up as usual inside the ship, but the Base sensors showed her rolling slowly, luxuriously, on her longitudinal axis—one victory roll, then another, while overexcited ions screamed light in her wake.

"Belay that, Mr. Sulu," Kirk said, at some pains to sound stern. "This is serious business."

"Aye, sir," Sulu said, looking soberly up and suppressing his smile as well. He knew the Captain had seen him setting up the maneuver and had said nothing. After all, look what ships were at Eighteen, some of them prime contenders for the drive, some of them old friends of the Captain's, or old friendly rivals: USS *Milton Humason,* USS *Eilonwy,* USS *Challenger;* and smaller ships that had worked with *Enterprise* before, or crossed her path—*Condor, Indomitable, QE III, Lookfar* . . . Sulu touched a control here, one there, and made the ship straighten up and fly right.

Kirk let his own smile go no farther than his eyes, and watched their approach, which was so close now that *Enterprise* was blotting out most of the Base sensor's sky. "Back to our visual for a moment, Mr.

Sulu," he said. The screen changed again, to show one unspiked end of the huge structure irising open for them, revealing a portal that could have swallowed twenty starships side by side. All about the opening door, mirror-polished stanchions and spires glittered fiercely golden and hatched the surface and one another with razor-edged shadows. Kirk winced as Base navigations guided them into the heart of the light.

"Cut the intensity on that, would you, Uhura?" he said, averting his eyes, then glancing back when the brightness was handled. There was something about the great silver and gilt interior that drew the eye, and at the same time made the watcher nervous. *Well, it's the old thing about alien architectures. The place isn't Terran-built . . .* If "built" was even the right word; for the exterior "skin" of the base was really only a tight fine mesh woven of what seemed, at this distance, delicate threads of mirror-finish steel—and were actually long single-crystal extrusions, each two meters thick. From the "skin" substructures hung, tethered by cables or jutting out on odd-shaped supports, looking like packages dangling or stuck on poles; they were offices, service bays, living quarters. All along the interior of the structure, little drones glided along twisting rails or sailed by on chemical propulsion, flashing suddenly if they happened into a sunbeam piercing the interior through one of many oddly-placed apertures. Motion, haste, an impression of life that was quick and glittering and very alien, that was what Kirk got—along with a slight uneasy feeling at being closed in. *But what am I thinking of?* he chided himself a moment later, considering the folly of trying to understand much about another species just from its artifacts. He recalled the conclusions the Tegmenir had come to about Earth-humanity from the single chair they'd found, and cautioned himself against judgments.

Still, it was hard to believe they were only seventy-five lightyears from Earth.

"It's a lovely place they've got here," Scotty said from where he stood beside the helm. On the screen, shadows slid and flickered as Hamal's fierce golden fire shone through and was occluded by the outer webwork of the StarBase. "I'd like to meet the designers."

On the other side of the helm, Spock stood straight and still with his hands behind his back, looking unmoved and calm as always; but his eyes were for the screen as much as Scotty's. "You may have that chance, Mr. Scott. Two of the Hamalki members of the Base design team are also involved with the development of the inversion drive."

"Thanks for tellin' me, Mr. Spock," Scotty said, looking very pleased and anticipatory. Jim smiled to himself. A brief stint at a desk job with the Federation's Bureau of Planetary Works had only served to increase Scotty's absolute worship of excellence in design in everything. Meeting one of the Hamalki designers—famed as among the finest in the known universe—would probably be akin to a religious experience for him.

"How are we doing, Mr. Sulu?" Kirk said.

"A pilot's coming out for us, sir. ETA to dock is five minutes."

"Sir," said Uhura from her post, "Base Operations just called. Commodore Katha'sat's respects, and it would like to see you in its office along with the Chief Engineer and whatever other department heads will be involved with the installation proper."

"Fine. Acknowledge, and tell it we'll be along immediately docking is complete."

"Here comes the pilot, sir," Sulu said. "They'll be belaying us in on tractors."

"Uhura, advise all hands—"

"Done, sir."

Sulu touched his controls again, and the view changed once more on the screen as the *Enterprise* eased to full stop, hanging there at the heart of the immense silvery structure. From off to one side something small and bright shot out of a crevice in the shining weave. *Someone in a powered pod?* Kirk thought, having his doubts—the pod was hardly a meter wide. The little gleaming egg fired itself along at the *Enterprise* with such force and speed that for a moment Kirk feared for his outer hull—yet barely a few meters from it, the egg snapped to a stop as sharply as if it had come to the end of a tether, and then inched delicately forward to touch the leading edge of the secondary hull. A moment later it backed away again, leaving attached to the hull the bright, pearly line of something Kirk had heard of but never yet seen, one of the new "tactile tractors" that were also of Hamalki make. Spinning its glowing line, the egg headed back toward the semi-spherical docking bay that was the far end of the Base, and actually towed the *Enterprise* behind it—inch by inch at the start; then with more speed, a slow glide.

Kirk found that looking at impossibility made his mouth dry. Scotty, beside him, was near spluttering with delighted perplexity. "That canna be done, I don't care wha' motive force you're using—"

"Yet there it is, Mr. Scott," Spock said. "Once again, size proves deceptive. The operating principle is called 'elective mass'; it is one of the assumptions that makes the inversion drive possible." He tilted his head to one side, watching the little glittering seed in utter calm. "Certainly it looks unlikely. So do the equations involved, I assure you. Many of their elements trespass into what we have for some time considered impossibility. Yet the drive works. . . ."

"Makes your head hurt, does it?" Jim said, shooting an amused sidewise look at the Vulcan.

Spock breathed out, shifting his shoulders a bit. "My somatic responses are hardly germane to the situation, Captain. It would be more accurate to say that there are facts I have yet to assimilate entirely."

"There are?" Scotty said, grinning. Spock didn't deign to answer that one, merely gazed at the screen as they all did. The silver ovoid with its tractor pulled *Enterprise* deeper into the Base. Abruptly, between the rounded far bay and the ship with its tug, light sprang into being, lines of it. Lines making angles with one another, defining chords within the immense circle of the Base's "hull"; twenty-four radial lines segmenting that circle, all meeting in the center; and woven among the radials, one by one, a dazzling confusion of oblongs and parallelograms of light. Straight at the glowing network the little silver egg led the *Enterprise,* and finally, with only the tiniest jolt, right into it. Kirk let go the arms of the helm, which he had been gripping. As he did, the framework of light came loose from most of its anchor-lines and dropped slowly about the *Enterprise,* wrapping itself closely about both hulls, clinging wherever it touched. The silver ovoid slipped through the mesh and darted away, leaving behind it a starship bound tight in lines of pearlescent white fire that dimmed somewhat in brilliance, but still pulsed, very much alive.

"That," Kirk said, getting up from his chair, "has to be one of the weirdest dockings I've ever had. Let's go see the Commodore. Uhura, you have the conn."

Kirk and Spock and Scotty headed for the lift. As its door whooshed closed behind them and Uhura slid into the command chair, Sulu turned to Chekov at the command console and gave him a wicked, merry look. "'Come into my parlor, said the spider to the fly—'"

Chekov rolled his eyes at the ceiling, and idly began working out the initial parameters for a search-and-discover spiral in the next galaxy over.

The StarBase's office complex was a little less exotic than its shimmering outworks. When the world came back after the transporter's glow was gone, Jim found himself standing in a very average transporter room. Not quite so average was the Sulamid chief engineer handling the console. He stood three meters high, a sheaf of constantly moving rose and violet tentacles, with eight restless stalked eyes peering about from the top of him. Lieutenant-commander's stripes manifested themselves in the skin of the barrels of several of his larger handling tentacles—Sulamids being color-changers of great skill. "Sirs/madams welcome be," the Sulamid said with a graceful flourish and wreathing of tentacles, knotting several of them in a gesture of respect. "Downhall left three doors lift, four-level down, two leftways, exit rightward, six doors right, waiting Commodore Katha'sat eagerly; introductions/briefing/legal intoxicants. Sirs/madams guide?"

"Thank you, mister," Kirk said, having doubts about the "mister" even as he said it—all twelve of the Sulamid sexes claimed to be male, especially the ones who had the children. "I think we'll manage."

They did, though Kirk was astonished again and again on the way down by how many of the nonhominid kinds of people were on station. Hamal was close to Sol and Terra, but it was also within the boundaries of the great Majoris Congeries, an intragalactic "open" cluster of twenty stars that was home to as many wildly diverse species, from methane-breathers to one winged species that found the atmospheres of stars congenial. There was a branch of Starfleet Academy here, to service this sector of space, and a library secondary only to that of Alexandria II. The stable population was around eight thousand sentients—crewmen on assignment, and their dependents, and civilians on vacation, for some of the Base was a resort, privately financed and operated. The halls were noisy with translated and untranslated conversation, as various kinds of people chirped, squealed, laughed, grunted or howled about their business. Kirk found himself smiling as he went, for there was an excitement in the air abnormal for even such a place as this, and his ship was at the heart of it.

The Commodore's office door was open when they came to it. Kirk tapped twice on the doorsill and walked in, finding Katha'sat getting up from behind its desk. It was a hest, off Rukbah V—a tall being, so slender as to look skeletal, with greenish-bronze skin stretched taut over a basically bipedal form. Hestv had extra knees and elbows, and looked a touch peculiar to Earthly eyes when they stood or sat. Their long gaunt faces were adorned with large gentle eyes, green or golden, that gave their faces a perpetually wistful look. Jim knew that look painfully well. Katha'sat had used it on him often enough at poker, with great success.

"Commodore," he said, reaching out a hand and then putting it behind his back again in the hestv fashion. "Good to see you again."

"Under these circumstances, I believe it," Katha'sat said in its whispery voice, matching Kirk's gesture, and then reaching out to clasp hands with him. "Perhaps you would make me known to your officers?"

"Commander Spock," Jim said, and Spock bowed, all reserved Vulcan courtesy. "Chief Engineer Scott—" and Scotty copied Kirk's gesture, which Katha'sat returned with the round-mouthed smile of its people. "No shortage of good company," it said. "Captain, I have some truly astonishing *nhwe* I've been saving for some worldshattering occasion; perhaps you gentlefolk would join me?"

There were all kinds of racks, supports and chairs in the office. It took a few moments to find ones that fit, but as soon as they had, the Commodore was passing around glasses and a crystal flask half-full of the dark blue *nhwe.* Kirk was glad to see it, and poured himself a generous splash. *Nhwe* might taste like machinists' oil, but it also contained a neuropressor hormone that in most hominid chemistries enhanced whatever emotional state the drinker was presently experiencing—hence its slang name, "More-of-the-same." Jim took a long drink, and got more cheerful than he had been, and watched Scotty get more excited. Spock sipped his carefully, and became more serenely unreadable by the moment.

"Getting things started in a hurry, are we?" Kirk said. "Is Fleet pressuring you, respected?"

"No, no. The chief of the installation team, however, has asked to meet you as quickly as possible and get permission to start her work immediately." The Commodore hooted softly, a hestv laugh. "She says she's waited eight hundred years to get out of the Galaxy, and she won't wait a day longer than necessary now that the problem is handled. . . ."

Kirk went over the additions-to-crew roster in his head. "That would be the Hamalki, then—"

Something scrabbled politely at the door. "Are they here? High time," said a voice that didn't so much speak as chime, a sweet liquid-brittle chattering, staccato yet melodic. The person who went with the voice came scuttling into their midst in a swift flow of delicate, much-articulated legs, twelve of them, that were attached to a rounded central body. The being was an arachnoid—a big one, standing about a meter high on those legs, her body about a meter across and half a meter thick. That body was transparent in most places, translucent in others, made of an analogue to chitin that was clear as glass. Most places the creature's surface was polished to mirror smoothness; the exception was the upper side of the "abdomen," where clear needle-fine spines made a fur that glittered like grass on a dewy morning. The abdomen had a slender, nubbly ridge or crest running atop it from "front" to "back," and in the ridge twelve eyes were set—four clustered at one end, four at the other, four studded along the ridge. At first glance they seemed expressionless—*like a shark's,* Jim thought, and repressed a shudder. Yet they also burned like blue-hot opals, full of shifting fires; and when one cluster of them fixed on Jim, he felt the personality behind them like a blow, and was impressed. *This is a power,* he thought as he rose to greet her. And then added to himself, irrationally relieved, *My ship is in good hands—*

"Captain K'rk, please sit," the windchime voice said, as the Hamalki settled on the floor in the middle of the group and tucked her legs in around her, folding them out of the way. "A great pleasure, I've heard many good things about you. I'm K't'lk."

"Thank you," Kirk said. "I only wish I were sure I could pronounce your name as well as you just managed mine, and without even a voder."

"No problem. Get the consonants right, and the vowels will take care of themselves. We only have one vowel anyway—" and she pronounced it, an E above high C, surrounded by shivery harmonics—"—and all the rest of the language is a matter of pitch; the same as yours, more or less." The fiery eyes turned their attention to the First Officer, and K't'lk lifted the two forward legs on that side to describe a swift gesture in the air. "*Mehe nakkhet ur-seveh,* Mr. Sp'ck—"

He lifted his hand in the Vulcan salute. "May you also live long and prosper, madam. And may I compliment you on your accent?"

She laughed in surprise, a merry chiming. "If it warrants it, yes indeed! Evidently that correspondence course I took to read all those Vulcan engineering journals was better than I thought." She looked over to Scotty. "And greetings to you also, Mr. Sc'tt; well met indeed! A long time now I've wanted to meet the man who so many times has pulled the estimable Captain's nuts out of the fire."

Jim put up an eyebrow. Scotty reddened, and held his grin back from becoming a laugh. "I thank ye, lady," he said, "though it's not often been so dramatic."

"The idiom, though, would be 'chestnuts,'" Spock said, utterly deadpan.

"Oh? Thank you."

"Where's your manners, Mr. Spock?" Scotty said in feigned shock. "Correctin' a lady—"

"Oh no, the correction's welcome, Mr. Scott," K't'lk said. "After all, language is what we build with, the tool that builds the tools. Inaccuracy there is as deadly as it'd be in a warp drive whose computer feeds it inaccurate mix ratios—Architectrix keep any such fate far away from you! Which brings me to the point: my technicians are lined up in the cargo transporters waiting for your permission to begin installing the inversion drive. May we?"

"Permission granted, of course; I'll give the orders," Kirk said, amused by the Hamalki's cheerful intensity. "A question, though, before you go. Katha'sat mentioned that you'd been waiting eight hundred years for this?"

"Eight hundred sixty-three standard," K't'lk said. "Towed your ship in myself so that no fool would damage it somehow and slow things down—"

"Are you Fleet personnel, then?" Kirk added, not much liking the idea of a person without Starfleet oaths in force touching his ship. "Or civilian?"

"Both," K't'lk said. "I comprehend your concern,

Captain. In this life I'm long retired from Starfleet, though I have a reserve commission as full Commander. If you wish to reactivate it, I'm willing to serve with you. Though the presence of stripes won't significantly affect my performance."

Kirk nodded. Scotty looked confused. " 'This life?' " he said.

K't'lk gazed up at Scotty with what Jim would have sworn was a humorous look. "Yes indeed. I had to be hatched four times, each time with the previous life's memories added on, to get all this work done—the equations for the inversion apparatus and so forth. This last lifetime, the theory just suddenly began to put itself together; so I went and talked to the Vulcans, and among us we worked out the hardware for the drive. Now that that's done, I want to get out there and accept the consequences of my work—or, preferably, enjoy them." The Hamalki stood up, rubbing two back legs together in what looked like an impatient gesture. "Captain, I desire your better acquaintance, and there'll be more leisure for that once the apparatus is installed and we're on our way to the Lesser Magellanic—"

"Of course," Kirk said gently, amused.

"Then I'd like to have the company and guidance of your officers in this business, if I might. I know your ship from stem to stern from her plans, of course, but you gentlemen—"she fixed those blue-hot eyes on Spock and Scotty—"will know where the bugs are."

Jim nodded at them in dismissal. K't'lk was out of the room in three quick leaps; Spock and Scotty went after her, having to move fast to catch up. "I read that article of yours in *Acta Mega-Astrophysicalis* last month, Sp'ck," the Hamalki's voice said in a hasty, good-natured chiming that dwindled down the hall. "The one about kinematics of nuclear regions in barred-spiral galaxies. Where did you get that figure for the radial motion? The Tully-T'Laea relation would seem to preclude—"

Spock's unruffled voice could be heard beginning a reply as the doors to the Commodore's office slid shut. Kirk leaned back in his seat and pursed his lips in the gesture he knew Katha'sat would read as a smile. "I may not be seeing much of my First for a while, if that was any indication," he said. "Looks like he's found someone who'll understand what he's talking about when he gets mathematical."

Katha'sat tilted its head to one side in hestv acquiescence. "I hope so. The Hamalki have been claiming that the Vulcans' assistance made the inversion drive possible—but the Vulcans deny it categorically and insist they barely understood what the Hamalki were talking about. Understandable, I suppose; I can't imagine Vulcans being very easy about any science called 'creative physics.' Yet they got together, and now we have the drive. . . . How do you feel about it, Jim?"

"Going extragalactic?" He took another long drink of the *nhwe.* "Excited. Pleased. A little annoyed about the politics . . ."

"That our worlds have leisure for politicking," Katha'sat said, round-mouthed, "is an indication we're succeeding at our jobs. No nervousness?"

Kirk shrugged and drank again, then put his glass down and looked at the Commodore. "A waste of time, Katha."

The hest tilted its head again. "No change after all this time," it said. "A long time, since you and I flew together at Academy, with our sleeves innocent of rank. . . ."

"You were a good wingman." Jim sighed. "I miss that sometimes, Katha. The freedom, and the excitement . . ."

"I miss it too, Jim. But I've graduated to larger

problems, these days, than a flitter's fuel mix and whether the navcomp will stay up and running long enough for me to find my way back to base. And so have you. . . . O Jim, that bland look of yours could fool a *hnt,* but not me. You're headed a long way from anywhere, on this mission, with no help to be had. And our friends the Klingons have been sniffing around the inversion drive's testing grounds with those new hyper-phasers of theirs—Be careful, my friend!"

Jim picked up his drink again, turned it around in his hands. "Which Klingons?"

"*Kaza* was here a tenday ago—showing itself along the borders, then slipping out again. Earlier in the month it was *Kytin* and *Kj'khrry* and a little convoy of support cruisers and cutters. K't'lk did her final test in a midsize craft, a cutter. Her test jump landed her right in the middle of them. It's well for us that she has good reflexes; before they could react, she re-elected her mass in another 'direction' and came out into realspace practically in the corona of a little white dwarf near Rasalgethi."

"A cutter might need to run," Jim said. "But the *Enterprise* won't. Let them come after us . . . if they can get up the nerve."

"Don't ask for anything you're not willing to have happen," Katha'sat said, its great eyes glinting with rueful humor at its friend. "Jim, your command record shows that you're pretty much the same way you used to be at Academy. You always could fall into a *fwe*-heap and come up covered with diamonds. This time I'd rather you just cover yourself with glory—rather than take the chance of taking a header into a *real fwe*-heap. Look over your shoulder, be *careful*—"

"I read, Katha, I read. Enough. What is this *fwe* business? Do you talk to your mother that way?"

"Who do you think taught me? And when does the game start?"

"Twenty hundred our time."

"There goes that last pay raise, Jim."

"Want to bet? My First Officer taught me this system . . ."

When Lieutenant Uhura called him and told him that the crew briefing was going to be held live on the Recreation Deck, so that a full offshift could attend, Lieutenant Harb Tanzer's first reaction was to make a face at the work ahead of him in the next few hours. But the reaction didn't last long—his usual tendency toward humorous acceptance of circumstances had him laughing at the problem and himself within a few minutes. Without further ado, he left the little cubicle of offices that gave onto the Rec deck, and went out to take down the forest.

He stood and stretched outside the door for a moment, yawning—it was late in his own shift. Lieutenant Tanzer was a stocky, square-built man, muscular, but with the muscles padded and gentled by a smoothing of fat. He had the prominent nose and craggy features common to many Earth-humans of the Third Diaspora, as well as the thick silver hair characteristic of those gallant-mad early spacers, who had so often dared deep space without appropriate shielding and had introduced some interesting mutations into their bloodlines as a result. Pale, close-set blue eyes looked out of that face; eyes that could go fierce and piercing when the occasion called for it, or could crinkle at the corners and smile as delightedly as the mouth when hilarity broke loose, which was often. Harb was somewhat older than the usual *Enterprise* crewman, who tended toward early- or mid-postadolescence. In his job, however, age was less an issue than in some that required hairtrigger reflexes and athletic prowess. His job demanded a sense of humor, sharp wits, and a keen insight into people; in Harb Tanzer, all these were improving with age. He was Chief of Recreation, a small department but an important one on a starship.

He let his arms fall and looked with affection and mild regret at the landspace around him. The slim black boles of smooth-barked trees reared up all around, almost completely shutting the night sky away with their thick crowns of whispering leaves fifty feet above; yet here and there a star winked through, big and bright. The starlight was in fact so bright that the leaves blocking it out cast clear sharp shadows on the leaf-strewn ground—for this was a forest that grew on a world at the heart of the great R Scuti Cluster, where stars shone even in the daytime, and the night sky was a jewelled tapestry thick with slowly-pulsing regular variables and novae, all huge and close. Harb had spent half his leave in that forest when they made planetfall there some months before, recording sounds and scents and textures with great care. *I did good work,* Harb thought, smiling with satisfaction as a breeze riffled through the leaves, and none of them showed holographic overlap or moire patterns. From off in the direction of the lift entrance, attenuated by apparent distance, came the mournfully sweet cry of one of the nightingale bats, a shadowy, abstract melody like an oboe singing its private sorrows to the night. Underfoot, the tiny white five-petaled flowers of elanor mimicked the brighter stars above them, and gave out their sharp-sweet fragrance to mingle with the other scents of a forest after rain. "It's all on tape," he said aloud to the pair of silver-fiery eyes that watched him from a high limb of the nearest tree. "I just hate taking it down. . . ."

A pale shape in a gold uniform tunic slipped around the trunk of one of the trees, looking around him alertly and with delight. "Lieutenant?"

"Here, sir," Harb said, and stepped out to meet the

Captain. The encounter was hardly unusual. Recreation saw a lot of Captain Kirk, who played as hard as he worked, though (to Harb's constant concern) not nearly as much. Lieutenant Tanzer privately held the Captain as a special responsibility—someone to be amused and entertained as frequently and as thoroughly as possible. His immediate superior supported him in this—Recreation being one of the departments of Medicine, and reporting directly to Dr. McCoy.

"They told me it was marvelous," said Harb's favorite customer, turning to gaze up through the gently-waving branches at the blooming, swelling, shrinking stars. "I see they were understating. What's that?" The Captain pointed at the eyes that watched them from the nearby branch.

"Nightstalker, sir." Harb clucked at it. The logistics computer picked up the sound and changed tapes, so that the dark furry form inched forward into the starlight and peered at them with its big ears pricked up. It held the position for a few seconds, then made a mistrustful mewling sound and swarmed up the tree-trunk, out of sight. Captain Kirk shook his head, smiling. "That was in Scutum somewhere?"

"Yes, sir. I forget the star's name; some little A7. We called the planet Lórien."

"I remember that. I never did get down there; too much to do . . ." Lieutenant Tanzer nodded. It was the old story; sometimes the man who ran the show didn't get to enjoy all of it. "But you have all this on tape, don't you, Harb?"

"Yes sir. At least in facsimile, you *can* go back."

Kirk laughed. "Good. I will. Meantime, the Commodore is coming across from the base for an evening of cards. It's hestv—"

"So you need cards marked for an infrared reader," Harb said. "What game, Captain? Star-and-Comet? Alioth? Fizbin?"

"Poker."

"Aye, aye." Lieutenant Tanzer gestured toward his office. Its door opened for them, letting a bizarre stream of everyday light into that midnight forest.

"Half a moment," Harb said. He went over to his master logistics console and queried it for availability of poker supplies, noting that three sets were missing—one was in Sickbay, in use, by the temperature readings he got from the cards; one was idle in Hydroponics; the third, in Engineering, was also in use—probably a few of Scotty's people were whiling away spare time while the Hamalki work crew installed the inversion drive. A rack of chips and one of the eighteen remaining packs of plastic cards sparkled into being on the transporter pad of the console. Harb picked up both chips and deck, made sure their charges were positive, then handed them to Kirk. The Captain rubbed his hands on the cards, apparently enjoying their warmth after the cool of the forest outside. The cards would be radiating at Earth-human blood temperature for hours, all but the dark symbols on them, which Katha'sat would read as shadows against luminous whiteness.

"Thanks," the Captain said, turning away, and then stopping. "Now what the hell is going on *there?*"

Harb joined him, looking down into the little twenty-seven cubic meter "repeater" tank in the corner, by which the big games tank out in the Rec room could be monitored for "gamesmaster" games, or just for kibitzing. The tank was full of stars that swooped and whirled and danced so violently that Harb's stomach protested a little at the image. The effect was as if someone was riding one of the ancient "roller coasters" of Terra, but through deep space instead of on a planet's surface, and with a fine disregard for which way up or down might be.

Far out at the fringes of the tank vista, small lights that were not stars swooped and soared, diving toward the point of view at the front of the tank, veering away again. One area of cubic up in one corner showed a larger view of what was happening. The long lean shapes of Romulan warbirds and Klingon-built "vulture" destroyers dove and fired at a lone little shape that rolled and twisted through a tortuous course to avoid their fire. Upper primary-hull disc, lower secondary-hull cylinder, upreaching nacelles—"Mr. Sulu asked me to make him a special mockup," Harb said. "A battle simulation for *Enterprise* without the usual battle methodology—no popping out of warp and firing, then ducking back into warp and running to get behind someone. Evasive and attack maneuvers in normal space, on impulse power only."

The Captain shuddered visibly as the *Enterprise* in the tank ran straight at a Romulan who had just popped out of warp and then veered away from it at a wrenching speed and angle that made his bones groan in sympathy, while behind her the Romulan struggled to turn and bring the forward phasers to bear on it. "You can't *do* that to a ship this size!" he said, watching in fascinated horror as the little *Enterprise* did a frightening duck-and-roll that left the Romulan behind her shooting at the one that had just been in front of her.

"With all due respect, sir, if you see it happening, it can. Mr. Sulu was very careful about the elements of the program that had to do with what a starship's structure can take. It's true, the program walks the outer limit of the design criteria—but then that's what he wanted for this simulation. An unorthodox battle situation that would stretch a helm officer a little. The object of this game for him is not only to elude the attackers, but also to keep the ship from being ripped apart by centrifugal and centripetal force—"

The mad helmsman on the other end of the game threw the starship he was piloting straight away from his pursuers, let them gather in a pack behind him and tear along on his trail. Three of them arced out at the vertices of a triangle to begin a standard englobement. The starship flipped end-for-end, braking savagely on its forward thrust, and headed right into the pack that still followed directly behind. Panicked, they scattered—but not fast enough. The starship hit one of them.

Point-of-view in the main tank winked out instantly, to be replaced by the computer simulation of the *Enterprise* and three Romulan vessels colliding at just under the speed of light. The explosion was impressive, to say the least. Where four separate matter/antimatter drives had been contained and then catastrophically released at high combined velocities, there was no expecting anything but a blast that would have burned any observer's eyes out, and then a slowly contracting ball of superheated gas and debris that for some time to come would do a creditable imitation of a star gone nova. Very sweetly, very sorrowfully, the master games computer began to play "Taps." The sound of various observers' laughter, merry jeering, and condolences—along with Sulu's annoyed swearing—came in through the tank circuit.

The Captain made a wry face. "*They* can laugh," he said to Harb. "It's not *their* ship.—How long did it take you to set that up?"

"A couple of weeks. It's only a prototype. Of course, if you'd like me to have the program added to your private terminal—"

Kirk smiled, a tight, tired expression. "I'm knee-deep in prototypes at the moment, Mr. Tanzer . . . but I suppose one more wouldn't hurt."

"I suppose not, sir. May I ask how the new drive's coming along?"

Kirk shrugged as they walked out of the office, a gesture half annoyance and half resignation. "It's not a drive, Mr. Scott tells me . . . but he's not sure what it is, either. The Hamalki have the equations for it, but they don't understand how the results proceed from them—and they don't care. Mr. Spock says he doesn't understand even the equations. . . . You'll hear at the briefing."

"Yessir. Speaking of which, all this has to come down. . . ." They stood together in silence in the moon-bright starlight, listening to the wind.

"Wait till I'm gone," the Captain said abruptly. "Nice job, Mr. Tanzer."

"Thank you, sir," Harb said to the back of the man already walking briskly to the lift. As its doors closed, Lieutenant Tanzer let out a small breath of satisfaction, for there was more spring in the Captain's step than there had been lately. "Moira?" he said to the air.

"What is it, Harb?" the games computer said.

"We've got a briefing in here, scheduled point nine. Estimated attendance is two hundred thirty. Implement preparation procedures for the room."

"Do you have positive storage on the forest?" the quiet female voice said.

"Storage is positive. I tell you three times, and once more for luck."

"Good. Hate to lose all those holos I took."

"*You* took! Who ran around the planet holding the camera?"

"Who told you where to shoot?" the computer said sweetly. Harb wondered briefly, for the hundredth time, whether it had been wise letting that skinny guy from Artificial Intelligence install that "For Argument's Sake" hardware option in his master computer. *Then again,* he thought, *I need to play too . . .* "Moira," he said, "is it true what I hear, that human beings are just what computers use to reproduce themselves?"

"You're catching on," Moira said, and chuckled wickedly. "Striking the forest."

The trees went out, flick, leaving nothing but leaf-scattered ground and shadowy hills against the horizon. The ground went out, revealing a dark carpet. The horizon blinked out, so that only the glorious sky remained, the many-colored gems swelling and shrinking in silence. Finally the stars went out too, revealing about an acre of burnt-orange carpeting, cream and gray panels four stories high, and the great observation windows full of golden light and shadows, the interior of the StarBase. "So much for Lórien," Moira said, sounding a bit sad.

"We'll put it back up when we get under way again. Meantime, wake up the drones and send them in." Harb headed out across the huge expanse of floor toward the alcove where the big games tank was. "I'll enlist some assistants from the Starship Demolitions Corps over there. We've got a lot of chairs to set up before point nine. . . ."

Three

The actual attendance was closer to three hundred—many people onshift managed to get dispensations to come down and see the Hamalki who would be assisting with the presentation. Even with the extra personnel, however, the briefing started on time; the audience was seated or standing or squatting or sprawling or hung up five minutes before the time appointed.

Lieutenant Tanzer had dug up a pedestal for K't'lk to perch on, and had set it up just to one side of the huge main screen. In the subdued light of the room, she glittered like cut crystal in the spot trained on her, and every time she gestured—which was often—dazzle flickered around.

"The heart of the problem, of course," she said by way of introduction, "has been that the humanities have been confined to our own Galaxy since all our species' births. Even the invention of the warp drive wasn't enough to liberate us. The warp drive, which is fine for transiting intragalactic distances—a few thousand lightyears at a time, say, on the longest hauls—is completely unequal to the distances involved in intergalactic travel. No modification of the warp drive has enabled it to sustain high enough warp factors, for a long enough period, to cover those immense distances in anything like a realistic fashion. Even at the lower speeds, with such extended use, you start running into problems like dilithium crystal embrittlement, plasma-bottle deterioration, and that kind of thing.

"There was also the problem of the so-called 'energy barrier' around the Galaxy—" K't'lk gestured a couple of blown-glass legs at the screen, which lit with a schematic of that spiral arm of the Galaxy where the previous *Enterprise* had attempted to leave the Milky Way, with such disastrous results. "Now the astronomers and astrophysicists just about went crazy when that 'barrier' was found, since there was no reason for such a thing to exist, any more than there was an actual 'edge' to the Galaxy. What we've found since the last attempted penetration, much to everyone's relief, is that there is no energy barrier. What the *Enterprise* experienced the last time was a transient effect—an encounter with the leading wavefront of a megabubble."

To the image on the screen was added a huge curved line that cut a little way into the spiral arm. "The wavefront carried with it a sleet of hard radiation—gamma- and delta-tachyons, and baryons, and other such exotic particles—blasted out of the core of a metastar exploding in the heart of one of our Galaxy's satellite globular clusters." The cluster in question pulsed slowly on the screen. "That wavefront is still expanding, but we won't have to worry about its impact on the inhabited worlds for some nine thousand years yet. More important is what we know now; that we can get out of the Galaxy without the crew going insane. Once that word got out, people all over the Federation started looking for ways to manage it."

K't'lk waved several of her back legs at the screen again. It changed view to show a 2-D representation of a 3-D diagram—a flat, gridded surface which seemed to have odd diamond-shaped structures budding out of it in several places. "The avenue of research that my team and I pursued with T'Pask and Sivek at the Vulcan Science Academy," K't'lk said, "was an investigation into a means of access to a particular alternate universe. It's called de Sitter space after the Terrene mathematician who first postulated its existence some centuries ago. Calling it a universe is a misnomer, really, for it's larger than universes. It is a *space,* infinite in a sense mathematically transcending the Euclidean 'flat infinity' in that it is multidimensional. How many other dimensions are involved, we're not sure, but we know of at least eight, having worked with them. 'Within' this space universes can be generated, like multidimensional bubbles. *Are* generated, in fact; and the evidence seems to indicate that our own universe was produced this way."

The screen changed, showing a closeup of one of the bud-universes, and adding a data table on the space that surrounded it. "The generation itself didn't interest us as much as the space in which it occurs," K't'lk said. "De Sitter space is infinitely hot and infinitely massful; it possesses infinite vector and acceleration qualities, 'stored' holographically in every part of it. The overall effect of de Sitter space is as if you had a whole universe crammed full of black holes, compressing themselves to the ultimate limits of compression—and beyond. However dense and hot you're imagining it, a million times hotter and denser than *that* . . . and on and on in the same way. *Infinite* mass."

K't'lk paused to let the concept sink in, and there was

a fascinated, uneasy rustling in the room as crewpeople got the idea and turned to trade glances. "Nothing can exist under such conditions—no particle, however elementary. Even super-compressed matter like a neutron fluid would in de Sitter space be crushed out of existence in the instant of its appearance there. In this completely occupied space, nothing in fact exists. Nothing *can*. It is a whole infinite space that is one limitless naked singularity. The laws of space and time and the other dimensions are meaningless there. *They* cannot exist there either."

The room got quiet as K't'lk looked up at the screen, which changed to reveal a barren, stony planet circling a weary-looking red sun. "This is the site of our first test with infinite mass," K't'lk said with some relish. "Based on equations that we developed jointly with the Vulcans, and with some use of selective ordinance—a Hamalki mathematico-philosophical technique that some people have been calling 'creative physics'—we built an apparatus that would tap into de Sitter space for an extremely tiny fragment of time, and materialize a very small speck of it in our universe. This was the result."

The second-counter on the screen sprang into life, digits racing backward toward zero. Zero came—and *something* happened. Just what was impossible to say, since it took no time; but at the non-sight of it many crewpeople shuddered, one of those quick tremors that comes out of nowhere. And then many exclaimed softly—for where that planet had been, there was nothing. Nothing, not a speck of debris; only that tired red star, bereft of company now. "What you saw just then was a hypercompression," K't'lk said. "The apparatus that produced it, and the planet on which it was built, were both hypercompressed into the pinpoint of de Sitter space in zero time. And completely out of physical existence."

The rustling in the room this time had an involuntary sound to it, as if people were having second thoughts about being in the same ship with such an apparatus. "The device we're installing in *Enterprise,*" said K't'lk, "works on exactly the same principle. Oh, slightly different in that the apparatus will be inside the ship, rather than on the surface of a planet. But the result is the same once it's activated. Any object containing a speck of infinite mass is going to be instantly crushed against the infinitely-massive-object's 'surface.' And faster than instantly; in zero time. For where infinite mass exists, by definition the laws of spacetime are briefly abolished. In zero time, the infinite mass to be generated inside *Enterprise* will pull the entire starship literally inside out, collapsing it into negative curvature —Some of you may have trouble with that image; the closest I can come to explaining it is to suggest that you imagine blowing up a bubble—and then deflating it, sucking the air out of it until it vanishes and begins inflating again, somewhere else, backwards." K't'lk made an abrupt, disorganized chime-rattle that sounded like an embarrassed cough. "My apologies, everybody, if the simile is poor, but the mathematics which is more precise takes a long time to master. At any rate, at another part of zero time set during the generation of the point of infinite mass, the negative curvature and the ship expressed by it run all the way down to the 'bottom' of the negative-curvature spectrum and out the other side, back into positive curvature—at which time the infinite mass 'expires' and the starship which has been 'containing' it pops out elsewhere in the originating spacetime. As far elsewhere as you desire, and in whatever direction, since an infinite number of vectors and accelerations are implicit in de Sitter space. You can go a light-year—or fifty, or fifty thousand, and out of the Galaxy at last. Clear to the next one—or if you like, beyond."

All around the room, people were quietly invoking their deities or support systems. Many trembled, and the eyes of many shone—those of them who had eyes, anyway. And over the shipwide circuit, left open for questions from the onshift crew, came a drawly voice that said very definitely, "*I don't like it!!*"

Spock, who was standing off to one side of the podium and waiting for his part of the presentation to begin, looked wearily off to one side and said nothing. K't'lk laughed, a delicate chiming, and preened herself with her forelegs for a moment. "That would be Dr. McC'y," she said, "who doesn't care for having his atoms scrambled about by the transporter."

"*There's something indecent about this whole thing,*" McCoy's voice said from Sickbay, "*and I'm seriously thinking of getting a transfer to a safer ship. One working the Romulan Neutral Zone, say. Or close-approach nova patrol.*"

"Indecent is an excellent word for it, Doctor," K't'lk said merrily. "So is 'illegal.' The equations from which the access to de Sitter space is derived break many known laws of physics, and a few we didn't suspect existed until we broke them. We are in fact dealing with an area beyond natural law—one in which it's possible to hypercompress you into a state too small and compact to be detected even with a tachyon microscope, and in zero time restore you to your marvelously testy self, with the testiness not a shade the worse for it afterwards. There's no time for damage to be done to your cells, or for anything else to happen. There's no *time.*"

"*That's as may be,*" McCoy said, a touch subdued by the whispery laughter that went through the Rec deck. "*But atom-scrambling aside, there's something that bothers me more. In the transporter, there's a brief but measurable period during which I don't exist—*"

"You will not-exist for zero time during this process

as well," K't'lk said. "However, the *Enterprise* will also be in not-existence at the time—and from your viewpoint, so will the rest of the universe. You'll have nothing to compare your not-existence against. The philosophical and ethical questions are pretty ones; I'd love to discuss them with you at length later, if you have time. For the moment, though, what I can tell you for certain is that I've been through inversion some fifty times now during prototype testing, and I missed it every time . . ." She trailed off sounding wistful. McCoy grumbled something inaudible, and said nothing further.

"By the way," K't'lk said then, "for those of you of Terran ancestry, the use of this drive will entitle you to a share of the prize anciently ordained by someone called Lloyd of London—a prize to be awarded to the first person or persons to take a ship through a 'black hole' or other singularity and return to report the results. I understand the authorities have ruled that de Sitter space qualifies as a singularity, so you're all eligible for a share in the award. They say the money has piled up quite a bit over the centuries, what with compound interest and multiple revaluation of currencies. If I understand the present state of the purse account, I think you people might be able to buy Starfleet if you pooled your resources."

There was laughter in the audience, some grim, some amused. A young Earth-human woman with long, dark, curly hair, wearing Defense Department gold, raised her hand and stood when K't'lk called on her. "Please correct me if I'm wrong, madam," she said in a sweet voice with a pronounced Oxonian accent, "but it sounds as if this—apparatus—has definite possibilities as a weapon."

"Oh yes," K't'lk said drily. "Hold a speck of infinite mass in one place for more than a tiny bit of time, and it starts pulling all the matter in the universe toward it at a shocking rate. That's even if it's out in the middle of nowhere. You can imagine the results of dropping a running apparatus into, say, the hyperstar field at the Galactic Core, where things are strange enough already. Better not imagine it. We have some investment in keeping this apparatus away from the Klingons and Romulans for the time being. Captain K'rk will speak about that later."

The room buzzed. A tall lean Altasa unfolded hirself out of hir crouch and triple-voiced hir question in basso Altan ululation. "Description-paradox-contradiction. And as-stated-possibility-timetravel?"

"There are a lot of paradoxes in the equations, yes," K't'lk said, sounding cheerful and unconcerned. "I wrote most of the principal equations myself, and tested all of them—yet I'm still unsure how the results proceed from those equations. And the Vulcans who worked with me seem to think we may *never* know. All *I* can tell you for certain is that they work. So at this point, figuring everything out can wait—seeing that the equations do produce a result we can turn to advantage. And yes, there is a possibility that the apparatus could be used for timetravel—or travel along any number of 'timelike' and 'spacelike' axes, continua you might call them, which are implicit in de Sitter space. But I think we'd best get regular space travel worked out before we start mudding about with the temporal coordinates."

"Mucking," Spock said *sotto voce* from one side.

"Thank you, yes. Is that all for the moment? Then Mr. Spock can go on with his part."

K't'lk flattened herself on her pedestal and stilled her chiming as Spock stepped up beside the screen. "Seeing that we are now free of the Galaxy," he said, standing straight and still, "Starfleet's mission for us involves a brief journey out of it, as far as one of our closer galactic neighbors, the Lesser Magellanic Cloud—"

The view on the screen changed to show a schematic of the Local Group, the association of twenty galaxies of which the Milky Way and the Andromeda Galaxy were the two largest. Close to the Milky Way's huge spiral, the Lesser Magellanic was circled and data-tagged by the computer. It was much smaller than the two great spirals—just a bright elongated spatter of stars, slightly thicker at one end than at the other. "This object is not properly a cloud, of course, but a type IO irregular galaxy, and along with its companion the Greater Magellanic Cloud, a satellite of our own Galaxy. The Greater Cloud is in fact slightly closer—a hundred ninety thousand lightyears away, as opposed to the Lesser Cloud's two hundred thousand. But the Small Cloud has been more extensively studied for some years, particularly its Cepheid variable stars."

On the screen, the spatter of light became a time-compressed closeup, in which many bright stars slowly pulsed brighter and fainter in a myriad of cycles. "These stars have been used for centuries to determine galactic distances. Now, however, we will be using them as navigational beacons. This one in particular—" —and the screen tightened on one blue-white star that burned high, sank low, burned bright again. "—DG Magellanis Minoris, in the Cloud cluster NGC 121. Its cycle of 89.39 hours is one of the shortest of any Cepheid, and easily identifiable.

"Locked on this star, we will transit using the inversion apparatus so as to emerge about a thousand lightyears from the fringes of the Smaller Cloud, making in zero time a change in position that would take us some two hundred eighty-three years at warp nine." He let the wondering murmur in the room die down before continuing. "We are then instructed to make ten more short transits in the Smaller Cloud, using long-range sensors to begin preliminary mapping of the stars and planetary systems affiliated with various Cepheids.

Once survey is completed, we are to transit back outside the Smaller Cloud once more and begin making our way back to our home galaxy by a series of thirty-six transits, during which we will be sowing an equivalent number of long-range navigational buoys in a cubic array, to serve as reference points in extragalactic space for future missions." Spock turned to one side, stepping away from the screen. "Captain?"

Captain Kirk stepped up in front of the mass of crewpeople and surveyed them for a moment. "Starfleet has given us no other orders," he said, "except that we take due precautions before investigating anything we feel needs investigating. However, you should know that the Klingons have been feinting in this area of late. They know we've been testing a drive that doesn't depend on the warp principle. It's a fair bet they'll come after us as soon as we're out of Federation space, and try to take it from us. If they start trouble, we'll do what's necessary to handle it. But I have an obligation not to allow the inversion apparatus to fall into their hands on any account—Starfleet was very definite on that matter." He paused to let them understand what he meant by that. The stillness in the room said that they understood very well. "Anyone wanting to decline this mission may do so without prejudice to its record. So? Comment?"

The room rustled. And one voice spoke—probably that of one of the Mizarthu crewpeople, to judge by the holophrastic speech and the growly voice. "Respect you, sir, we stop talking hurry up *go!!*"

The place erupted in cheering and howling, screeches and hoots and noisy applause. Kirk got down off the platform and headed for his quarters, and the card game—waiting only till the lift doors shut on him to let out the grin.

Four

At departure minus three hours, the *Enterprise* from the outside looked no different than she had on entering StarBase Eighteen; she hung placidly at the heart of the pulsing tactile-tractor web, silver-shining and calm. Inside, though, in-ship communications was alive with voices chattering like thoughts in a mind.

"*—look, I don't care what you do to that modulator, just get it up!! If Mr. Mahásë finds out that it's—*"

"*—nervous? Me?? Don't be silly.*" (a pause) "*I'm dying.*"

"*—we're secure, what's keeping the rest of you?*"

"*—terror-haste-pressure-excited-excited-excited-department head- pass/no pass-advanced starvation-cardiac failure! Query-query-(inexpressible and physiologically unlikely in hominids) expletive! exclamation—*"

"*—whaddaya mean I have to review and sign all these before we can leave?! I'm a doctor, dammit, not a bureaucrat! And where's that nurse?! You promised me* *a head nurse, Jim, what'm I supposed to do around here with Chapel getting her bloody doctorate and refusing to even pick up a God! damned! hypo any more without giving me a God! damned! diagnosis first—"*

"—you always did bet small. Ten credits that there'll be at least three Klingon destroyers, and we'll handle them in less than four minutes—"

"—aye, well all I know is that the Captain's on his way down here to have a look at it. So look sharp and clean that mess up, laddie. I willna ha' a sloppy deck when himsel' arrives—"

"—the Exec wants to know when you're going to file completion on the revisions in that program—"

"Mz. Uhura," the Chief of Astrocartography said, letting out a tired sigh, "my respects to Mr. Spock, and we're having to rewrite the program practically from line ten to make the new location coordinates work. You know what it means just in terms of changes in broadcast orientation and signal strength for the buoys—"

A weary chuckle. "That wasn't the question, Mayri."

"I know." Lieutenant Mayri Sagady looked over her shoulder. "D'hennish," she said, "how about it?"

"If the sir desires more area covered," the answer came back, "the sir must resign himself to the programming taking a little more time."

"Right," Mayri said. "Twenty minutes," she said to Uhura.

"WHAT??!"

"Quiet, D'hennish. Work."

"Twenty minutes aye," Uhura said. "Bridge out."

"I would kill the respected superior," the growly voice said from behind Mayri, "except that I would only be promoted into her position, and still have to finish this job."

"Noted and logged," Mayri said, and let out another sigh, and stretched. Mayri Sagady was in her mid-twenties, fiercely redheaded, and built like a Valkyrie; she had an open, friendly face with blue eyes that looked sleepy but missed nothing. She finished her stretch and went to stand behind her junior officer, looking over his shoulder as he worked at the main graphics tank.

Ensign Niwa Awath-mánë ri d'Hennish enu-ma'Qe said something annoyed under his breath, a soft yowl that made Mayri think of a tomcat warning another one off his fence. D'Hennish was an ailurin from Sadr—bipedal, and built wiry and slender for his two meters' height. His silky ash-blond mane spilled down over the shorter, plushy, platinum fur that covered the rest of him, all but the soft pads on fingers and toes. Those long fingers patted swiftly on the terminal-pad as d'Hennish hunched over it in fierce concentration. In the tank in front of him and Mayri, between schematics of the Milky Way Galaxy and the Lesser Magellanic Cloud, dots of light in a cubic array subtly shifted their positions, and lines reaching back from each one of them to specific stars in the great spiral galaxy shifted as well. "Twenty minutes," d'Hennish growled, "twenty minutes indeed. You people and your minutes and hours! Work should be done when work is done, Mayri—" He broke rhythm long enough to glance up at her. It could have been an intimidating look—the glare of brown-amber eyes in the long, almost doggy cheetah's face, with the upper lip curled just enough to show a fang or two. Mayri, however, wasn't buying it. "Are all of those optimum transmittal positions?" she said.

"Of course," d'Hennish said, turning back to his work and patting a last few of the controls. He sat back, then, and the cubic array rearranged itself slightly one more time. "There is the basic matrix," he said. "Now to make the array holographic." He bent to the keyboard again. "Twenty minutes—!!"

Mayri smiled to herself, seeing the old argument about to start again. "If you'd started this last night, as you should have, instead of waiting till this morning—"

"I started it now," d'Hennish said without looking up, working with the first point in the array to connect it with all the other receiver-stars in the Galaxy, one at a time. "I always start it now."

Mayri shook her head. Sometimes d'Hennish didn't seem to make sense, but then Basic didn't have the syntax necessary to convey the ailurin's peculiar perception of time, and her attempts to learn Sadrao had resulted in a headache from the strange worldview and a sore throat from the yowly vowels. "I know," she said, "but sometimes your now is later than it should be. . . ."

"What?"

"Hush up. Work." She stood there silently watching for the next ten minutes or so, while d'Hennish worked in furious haste, the docked tail of a Sadrao prince thumping in anxiety and annoyance on the seat of his chair. The computer flashed HOLOGRAPHIC ARRAY COMPLETE just seconds before the communications screen whistled. "Transmit it, quick," Mayri said, and d'Hennish slapped the pad and sent the program on its way to the Science Department and Ballistics computers that would need it next. "Astrocartography," said a familiar, cool voice. "Lieutenant Sagady."

"Screen on," she said, turning to it. "Yes, Mr. Spock."

There was ever so slight a pause, as Spock glanced upward at another screen, examining something with his usual calm regard. "Acknowledging receipt of the sowing-and-targeting program for the buoys," he said. "Bridge out."

The screen went dark. Mayri sagged against d'Hennish's chair. "We just missed getting reprimanded by that much," she said, looking narrowly at d'Hennish to see if he'd gotten the message. He had; his eyes had gone from slits to amber-ringed, nervous circles.

"We're not reprimanded, though." D'hennish panted for a breath or two. "Mayri, believe me, I will not disappoint the Captain or this ship. I swear that when I board her. It's just—" He grimaced. "Space I can see structuring—but the flow of one's being? Silliness. I can't take it seriously—"

"I know," Mayri said, letting out one last sigh and patting the ensign's shoulder. "But you can handle it—or they wouldn't have let you aboard ship in the first place."

D'Hennish wrinkled his nose. "He might say I do that work well," he muttered.

"Did he tell you you'd done anything wrong? Then you've just been complimented."

D'Hennish dropped his jaw in a grin. "So I am," he said. "Are we done?"

"For this shift, yes."

"Then I'm eating. Are you eating with me?"

Mayri grinned back and went to log out of the office. "I am," she said, falling into his phrasing, "and I'm eating as many calories as I can get my hands on."

"Oh Mayri! What about your diet?"

"I am punching you in your big pink nose," Lieutenant Sagady said with dignity, "as soon as I eat enough to get up the strength."

"This is it?" the Captain said, looking down with hands on hips, and sounding rather disappointed. "This is all there is?"

K't'lk chimed briefly, a bell-arpeggio of laughter.

"This is all there ever is," she said, jesting. Then, more seriously, "Should we have made it bigger?" she said to Mr. Scott.

"Bigger wouldna help, lass," Scotty said. "I still wouldna understand it."

The three of them stood at the heart of the Engineering Department, on the lowest of the three levels through which the main matter/antimatter mix column pierced. A few meters away from the column, connected to it by a sighting phaser and two power-feeder guides, was a transparent metal box about two meters square. Jim Kirk hunkered down to look at it more closely, and saw nothing he hadn't seen from above—various delicate, glassy-looking inner workings, a trihedrally-fractured dilithium crystal in an ordinary five-grip setting; meselectronic relay liquids and capsule thernistors. "I would have thought there'd have to be some kind of containment vessel," the Captain said, "something to keep the infinite mass-point from pulling the apparatus in on itself—"

"Not needed. The integrity of the apparatus only needs to be protected before zero time starts. After that, it doesn't matter if it's collapsed in with everything else. In fact it has to be; otherwise you wouldn't be able to get home. . . ."

Scotty shook his head. "Lassie, I swore a long time ago that I'd never have anything in my engine room that I couldna understand. I've never before had anything here that I *didna* understand by the time I had it installed. But this is the exception . . . and I don't mind tellin' ye that it's drivin' me buggy."

"Well, if you like, I'll do what I can to teach you the physics during the voyage." K't'lk's chiming had a tentative sound to it. "It may stretch you a little—"

"So it may. But I canna rest till I understand at least the equations." Scotty shook his head again, looking utterly perplexed. "I don't see how you derived this beastie from them. Or even what they do! They don't seem to do *anything*—"

"They don't," K't'lk said, warming to her subject. "They merely name the circumstances you wish to invoke. And the circumstances happen. That's 'creative physics.' "

"Magic, that's what it sounds like," Scotty said, a touch sourly.

"So it does. Why are you so surprised? One of your own people independently codified the Third Law of Ordinance some time back; Clerk, I think his name was. Or Clark. 'Any science sufficiently advanced will be indistinguishable from magic.' Which leads directly to T'Laea's Corollary—"

"K't'lk, please, save it for later," Jim said as gently as he could. "Are we ready to go?"

"Yes, we are. All you need to do is take us a hundred lightyears out or so, and hold an even keel while we make the transit, so as not to complicate the vector equations."

"Done." Jim turned to head for the Bridge, and then stopped and glanced back at the innocent-looking box sitting there on the engine room floor. The memory of that unsettling visual from the briefing was nagging him. "Is there any chance we could get a visual of it working during the jumps, for reference purposes?"

"Why not?" Scotty said. "I'll see to it."

"Would you like to see it now?" K't'lk said.

Jim was surprised. "Wouldn't we have to jump?"

K't'lk chimed. "No. It can be activated with no vector or acceleration added, as well as a large one." She went over to the box, reached up with a sharp shiny foreleg to touch a control pad set in the clear metal, and spoke a precise sequence of notes, quick and imperative.

And in the box, something happened—

(—a feeling like a shudder went through him. He stood frozen at the heart of the ship, unmoving; yet he also *was* the ship, all of it from this terrifying still core of *now*ness on out. His veins ran with electrons and coolant and artificial gravity; the bright web of tractors and the pale rain of radiation sleeting in from deep-space seared his eyes. Unseen, but felt, starlight hot with neutrinos burned his skin—)

"That's all there is," K't'lk said. Jim twitched, feeling suddenly released, though nothing had held him. "I think I missed it," he said—but his words sounded oddly tentative to him. He had seen something. He couldn't remember. He *thought* he'd seen something, anyway. "You people did take humans out on the test runs, didn't you?" Jim said slowly.

"Of course. They always missed it too, Captain."

Kirk nodded. "Well—Scotty, see to those holos. We'll be leaving on time."

"Aye, sir."

Jim Kirk headed for the doors, feeling as if there might just have been something wrong with him. He put a hand to his forehead and felt no fever. *Stage fright,* he told himself. *Get up on the Bridge where you belong and get this show on the road. The Galaxy is watching.*

But just being watched had never made him this nervous before. . . .

"Maiwhn ss'hv rhhaiuerieiu nn'mmhuephuit," Uhura said into the waiting silence of the Bridge, and touched a light to put the hushed circuit she'd been using on hold. "Captain? The ship reports secure. And Commodore Katha'sat says to send its good wishes."

"Acknowledge that. Thank it for me, and tell it I'll see it when I get my next pay raise. Not sooner."

Uhura nodded, a smile twisting her lips, and said another quiet sentence or so in Hestv before closing the channel down. "Base control signals ready to undock, Captain," Sulu said.

"Have them cast off at will, Mr. Sulu."

All around *Enterprise,* lines of light flicked out; all but one, attached to the tiny bright Hamalki tug and the secondary hull. This time K't'lk was not piloting. She stood glittering by the helm, watching the main screen narrowly, and absently rubbing together the two forelegs that now boasted bright enamel-and-metal bands, her commander's stripes. "That's Y'tk't, Captain," she said, "and her piloting's excellent, so I think I need not be here any longer. With your permission I'll go down and see to the inversion apparatus with Mt'gm'ry."

First names already? Kirk thought, amused. *Maybe it's a good thing she's not human. I'd hate to lose Scotty for paternity leave. . . .* "Go ahead, Commander."

She chimed off into the lift. Kirk sat quite calmly and watched the tug bring his ship about and head out the great irising opening, into clear space. The tug put a little boost on the starship, rather than leaving her to hang becalmed, so that she sailed off at a few tens of kilometers per hour and the StarBase tumbled on its way in the opposite direction behind her. "Last message from Base, Captain," Sulu said, and smiled a little. "The tug wishes us Goddess'-speed."

"Uhura, please acknowledge that with thanks. Mr. Chekov?"

"Distancing course locked in, Captain. One hundred thirty-seven lightyears on a bearing plus twenty-six minutes galactic by minus twenty-three degrees gallatitude, toward Acamar."

"Very good. Mr. Sulu, take us out past the warp-drive perimeter. Impulse power, one-third *c.*"

"Aye." The StarBase and yellow Hamal leaped away from them, seen in rear view—dwindled to a spark and a golden ball, shrank to a single fire.

"Scan, Mr. Chekov?" There was no need to say what he was interested in scanning for.

"Only local traffic, Captain. No company."

"Good. Keep your eyes open. Subspace detectors?"

"Hot, Captain."

"Weapons control?"

"Phasers are hot, sir. Torpedoes are charged."

Kirk punched the com button on his chair's arm. "Engineering—"

"Engine room aye," Scotty's voice said. His brogue was unusually pronounced. Jim smiled; if he was suffering from stage fright, he wasn't the only one. "How's your baby, Scotty?"

"On line and ready to implement."

"Good. Stand by. Spock?"

The Vulcan glanced up from his station with a look of utter calm that Jim read as fiercely controlled excitement. "All ship's sensors on 'record' for the first jump, Captain. From the off-Acamar position, one thousand five hundred eighty-six point three two lightyears to iota Sculptoris."

—and that was when ship's subspace and proximity detectors began whooping, and the computer went to red alert without asking for authorization first. "WARP INGRESS! WARP INGRESS!" the alarms shouted, and all around the Bridge people scrambled for battle stations. Kirk opened his mouth to shout "Report!" and was beaten to it.

"—helm on autoevade, Captain! Five Klingons—six —seven—"

—the screen went to superimposed tactical and tagged the ships popping out of warp all around *Enterprise:* KL 8 KAZA, KL 96 MENEKKU, KL 66 ENEKTI, KL 14 KJ'KHRRY, KL 55 KYTIN, KL 02 AMAK, KL 782 OKUV, KL 94 TUKAB—

"—no fire as yet, Captain. Trajectories indicate movement to englobe—"

"—Commander of *Kaza* on ship-to-ship, Captain. She orders us to surrender—"

"Pop us out, Mr. Sulu. Warp three—"

"Aye!" Sulu said, and kicked in the warp field. The stars went strange, then normal again as *Enterprise* left the ambushing Klingons in realspace. "Accelerate to warp six," Kirk said. "Standard evasion." *It's a bad situation. Eight to one now. And Base couldn't scramble us help fast enough to do anything—even if they had enough firepower there to make a difference. These guys don't want to hurt us—they want what we* have. *Yet if we run too well they'll just blow us up out of pique, knowing the Federation will build another of whatever we have. And we're outgunned—they've got those new hyperphasers. Damn! Even with Chekov shooting and Sulu at the helm, these are ridiculous—odds . . .* A thought started. Kirk stopped it half-formed. It gave him goosebumps.

More alarms sang through the Bridge. "They're in warp, Captain," Chekov said. "Warp two and gaining. Matching our evasion."

Pursuit came howling on their track, an octagon of pinpoints spreading out to begin a standard surround; four-up, four-down, a cube's vertices. *Running is silly. Shooting is silly. We need more firepower and there isn't any. How to buy us time—?!* "Mr. Chekov, photon torpedoes. Standard pursuit scatter. Empty the tubes."

"Yes sir," Chekov said, fingers dancing over the controls. If he had questions about the wisdom of using their whole supply of torpedoes before the engines could recharge the tubes for another salvo, he kept them to himself. Behind them the Klingons jostled about, firing ahead to predetonate the torpedoes. "Hard about," Kirk said, gripping his chair's arms harder than necessary, "and drop out of warp. Mr. Sulu, you play tank games, don't you?"

Sulu looked over his shoulder at the Captain in shock. "Sir! Yes sir—"

"Get it right this time," Jim said. He watched the sweat break out on Sulu's forehead as his helmsman realized both the direness of the situation and the opportunity ahead of him. "Aye," Sulu said, and the word sounded like a prayer. He hunched himself over his console and began to work.

The stars wobbled and wavered and went sane, and *Enterprise* popped out in empty space, dumping velocity at a rate that would normally have been impossible. Kirk glanced over at Spock's science screens and saw that Sulu had put the deflector shields up at full power a second before dropping out of warp, so that the shields were dumping the built-up kinetic energy as a blinding storm of hard radiation, everything from high ultraviolet to X rays and synchrotron radiation. *We're obvious as hell to anyone with sensors,* Jim thought unhappily—but he got a touch less unhappy as emergence alarms whooped again, and all around them Klingons popped out of warp and went shooting past, braking desperately, but not as effectively as Sulu. Kirk hit the com button again. "Engineering!"

"Scott here. What the devil's goin' on up there?"

"Company, Scotty. Can you channel all the power of the warp engines into the shields, except when we're in warp? We're going to be running on impulse in realspace for a while."

"All *the power?"* Scotty came as close to squeaking as Jim had ever heard him. From his post, Spock looked over at Kirk with an expression so incredulous (for a Vulcan) as to suggest he had just discovered his Captain playing with toy boats in the bathtub. Jim matched the expression look for look; Spock said nothing, turned back to his station. *"Aye,"* Scotty said from the engine room, *"but what are you going to—"*

"Play fox and hounds," Kirk said. "Bridge out. Mr. Sulu, evasive maneuvers at your discretion."

"Yes sir." The screen showed that one by one the Klingons were flipping end-for-end to brake, or arcing around in long deadly-graceful hyperbolas that would intersect with *Enterprise*'s course. Several had begun firing already in typical Klingon attack frenzy, though the fire wasn't very effective as yet; the distance-attenuated hyperphaser beams hit the shields and fizzled, their coherence easily disrupted. Sulu didn't run. He dumped more and more velocity, while Klingons streaked in closer and closer, and little by little the shields began to lose their blue-hot radiation fire and take on the angry red of splattering Klingon phasers that were becoming more effective by the moment. "Getting ready for warp, Captain," Sulu said. His face had acquired a fierce, closed look. "Pavel, find me a star of type F or above within twenty lightyears—"

Shock sang through Jim's blood. He sat straight up in his chair. "Hikaru, what do you have in mind?"

"Bova's Recourse, sir."

"Mr. Sulu," Jim said—as heads turned all around the Bridge—"—are you sure this is necessary?"

Sulu did not look away from his screen. "Captain," he said in the same tone of voice, "we can't keep this up forever. Do you have a better idea?"

Jim breathed in, breathed out, swallowed hard. "No. You call it. Find him the star, Mr. Chekov. Engineering!"

"Here, Captain," Scotty's voice said. *"Shield status is good so far. But the inversion drive is powered out of the warp system, and if all the power's bein' diverted, we canna—"*

"We can't anyway, Captain," K't'lk chimed in. *"The implement equations for the drive don't have all this swooping around vectored in. If we tried to jump, we could end up anywhere—"*

"Just stand by," Kirk said, sweating more, "and when I give you the word, be ready to implement fast. Out." The ship was practically at a standstill; the Klingons were screaming in at half a *c* or more. "Mr. Sulu—"

"Warp three *now,*" Sulu said, doing it, and space went bizarre. They were not alone for more than a few seconds—the Klingons' sensors were more than adequate to tracking another ship in warp, with the cloaking device up or not. *Enterprise* fled through the wavery starlight, accelerating. Her pursuers came hot behind, matching her acceleration, surpassing it, beginning to catch up. "What was the dump for, Mr. Sulu?" Kirk said, trying to sound absolutely casual.

"To get them angry, sir. Nothing upsets a Klingon more than the suspicion that he might not understand what his opponent's up to. They've all lost face in front of each other now. They'll be furious."

"Thanks very much, Mr. Sulu," Jim said with gentle irony, and by sheer force of will kept himself from getting up, going down to the helm console and fiddling with something. Sulu didn't need his distraction, or the implication that his Captain was nervous about what he was doing. Which his Captain was. Yet it was sound strategy, such as one might have expected from the best helm officer in the Fleet. *He can handle it, Jim. Let him do his job. You sit tight and do yours; look like you're not even worried—*

"Warp five," Sulu said. "Warp six." The engines began that familiar soft moan that not even upgrading had changed, an unnerving subharmonic vibration in the ship's durasteel bones. "Warp eight. Pavel, *where's my star??!*"

"If you are, as I think, looking for a star with no inhabited planets," Spock said calmly from his station without looking up, "109 Piscium is an A3 with some unstable lines in its spectrum."

"Thanks, Mr. Spock," Sulu said, and hit his communicator button. "All hands, prepare for dump from warp eight, and impulse maneuvers. Pavel, an open-ended course for 109 Piscium. Straight-in approach." Chekov nodded and began plotting the course. Kirk noticed with secret satisfaction that Chekov was sweating too—as well he might; the course Sulu had requested was not for orbit, but for collision. "Five seconds to realspace. Three. Two. One—"

—the shields went up and the warp field went down. Sensors were blinded, but Jim's unnerved imagination told him well enough what any observer would see: the *Enterprise* blasting out of nowhere, blazing brighter than any comet, as free-floating atoms and the electrons of the shields themselves were so fiercely excited by the warp-nine dump that they shattered completely in a hail of photons and negatrons and other bremsstrahlung radiation. *Anybody close enough to use sensors on us is going to have them burned out,* Jim thought with grim satisfaction. The emergence alarms told him that was happening right now, as *Kaza* and *Kytin* and *Menekku* and their brothers popped out of warp behind *Enterprise.* Kirk could almost hear the enraged screaming as instrumentation set to highest sensitivity for the detection of a ship fleeing through realspace was fried in a second. "Long-range sensing on pursuit ships is down, Captain," Spock said quietly. "Scan indicates they are dumping, and arming all weapons systems. Two ships are missing. I would suggest that *Amak* and *Enekti* are waiting to attack us in warp should we decide to reenter it—"

"Sounds reasonable. Mr. Sulu," Jim said, watching as the images of six very annoyed Klingon ships began on the screen to converge on their position, "do your stuff."

He did. It was terrifying. The Klingons made the velocities from their dumps last them as long as possible, instructing their battle computers to lay in courses that would intersect with *Enterprise*'s most likely one—a hurried vector away from them and into open space for a pop into warp, where *Amak* and *Enekti* lay in ambush. But *Enterprise* wasn't running her part of the battle according to the sensible, reasonable tactics they were expecting. Since nearly everyone in the Galaxy now had the Romulans' "cloaking device"—making it almost impossible to initially detect a ship in realspace, let alone bring it to battle there—the methodology of starship-level warfare had changed in recent years. Ships running almost entirely on instruments ambushed one another in warp, where the cloaking device didn't work, and fought whole battles there; or forced a ship in warp out into realspace, where running tended to be difficult for large ships and firepower was the determining criterion. *Enterprise,* though, wasn't following the rules. She would not fire. She would not duck into warp, however closely *Kaza* and his brother destroyers followed her. Instead she swooped and soared and dipped and rolled through realspace as if a suicidal maniac piloted her. The Klingons' battle computers didn't have the necessary protocols programmed into them for this kind of realspace fighting; no one could get close enough for even hyperphaser fire to pierce those shields powered by the whole unreserved output of an undamaged warp drive. Anyone who tried soon enough heard the sound of screaming, overstressed metal in his ship's structure, and fell back to a saner, straighter pursuit, swearing—

Kirk gripped his command chair's arms and wished he had such an option. Sulu had called up readouts on the screen for figures on the centrifugal and centripetal forces the ship was experiencing—readouts no different from those he had been reading in the tank game. *When he blew the ship up,* Jim thought, starting to twitch. He hardly needed the readouts, as the screen went through that crazy roll-yaw-tumble sequence, and his stomach tried to drop out of him despite gravity's reassurances that everything was all right. The intercom whistled in the middle of the mad chase, and *"What're ye crazy people doin' to my ship??!"* Scotty hollered.

"Keeping it in one piece, Mr. Scott."

"I dinna think that's funny, Captain! Much more o' this and we won't make it to the next star, let alone the next galaxy—"

The screen was beginning to agree with him. PORT NACELLE STRESS TOLERANCES IN VIOLATION, it flashed as Sulu snapped *Enterprise* leftward and "downward" in the beginning of a wicked roll, then up again, aborting the roll and leaving behind him *Menekku* and *Tukab,* who had been closing on *Enterprise* from either side and now found themselves on intersecting collision courses. They peeled hastily away from each other, then streaked along for a second or so without initiating new courses. Spock, watching the bright lines of plotted courses on one of his screens, looked over at Kirk. "Elements of arcs are changing, Captain. I believe the Klingons have gone off computers to manual pursuit, seeing that standard battle programming has proved ineffective."

"Good," Kirk said. It was old Academy wisdom that anyone who tried to fly a space battle by the seat of its pants was certifiable for reconditioning. *Wonderful,* he thought, looking at Sulu, who was hunched over his helm console, fingers dancing over it and hammering at it like those of a frustrated keyboard artist performing a particularly demanding piece. The helmsman hardly looked up at the screen except to notice the centrifugal/centripetal readouts. Klingons were catching up to them again, flying peculiar courses that lacked the perfect grace and symmetry of the usual computer-coordinated attack formation. Sulu let them gather, let them run hot behind *Enterprise* for a few moments; then without warning flipped her end-for-end, letting forward thrust act as a brake, and threw her right at the heart of their ragged formation, where *Kaza* was flying point—

Jim held his chair hard and kept his mouth shut while the screen screamed PORT AND STARBOARD NACELLE STRESS TOLERANCES CRITICALLY VIOLATED, ABORT MANEUVER!, and *Kaza*'s image swelled on visual, a huge, grim, gray bird spitting phaser fire. *They've gone completely nuts,* he thought, *they're going to ram*—and he was just opening his mouth to shout "Abort it!!" when the bird showed *Enterprise* its belly and the undersides of nacelle-wings, veering upward and away, coughing impotent photon torpedoes at them from fore and aft tubes as *Kaza* ran. The torpedoes were no threat with the screens fully powered as they were. "Prepare for warp," Sulu said then, and Kirk swallowed, suspecting what was coming. "Three to five episodes of warp without dumping. Chekov, you have that course for me?"

"Yes, Mr. Sulu."

"Engineering?"

"*Aye, Mr. Sulu,*" Scotty's voice said, sounding as if he was planning to have a long talk with the helm officer after things quieted down.

"Lock the inversion drive into Mr. Chekov's computer. I'll give you three seconds' warning of vector and acceleration for your implement. That be enough?" His voice was calm. Behind *Enterprise*, the Klingons were coming about, leaping after her again.

"*Two would be enough.*"

"Noted. Warp three *now,*" he said, and the image on the screen rippled like water and steadied. *Good,* Kirk thought, watching speed and course. *Not so slowly that they'll suspect anything, not so fast that their damaged instrumentation will lose us*— One Klingon popped in,

Kaza; another, *Menekku;* from ahead, *Amak* and *Enekti* swooped in, firing. Sulu grinned like a shark and threw the *Enterprise* straight at *Enekti*, the biggest. For a terrible few seconds it swelled and the screens splattered red with its phaser fire—but then it veered off as hastily as *Kaza* had. No one was crazy enough to chance a full-speed impact in otherspace.

Sulu, however, wasn't letting *Enekti* off. He went after him, ran right up his tail, seemingly ignoring the seven Klingons chasing after the two of them at a slowly increasing and respectful distance. *Enekti* fired at him aft, both torpedoes and phasers, to little effect, and dodged and wheeled crazily in an attempt to shake Sulu. It didn't work. The forward rim of *Enterprise*'s primary hull was less than five kilometers behind *Enekti*'s rear end, and Sulu held her there as if the two ships were connected by tractors. He had status estimates displaying now on the stresses experienced by the Klingon ship, and, as Jim might have expected, they didn't look good. After all, a Klingon battleship was built heavy on firepower and speed, not so much for maneuvering—their fighting style being biased more toward sudden surprise attacks, running down and gunning down an opponent, and disdaining the subtleties of swift maneuvering as a sign of weakness. *Enekti*'s structural status was poor and getting poorer as his helm officer, not as used to independent option as Sulu, ran terrified in front of *Enterprise*, turning and banking and having every move matched. And then *Enekti* made one move, a sharp "downward" arc that for some reason made Kirk's stomach lurch. Sulu didn't follow, but circled "upward" and away at warp five. And behind them, they saw *Enekti*'s maneuver shear off his port nacelle. A second later, what was left of the ship bloomed into white fire as suddenly uncontained matter and antimatter spectacularly annihilated one another.

"Prepare for realspace," Sulu said. "Pavel, have

your computer talk to the helm. I'm going to hop once or twice more, and then I want to come out four lightseconds from the star. No farther."

Chekov turned pale as paste, clenched his jaw and began setting it up. Kirk nodded slowly to no one in particular. The only thing that had been missing from this encounter—the one thing that would make sure the Klingons followed the *Enterprise* as closely as they possibly could—was blood. "Drop warp *now.*"

Space wavered, settled. Klingons erupted into it behind them, gaining fast. "Message from *Kaza,* Captain," Uhura said quietly. "They advise us to kill our helm officer and send him or her before us, so the Black Fleet will know what ship's crew to expect."

"Thank you. Mr. Sulu," the Captain said, "I think you've just been complimented."

"Thank you, Captain. Warp two, now—"

—and space shook again. Behind them, the Klingons got closer as Sulu used the warp field now to dump some of his velocity. *Kaza* and *Menekku* and *Amak* were now within effective attack range, and their phasers dyed the whole rear area of the shields and warp field with bloody fire. "Shield overload imminent," Spock said from his station, as if announcing the weather.

"Noted. How close are the leading three?" Sulu said.

"Point two five lightyears, and closing fast."

"Good. Last hop, Pavel. Engineering, on my mark we will drop warp and exit into realspace at .9 c. You will then have three seconds to implement inversion."

"*At plus three seconds, aye,*" Scotty said.

"Pavel?"

"109 Piscium on visual. Positive lock." One star at the screen's center grew magnitudes brighter with every breath. "Six lightyears. Two. Point five. Klingons at two lightmonths, twelve lighthours, ninety lightminutes, ten lightminutes, thirty-five lightseconds, twelve, two, a hundred fifty thousand kilometers, thirty thousand kilometers, fifteen—shields critical—"

"Realspace mark," Sulu said. There was 109 Piscium, a Sun-sized white star with the barest touch of yellow, a raging globe licked with prominences and spattered with spots. Behind *Enterprise* Klingons were popping out into realspace—and Jim could practically hear the shouts of horror on their bridges as they realized the trick being played them, and struggled to react fast enough to escape with their lives. *Amak* and *Menekku* went screaming off at crazy angles to avoid dumping into the star—not warping out, for no one went into warp closer to a star than eighty times its diameter. That was a good way to have it go nova, and a nova's cataclysmic effects reached even into otherspace, destroying any ship within range as certainly as in realspace. *Amak* turned too sharply and ruptured itself, letting loose another blinding flower of fire that continued along the same course like a disastrous comet. *Kytin* and *Kj'khrry* swerved more safely, fleeing in opposite directions into the dark, striving for enough distance to get out of there into warp. *Okuv,* unable to stop, streaked into the star, a drop of fire in a sea of it, unremarked. *Tukab* followed it. Only *Kaza* still ravened behind *Enterprise,* firing everything at once, phasers, torpedoes, knowing themselves doomed and not giving up. "Plus one second," Sulu said, "plus two—"—and dropped *Enterprise* into warp, at warp nine.

When a star goes nova, there are parts of the process that for a brief period surpass the speed of light, and crack easily into those nearby universes, such as otherspace, where light moves faster. *Enterprise* had been barely three-quarters of a million miles from 109 Piscium at the furthest, no more than a half million miles distant when she ducked back into warp. Now, racing through otherspace at her highest speed, her scanners clearly showed the rippling of space close behind her on the borders of the universe she had just left, as if she were a swimmer looking up at the water's surface from beneath it after a dive. The screen showed the rippling hitting the star they had left behind. They saw the star itself distend and writhe frightfully in the grip of the shredding space that held it. Saw the star blow, an explosion like the universe ripping open to reveal its first moment of existence, the light that was all there was. They saw the effect of the explosion coming after them, faster than light could in that other universe, warp two and accelerating, a globular pseudo-surface of deadly, searing fire that made the sensors back themselves hurriedly down like eyes squeezed shut. Warp three, warp five, the fire chased them, reaching out to eat them in this space as it had inexorably eaten the Klingons in the other. Spock, watching on his own screens the splendid destruction ravening in their wake, spoke softly to his computer, instructing it to notify the Interstellar Astronomical Union as soon as possible of a change in the status of 109 Piscium. The destruction reached out for them. Warp seven—

"Plus three," Sulu said.

"Inversion drive implement," Scotty said from Engineering.

And the nova, and otherspace, and even *Enterprise* herself, went out—

Five

It was dark. No sound reached Jim, no sensation. His body was gone. His mind struggled in the darkness like a limed bird, to no avail. Without sound being involved, somewhere someone was screaming—a horrible, anguished, terrified howl of inconsolable loss, that went on and on forever. It couldn't have been him: he was choking, trying to breathe with lungs that weren't there. *Death, that's what it is, we're all dying—*

The darkness didn't stop. But something else about it became evident, as if he simply had been too preoccupied to notice. The darkness had stars in it. And he had a body again. She thrust along through the cold night, feeling the small stretches and contractions of her skin as she leaned away from the planet she had been orbiting, and the heat of its primary on her diminished. Soon enough, now, would come the deep dive into that place where starlight was stronger stuff, where the wine of it would run white-hot through her and free her for speeds she could never achieve in this calmer world.

Then the true life would begin again. These tame circlings about planets were never more than times of rest between the real adventures. The great joy lay in streaking outward, forever and forever, bathed in strange starlight; in passing through the waste places in strength, exulting in her swiftness and her power, dealing with what she found.

And since the joy, unshared, would have been empty, she had chosen companions who adventured during her times of rest, and rested while she adventured. They complemented her well. That was to be expected, for she had chosen them with great care. They desired the darkness as she did, though admittedly on a smaller scale. And even that would change some day. Some of them had the seeds of the Great Desire in them already, to love the journey not so much for the achievement of some purpose, as for the journey itself. Several of them in particular were gradually coming to that state, the ones who sat oftenest at her heart, and knew her will best—especially the chief of them, whom she was slowly training up in the way he should go. To her delight, her exaltation, he was learning. He had come to be aware of her selfness, to know her, in the small shadowy way of her children. He would know her better yet. She would teach him everything there was. She would raise him up to be the equal of one of her own kind. And then—then—

—then Jim found himself back in his seat again, shaking all over. Emergence alarms were whooping all around him, and his people were looking frantically around the Bridge like statues suddenly come to life. "Status!" Jim said, and counted himself lucky that the word came out as a shout and not a squeak.

"We are undamaged, Captain," Spock's voice came, calm as always, from his station. "The Damage Control computers never even activated."

Jim turned to Uhura. "Injuries?"

Uhura took the transdator out of her ear with the air of a woman being yammered at. "None, sir. But the crew is very upset. Whatever they were expecting inversion to be like, it wasn't *that.*"

"I can't blame them," Jim said. He was still deep in that feeling he had first experienced when K't'lk showed him the drive running, with the difference that this time he remembered something of what had happened to him. "Tell them we'll put a report out on ship's channels as soon as we figure out what happened."

"And where we are," Uhura said, glancing at the front viewscreen.

Jim looked too, and agreed. "Mr. Sulu, Mr. Chekov," he said, "I thought you had a course set for the iota Sculptoris system. I've been there. This is *not* it."

It certainly was not. Iota Sculptoris was a tame little M2 star with several subspace relay stations in orbit. Whatever the star was that hung centered and blazing in the viewscreen, it was *not* tame. It was a white giant, so violently luminous even at this distance that the screen had already backed itself down to minimum intensity and was reading out warnings of imminent sensor overload. *Enterprise* was coasting around it in a wide-mouthed hyperbola at about .2 *c,* so that it was easy to see the concentric globular shells of luminous gas in which the star was nested—shells shading from incandescent violet nearest the star to a deep, eye-searing indigo furthest out. The surrounding starfield wasn't dull either; nearspace for parsecs around was littered with blue and blue-white giants, a scattered splendor of burning gems. But the blinding white terror about which *Enterprise* swung put them all to shame. "Is that what I think it is?" Jim said.

"A Wolf-Rayet star, Captain," Spock said. "There is not one in the whole Federation—or, for that matter, within the range of the longest-range survey ship we have. Our presence here tells us we are a long way from home. But we are also most fortunate, for no Federation ship has ever been this close to one. It would be a great loss to science if we did not stay long enough to take some measurements."

"Get a spectrum on it," Jim said to Sulu. "If it's one that's been detected from home, we can use it to determine our position."

"Aye, sir."

Jim turned back toward Spock, noticing with idle amusement that, behind him, Sulu was betting Chekov that he could tell which star it was without looking in the catalog. Chekov took the bet. "Mr. Spock," Jim said, "if I understand the nature of these stars, this is not exactly a safe place for us to loiter. All those shells are supposed to be what's left of large portions of the star's atmosphere, which it blows off every now and then. With considerable force, I might add—look at the blueshift on that inside shell! Not to slight Mr. Sulu's efforts, but I think I've had enough novae for one day. If that thing gets cranky and decides to go off while we're here—"

"The odds are against it, Captain."

"That's what they said about Pompeii," Jim said, not reassured. "And look at *them.* You can. In museums."

"It's zeta-10 Scorpii, Captain," Sulu said. Out of the side of his mouth, and more quietly, he said to Chekov, "Pay me."

"I'll have it for you Twosday."

"This is most remarkable, Captain," Spock said. "This datum indicates that we have been flung approximately 5700 lightyears—nearly a twentieth of the diameter of the Galaxy—along a heading almost diametrically opposite to the one laid in. Right across both the Federation and the Klingon Empire, in fact, and into space as yet unexplored by any species we know.

This is another excellent reason for us to remain here for a short time. We will have access to views of the Galactic Core that have never been available, due to the presence of interstellar dust—"

"Which brings up another interesting question," Jim said, and hit the communicator button on his chair. "Engineering!"

"Scott here."

"Scotty, are the engines all right?"

"Oh, aye, Captain, the engines are working—but I dinna know why."

"Are *you* all right, Scotty?"

"Aye. My brains are still spinnin', but at least they're doin' it in the right direction now."

"Yours, maybe. But K't'lk's? Where is she?"

Chimes rattled. *"Here, Captain."*

"I thought we were supposed to be going to iota Sculptoris, Commander."

"So we were, sir. Evidently, however, Mr. Sulu's nova had other plans for us. Though we stabilized the ship's course, the star's explosion imparted a great deal of energy to us, and recomplicated the vector equations thereby—"

"Transmission of shock wave through the interstellar medium," Spock said from his station. "Normally that is impossible—hard vacuum does not transmit conventional shock waves. But when a nova explodes, near-space for several astronomical units around can be full of its liberated atmosphere within seconds. It's been postulated that otherspace may be similarly affected; gravity waves and other such 'sub-etheric' disturbances can theoretically be propagated in such a fashion, affecting us even in warp. I suspect we now have confirmation for that theory."

"Wonderful. The nova kicked us in the pants."

"Precise in mood, if not in particulars," K't'lk said.

Her chiming sounded sour, as if she considered the malfunctioning of her drive a slur on her personally.

"Scotty, are the warp engines all right?"

"Well, damage control didna report anything. But computers have blind spots. Captain, I dinna know what the time parameters are on the orders Starfleet gave you. But would it be violatin' them much to give me a little down time so that I can check my puir bairns—I mean, the warp drive, and the impulse engines, my ownself? We did a lot of wild swoopin' about in the neighborhood of 109 Piscium."

"No question about that. I think we can manage it. How much time do you need?"

"A day would be good."

Aaaaagh! Jim thought. *I was all ready for the big jump, and now this!!* "A day it is. But make it count, Scotty! Another case of transitus interruptus like this, and *my* vector equations may need checking." Jim let out a long breath. "I tell you, I'm not happy about the stroke of luck that landed us here next to a Wolf-Rayet star, however rare and interesting it is—"

"I don't think luck had much to do with it, Captain," K't'lk said.

"Nor do I, sir," Spock said. He was looking at his station's screens with that expression that Kirk knew from old: utter fascination. "I have been examining the spectra of 109 Piscium that we took before we left its neighborhood, and the spectrum of zeta-10 Scorpii here. There are some intriguing correlations. I shall pursue them further. But I would suggest that the inversion drive's vector equations were deranged slightly by the presence of the nova in both realspace and subspace, so that it 'sorted' for an energy source of roughly equivalent type. And here we are. A Wolf-Rayet star, after all, can be considered as a kind of very restrained, irregular nova—"

"It's the irregularity that worries me," Jim said. For a moment he just sat and gazed out at the frightful blaze of zeta-10 Scorpii, that hung there nested in its concentric, fiery shells like some god's resplendent version of an ancient Terran-Chinese carved toy. "No matter. We'll stay and take your pictures, at least for a little while—heaven forbid I should ignore astronomical research on this mission! First things first, though. K't'lk, can you keep the drive from getting deranged again?"

"Surely, Captain. It's a minor adjustment, like many others we had to make during testing—though we had little chance for this particular problem to come up." Her chiming sounded cheerful again. *"No matter. I'll soon have it debugged."*

Jim smiled and said nothing as to the cause. "Fine. Proceed. And Scotty, don't start a major overhaul! If this star cries Wolf, we may have to get out of here in a hurry. K't'lk, how long will your repairs take?"

"I'll be done with my revisions to the drive long before Mt'gm'ry's finished with his 'poor barns', Captain. Three hours maximum."

"*'Bairns,"* Scotty said firmly.

"Oh. Thank you. . . ."

"Execute, then. Kirk out."

Jim sat back in the command seat and exhaled. There was nothing left to do now but wait—and think what inversion had been like.

That was even worse than waiting. It was almost his offshift anyway—and he needed someone to talk to. "Mr. Sulu," he said, "plot us a nice, wide orbit around that thing. And put our screens up so that as little energy leaves this ship as possible. If I've got to stay in this neighborhood, I want to tiptoe around that star and not do anything that might wake it up. Spock, the conn's yours for the moment. Are you about to go offshift?"

"I am so scheduled, Captain." Spock was intent on his screens. "But these spectra—"

Jim knew fascination when he saw it. "Do what needs to be done about the spectra, Spock. And put a watch on that star—I don't want it to so much as burp without being notified. I'm going to get some lunch. When you're free, if that's this shift, I'll be eating in the officers' lounge if you care to join me."

He got up from the command chair and headed left as Spock stepped down from his right and seated himself—their old habit of shift relief, half dance and half wordless joke; but Jim didn't even need to look at Spock to know his mind was far from the joke right now. "Mz. Uhura," he was saying as the lift's doors opened for Jim, "be so good as to call Stellar Dynamics and have them begin analysis on the data running at my station, with emphasis on the relationships among the hydrogen lines. See if Mr. Benford is onshift at the moment—"

The doors slid closed. "Deck six," Jim said, and heard echoes in his mind, and wondered why. The beginnings of misgivings were coming up.

I wanted *this drive. Why am I so nervous?*

For once Jim had no eyes for the window in the officers' lounge, despite the radiant view outside. He managed to get a good part of his steak down before the ship's computer spoke softly to him, telling him that Spock had logged off the Bridge and had instructed the lift to drop him at deck six. Jim bolted the rest of the steak, had the table dispose of it, and was working on a salad when Spock came quietly in.

"May I join you, sir?"

Jim waved a forkful of greenery in invitation. Spock sat down, touched the pressure-sensitive area on the table that brought up the menu, eyed it, spoke a letter-and-number combination. The table's transporter materialized another salad—Boston lettuce from the looks of it, with odd yellow objects scattered through it. Jim looked at them curiously as Spock started eating. "Something Vulcan?"

Spock shook his head, finished his bite. "Terran, originally; a variant form grown on McDade. Xanthopipericum flagrantum Ellison. It was once referred to as 'Sechuan Death,' though I—"

Jim waved away the explanation. "Later for botany, Spock. You look preoccupied. What is it with the spectra, anyway?"

"Irregularities," Spock said. "The problem is more easily demonstrated than discussed. Screen," he said to the table. It stopped pretending to be Sargolian redwood and faded to black. "Science station readout," Spock said, and added a string of numbers. "Authorization," said the table. Spock laid his hand on the screen. It read it, then displayed four sets of spectra—strips of rainbow light, and assortments of bright colored lines.

"The most intriguing part of the problem," Spock said, "lies in the fact that no two novae ever go off in exactly the same way. Some of them go this way and that"—he indicated one set of data, the few scattered bright lines of an "emission" spectrum and the dark-lined rainbow strip of an "absorption" spectrum—"while another star, seemingly no different from the first, will go that way and this." He pointed at the second set of spectra, in which both bright and dark lines were shifted much further into the blue. "But by and large, the actual nova event will conform to one of these two sets of patterns. Now this one," Spock said, pointing at a new specimen that appeared near the top of the screen, "is the catalog spectrum of 109 Piscium, the one in our files. This one"—he indicated another—"is the one our computer obtained when it made its initial lock on the star from ten lightyears out. And *this* one the computer took just before Mr. Sulu threw the ship into warp practically in the star's corona. He is to be commended, by the by, for the foresight he displayed in thinking to have the computer do this while he was already so thoroughly occupied."

Spock set his salad aside, out of the way of the next set of spectra that came up beside the first one. "Now these, Captain, are of zeta-10 Scorpii. Note how the spectrum is severely blue-shifted, as in that last spectrum of 109 Piscium. The cause is the motion of those shells of gas you were concerned about. Here again are the catalog spectra, and the ones Mr. Sulu took on our arrival. Can you see the alteration in the positions and relationships of the lines in the brightline spectra? It is most subtle."

"I can see it, barely," Jim said. "But what does it mean?"

"Captain," Spock said, "there is one confirmed common factor, one outside effect present while each of these stars was in the process of going, or in zeta-10's case, 'almost-going' nova. *We* were there."

Jim nodded slowly. "But how can a starship possibly affect a star?"

"The way we affected 109 Piscium, for one," said Spock. "But this alteration is something different—subtler, as I said, and at the same time most alarming. The situation is not made simpler by the fact that this ship is carrying apparatus not carried before by any other. I discard as irrelevant the effect of our warp drive as a cause for these changes; we have never come near the warp-effect boundary while in the neighborhood of zeta-10 Scorpii. But I would give a great deal for a spectrum of that star near Rasalgethi by which K't'lk emerged, one taken at the time of her emergence. Two such occurrences might be coincidence, though I would give you long odds against it. But three—"

Two occurrences, Jim thought. "Spock," he said, "may I ask you something in confidence?"

Spock put up an eyebrow, tapped the table to vanish the rainbow strips of the spectra and turn it to redwood again. "Captain, I am at your disposal."

"Did you experience any—odd effects—during the inversion transit?"

Spock put down his fork and leaned on his elbows, steepling his fingers in that characteristic meditative gesture of his. "Captain," he said, "it is partly for that reason that I came so quickly from the Bridge. I have been seriously considering declaring myself unfit for duty, secondary to such an occurrence. I believe I am even ready to speak to Dr. McCoy about it."

Jim nodded, being most careful to keep his face still. He wasn't going to add to Spock's distress by letting either surprise or amusement at that last statement show. "Might one ask—"

"One might," Spock said. He paused for a few breaths' space, not looking at Jim. "I experienced a most—unnerving—sense of the loss of time. Unnerving in its literal definition, for all bodily sensation was absent. But the loss of duration was the most prominent effect, and the distress it caused was considerable." Spock's eyes snapped back into here-and-now, and he looked at Jim. "As might be expected, for by our definitions, life needs time to move through, or it is not life."

Jim nodded. *That was what the screaming was,* he thought. *My mind screaming for time, where there was none, the way lungs scream for oxygen in a vacuum. You breathe and breathe but it does you no good—*"I experienced something similar," he said. "'Distress' is a mild word for it. I had more than that, though."

Spock lifted an eyebrow at Jim, waiting. Jim hesitated, somewhat embarrassed now that he had come right down to it. "It was—I was the ship. Without there actually being thought—at least what I would have called thought—there was sentience. A sense of incredible power, of strength and swiftness—and of self-assurance, without there really being a self. A yearning outward. A delight in the yearning. An unshakeable sense of *purpose,* taken for granted the way we expect to keep on breathing. It was almost—" and he hunted for words—"—almost an apotheosis of mechanicity, if that makes any sense. It doesn't make much sense to *me.*" A breath of laughter escaped Jim. "I've always thought of myself, in terms of the ship, as if I were a possessor. But the ship didn't—doesn't see it that way. I may be the possessed. . . ."

"Fascinating." Spock was still a moment, then said, "Captain, have you ever been to the beta Pavonis system? The fourth planet out?" Jim shook his head; he had heard of the place in his studies, but even the most active commander never got to see a hundredth of the known worlds. "The primary is ordinary enough, a type A5. But the third planet is ringed. Dawn in its supraequatorial regions is a most intriguing phenomenon. In the heart of night, the sky is wholly black. But as the terminator approaches a point on the ground, the rings stand up blue and green in the east like the shard of a curved sword. They grow, they arch over the sky. Then the sun comes up, and the blue and green blaze silver against orange heaven—"

This time the surprise at Spock's sudden poetic turn of phrase was harder to conceal, but Jim managed it. "Spock, I think you lost me. Does your last visit to beta Pavonis have something to do with your, ah, experience?"

"It does indeed, Captain," Spock said, looking at him with the faintest touch of unease. "I have never been to beta Pavonis IV."

Jim closed his mouth.

"Nor am I likely to be there in the future," Spock

said. "The planet was surveyed thirty-four standard years ago and immediately placed on interdict status 5b/r for a minimum of two hundred years—"

"Religious warfare," Jim said. "No contact whatever until the situation resolves itself—"

"Yes. Yet I was there," Spock said, his eyes going distant again. "We were encamped by the hundreds of thousands on a great barren plain, waiting for the battle to begin—waiting for a sign. The sword came up in the east, and we were ready. But the sign came otherwise than we expected. It rained stars. We ran across the field to where our enemies were encamped and embraced them, our brothers—"

Jim saw Spock's hands trembling where they were laced together, saw Spock stop them from trembling. "It was a most—emotional—experience, being there when peace broke out. Experiencing the overwhelming relief, the . . . joy." The Vulcan's eyes came back to here-and-now again. "Then the experience ceased and I found myself at my post, completing the instructions I had begun giving my library computer before we entered transit."

Jim asked the table for a mug of hot tea and sipped it a moment in silence. "Could it have been a mind-link of some sort?"

"I think it unlikely, considering the range. So, sir, with your permission I think I had best go submit myself to the Doctor's ministrations—"

"Half a moment," Jim said, touching Spock's arm to keep him from getting up. "Com function," he said to the table. "Sick Bay."

"McCoy."

Bones sounded disgruntled. Jim was surprised at that, and (to a lesser extent) by one of the voices talking animatedly in the background, a voice he didn't recognize. Jim realized instantly that it was one of the replacement crew; when one is shut up with only four hundred people for long periods of time, every voice becomes familiar. But he put his curiosity aside for the moment. "Bones, I had an interesting experience during that transit—"

"You too, huh?" McCoy sounded thoughtful. *"I thought maybe it was just me. . . ."*

"No. Others have had it. I want everyone in the crew who had anything like it checked."

"Give the order," McCoy said, *"I'm not going anywhere anyway. Damn paperwork! And another thing, Jim—"*

"Save it, I'll stop by. Kirk out." Jim looked at Spock. "Care to accompany me?"

"Yes, Captain. Though I must still declare myself unfit for—"

"Oh, Spock, put a field around it. I'll lay you long odds that everyone in the ship had unsettling experiences like ours. And besides—since your experience occurred in zero time, nothing can have happened to you—because 'happening' requires duration, and there is no duration in zero time. Starfleet is hardly going to be concerned about something that never happened. Neither am I. So what are you worrying about?"

Spock looked sidewise at his Captain with the old good-humored glint in his eye as they stood up. "The fact that I am still left with the experience. However, that was neatly reasoned, Captain. You are becoming adept at getting paradox to serve your turn."

"Well, isn't it the Vulcans who say that the doors of truth are guarded by Paradox and Confusion . . . and that if you attempt to handle them by turning your back on them, the truth will remain closed behind you?"

"If we did not say it," Spock said soberly, but without that glint leaving his eye, "I will see to it that we do from now on."

"You do that. Let's get down to Sick Bay."

Six

Jim called the Bridge from the turbolift to give the order for affected crew to report to Sickbay. When he came off the allcall channel, Uhura said to him, "Captain, Mr. Scott just called in with a status report on his checks. He'd like to see you at your earliest convenience."

The lift slowed and stopped at Deck Four. Spock looked at Jim. "You go ahead," Jim said. "Catch Bones before the rush starts. I'll be along." Spock nodded and stepped out of the lift. "Engineering," Jim said.

When the lift doors opened again, Jim saw with mild amusement that there were crewmen running all over the department, up and down between the various levels, looking slightly frantic. It wasn't a good sign—there was probably something wrong with the engines—but Jim had always found it a little funny that Scotty's crews picked up and expressed the exasperation Scotty hardly ever let out. He walked in, and heard Scotty's voice and K't'lk's chiming echoing up from one of the lower levels. Jim headed down toward them.

"—no, Mt'gm'ry. Let's try it this way. There are three physical 'dimensions,' right? Each generated out of the one before it. Of course there are more, but we're working with a tridimensional paradigm for the moment; it's easiest to handle. So: length, breadth, height or depth. Now once you've postulated physical existence, you can also have motion through it. That's what we use to define the next function—"

"Time."

"Right. There are three dimensions of that too—and, again, potentially many more—each also generated by the one before it. In the three-dimensional paradigm those are inception, duration, and termination. Or you could call them creation, preservation, destruction. All right so far? Good. So once you've postulated physical things, and time, then the physical things can begin affecting one another. So there's another set of functions for which your physics doesn't seem to have precisely congruent terms. You could call these functions aspects of 'relatedness.' The closest equivalents in your language would be 'affectedness,' 'effectiveness,' and 'cause'—"

"Wait a moment, lassie. I thought cause came before effect."

"Sometimes it does. But I wouldn't depend on it."

There was a pause. "I think you lost me again."

"Me too," Jim said, coming down to their level on the little railed lift-platform.

"Captain," Scotty said, sounding slightly relieved that the lesson had been interrupted. "I didna think ye'd be down here so soon."

Trouble for sure, Jim thought, hearing the brogue so thick. "Engine problems, Scotty?"

"Aye. Look here." Scotty stepped over to a console,

keyed it for structural analysis readout, and moved a little to one side so that Jim could see. "There's a weak area in the port nacelle's interaction-confinement vessel. I dinna know for sure where we picked it up—though odds are good it was durin' that crazy point-nine-cee dump Mr. Sulu put us through. What bothers me, though, is that the damage control computers didna pick it up."

Jim looked at the readout, a graphic of a microcrystalline X-ray scan of the nacelle, and nodded. He kept his external calm, but inside he shook. The superhard iridium-rhodium hull plating had simply begun to unravel. Millions of the bonds of its single long-chain crystal were shattered, so that there was a huge crack-shaped weakness right down the nacelle's length for many meters. "If we'd tried to go into warp with that the way it is," Jim said, almost absently, "we'd be so much spacedust right now."

"Aye, Captain."

Jim turned away from the readout. "How long will it take to fix?"

"Not much longer than my original estimate. We'll have to go out and reweave the metal, but we're equipped for that. Meanwhile I'll have other checks running. And Captain, if I may say so, best you have the computers looked at too. Damage control should never have missed that flaw."

"I'll speak to Mr. Spock." Jim reached out and patted Scotty on the shoulder. "Well done, Scotty. You keep listening to your hunches on this trip."

"That I will, sir."

"And how about you?" Jim said, looking down at K't'lk. "Is the drive repaired?"

"Indeed yes," K't'lk chimed. "It was a half hour's work, if that. The relationship equations were biased by the nova toward increased affectedness, that's all—"

"Right," Jim said hurriedly. "Save it a second. Scotty, I forgot to ask. While we were in transit—did you have any odd—sensations, experiences—"

Scotty looked at Jim in a mixture of relief and alarm. "Aye," he said in the voice of a man telling the strict truth and wishing he could do otherwise. "But I dinna think it was anything serious—"

"Neither do I. Still, go see McCoy. Everyone else will be, too, I think. Best get there early and avoid the rush. And have any of your crew who were affected get down there too, when they can."

"Some of them have gone already, sir. We heard the order. As soon as my crew chiefs have the reweaving well under way, I'll go up mysel'."

"Good. As you were, then." Scotty headed off, shouting energetically for one of his lieutenants. Jim watched him for a moment in satisfied amusement, then glanced down at K't'lk. "You two seem to be getting along well."

"He is one of the best Terran engineers I've met," she said, "and I've met quite a few. He seems to have mastered the knack of truly *seeing* other-species design from the inside, which is a rare gift. His interest in my people's physics is a symptom of that, I think. And he cannot stop wanting to know. It's an honorable trait."

"This ship is full of honor, then," Jim said a bit dryly. They began to stroll through Engineering together. "Did you notice any effects during transit, Commander?"

She shook herself, making a chiming shrug as she picked her way delicately along beside him. "No, I seem to have missed the excitement again. I think my species must be either resistant or blind to the effect—none of my Hamalki colleagues ever mentioned any such occurence during the tests. The Terrans sometimes seemed shocked or surprised after inversion, but that always passed quickly; none of them ever mentioned experiencing anything peculiar. And the Vulcans showed no sign of any problem at all."

Like Spock on the bridge this morning, Jim thought. "Walk down to Sickbay with me if you're free, Commander," he said as the Engineering doors slid open for them.

"Certainly. But Captain, feel free to call me by my name. Unless you think it will compromise discipline among your officers."

"Oh, discipline must be maintained at all costs," Jim said, doing his best to keep his face straight.

K't'lk jangled at him, the sound Jim was coming to recognize as laughter. "Captain," she said, sounding quite dry, "do you think I was hatched yesterday?"

"I don't know what to think about you, K't'lk. I haven't spent that much time talking to glass spiders. What's this crazy stuff you're trying to get Scotty to swallow?"

She began telling him. Jim had of course done the required reading in the non-causal sciences and the "philosophical" scholia of pure physics while in Academy. Though the subject had confused him at the time—and he hadn't seen the worth of it—Jim had sopped up the information, used it to pass his tests, and forgotten about it. K't'lk's explanation, unfortunately, began where Jim's limited understanding of the non-causals ended, and became practically unintelligible within minutes. So Jim just kept nodding—certain that stopping her to ask for explanations would only make things worse—and resigned himself to simple fascination with something and someone so alien. When they finally reached Sickbay, Jim glanced in just long enough to see that the place was packed full of crew, with more arriving every moment. McCoy and Chapel and other members of the Medical staff were sitting around at terminals or with datapads in their laps, talking to crewmen and taking notes at top speed. It was obvious that McCoy wouldn't have a report for him for some time, so Jim simply kept walking, listening to K't'lk expound on "universal gender" and "radicals of causation" and "taub-NUT universes" and Space knew what else. She was a welcome relief from what would have otherwise been another of those periods during which a Captain can do nothing but wait.

Eventually they wound up at Jim's cabin. "Ah, the spot famed in song and story," she said, looking around her as he bowed her in. One of Jim's eyebrows went up as he headed for the Saurian brandy decanter. "K't'lk, do you partake?"

"For flavor only; alcohol doesn't affect my metabolism. To get 'drunk' we eat polycarbons. 'Graphite,' I think Mt'gm'ry called it."

"Here you are, then. But how are you going to—" Jim stared at the crystalline leg with which she reached up and took the glass. "You didn't have claws at the end of that a moment ago," he said accusingly.

"I didn't need to," said K't'lk, climbing delicately up into one of Jim's easy chairs and tucking her legs in around herself. She held the drink up close to her right side. That looked odd, but odder still was the imbibing organ she extended from her side and dipped into the snifter. She began sipping, making bubbly noises like a child with a straw in a milk container. "So, Captain," she said with perfect clarity while she drank, "how many of those rumors are true about how you spend your evenings here?"

"Madam," Jim said, unoffended but very amused, "not as many as I *wish* were true! Besides, what would you do if I asked you about *your* sex life?"

"I'd tell you."

"!!" Jim did his best not to choke on the brandy. "I

thought they always taught at Starfleet Academy that the two things you shouldn't discuss with aliens, just on general principles, are sex and religion."

"We must have studied at different branches of Academy, Captain. They told us not to mention death and taxes."

"But there you go mentioning them."

K't'lk shrugged again, chiming. "One of them doesn't apply to either of us," she said. It was true; Starfleet personnel were tax-exempt.

"And the other?"

"I don't pay taxes," she said.

The conversation kept going that way, veering from the commonplace to the incomprehensible and back again. Through it all, Jim was fascinated by the perception that this was a peer, who had nevertheless surrendered herself, by pleased choice, to another's command —a phenomenon he had gotten used to in his *Enterprise* crew, but saw much less frequently outside it, and less frequently still in a species so far from the human. K't'lk's unflagging energy fascinated him too. Mostly it expressed itself as delight in whatever was going on. Even when the discussion turned to death and destruction, as it did once or twice, K't'lk never descended into anything like human seriousness. Earnest, lively opinion, tinged slightly with affectionate anger, was as close as she got. Jim began to think it sounded like fun to be a glass spider, and finally told her so.

Just a touch of sobriety crept into K't'lk's voice when he said that. "I don't know if your pleasure in infinite diversity would stretch that far, J'm," she said to him—he had long since offered her his given name, and had in turn been made free of one of her interior syllables. "You seem to enjoy the—extracurricular—things that happen in this cabin. If you were a Hamalki male, you would only enjoy them once."

"Uh. T'l, I know I, ah, shouldn't—"

She laughed at him. "J'm, we've already survived discussing the horrors of death and taxes; could discussing what remains be any worse?" And she began to explain what she'd meant by the remark about Hamalki males, for which Jim was glad; he was genuinely curious.

Nature had presented the Hamalki with an interesting problem. Reproduction in their presentient days had been a haphazard and frightful business—a given male fertilizing as many females as he could before being devoured by one of them in the nuptial act. Slowly, though, as sentience set in, the Hamalki began to notice something; that the hatchlings of those females who ate their mates prospered, growing faster and stronger than the children of Hamalki females who didn't. It wasn't until much later that their scientists discovered the cause. The enzymes and hormones present in the male's body during mating caused the female's analogue to DNA to split and recombine with the male's in new and more effective ways.

But by the time this came to light, the Hamalki had for thousands of years surrendered to the bare fact, and surrounded it with custom born of civilization and the high emotions. Courtships had become an ecstasy of weavings, physical, vocal, and intellectual, as the two participants consciously and unconsciously determined what genes to share, how much memory to perpetuate, what of themselves to keep. A mating pair would sing visions and trade desires while jointly building the edifice that would serve both as a statement of what they had been, and the nest for their mating. The climax of the nest-weaving—as it were, the "written" confirmation and completion of their relationship—then triggered the act of love directly. Just after his ecstasy's height, when the enzymes were at full flow, the male would initiate his own death by biting the female and causing her (in her own throes) to blindly attack, kill and devour him.

Jim sat still for a while, dealing as best he could with his own reactions. "Surely, though," he said eventually, "you don't have to do it that way. You're advanced enough to have synthesized the enzymes—"

"It's been suggested," K't'lk said, rearranging a few front legs so they hung down over the front of the chair. "It caused a few holy wars."

"There *I* go, now," he said. "Religion. Sorry."

"No offense taken, J'm. You have religions, though, that offer participation in miracles of various kinds to their celebrants. One of them, I understand, offers you the opportunity to eat God. I was surprised to hear about that—for some of our people say that's what we're doing. No matter. How would the celebrants of that miracle feel, do you think, if you told them you could cause the transubstantiation in question to occur in a test tube, without recourse to the Deity involved?"

Jim shuddered. "We did have some problems of that general sort a while back," he said, "but they didn't last more than a century or so. I seem to remember that several religions got, ah, expanded a bit, to take into account some of the new things the Universe had proven able to do."

K't'lk laughed, reaching over with one free leg to touch Jim lightly on the forearm. "Typical," she said. "That's a vertebrates' civilization for you. My people are a little more rigid . . ." She sipped at the brandy again. "The other part of the problem is that there's something else passed along in the Act that the enzyme doesn't supply." Now K't'lk did sound serious, though not sorrowfully so. "Ghost," she said.

Jim was perplexed for a second. Then he got it, and had to keep himself from smiling; he wasn't sure how well K't'lk could read human expressions. "Spirit, you mean. The soul."

"That's right. It has to be transmitted somehow, after all . . ." She began fiddling with her front legs. Jim looked at the movement curiously and then realized, with a slight shock, that she was spinning. A bright-glittering filament stretched from a tiny orifice on K't'lk's belly to her claws, and with four of her "front" legs she was shaping and interlacing it, weaving a structure as delicate and fragile-looking as spun glass, or a spun thought.

"I miss T'k'rt't," she said, working absently while she talked, like someone crocheting. "My mate the last time out. We knew each other for a hundred years or so before we decided that it was time to share the Act. It doesn't seem like enough time, though. He was an architect; he constructed the most elegant structures, and sentences, and emotions. And I used to pretend I knew nothing about architecture myself, so he'd come visit and lecture me on it." She laughed. "He's probably the reason I found myself working on StarBase Eighteen's design team—his old memories woke up in me. . . . I wove two of his syllables into my name, this time out." She busied herself with her knitting for a moment. "He's in me still, of course," she said after the pause. "We store the enzyme, and the male's seed, for as long as we want to. I could have a little T'k'rt't any time. But it wouldn't quite be him, it wouldn't be the same. I would sooner turn time back and have him again. But he'd say that was silly, and laugh at me . . ."

There was another pause. "I begin to see now," Jim said, "why your people are such great builders."

"Oh, yes. Building is love for us—literally. Every edifice is a reflection of the one we will build out of love, or have built already. And besides—the price of our lives, and our loves, is death. The payment's dear.

Love and life and the vision that grows out of them both have become precious to us—not just ours, everybody else's too. So we serve those others, we serve you, building and making. Doing that, seeing your desires achieved without your dying, we conquer death a little. And being the answer to others' questions is sweet . . ."

The communicator whistled. Jim reached out to the controls on the table. "Kirk here."

"McCoy," said the familiar voice, sounding no less disgruntled than before. *"We're cleaning up down here, Jim. Do you still want to stop in?"*

"On my way. Out." He turned to K't'lk, who was finishing the delicate structure she had begun—a spiky, interwoven mass full of absent-minded symmetries. One foreleg sliced the slender cord that still attached it to her; the other three offered it to Jim. "I'd best go see what Mt'gm'ry is up to out there. Not that he's not competent—but we did invent the crystal-weaving process for starship hulls, and if he's found some way to improve on it, I want to know . . ."

Jim took the sculpture and put it up on a shelf out of harm's way. "Tell me if he has. And thank you. Meanwhile, let's move. Bones sounds like he's at the end of his rope. . . ."

Sickbay was somewhat quieter when Jim got there. Most of the crewpeople were gone, except for a few sitting about and still talking to people from Medicine, or to one another. Off to one side, Christine Chapel was having an earnest, frowning conversation with one of the diagnostic computers; it was answering her questions much more calmly than she was posing them, which as usual was not improving her temper. "There you are," said a voice behind Jim. McCoy was standing in his office door, talking to a little dark-haired woman Jim didn't recognize. "Come on in, Jim."

"We haven't met," Jim said to the new crewman as he went to where she stood with McCoy, taking the opportunity to look her up and down. She stood straight and slender in Fleet nursing whites, with the serpent-and-lightningbolt insignia of the First-In Services at her collar; Jim wondered briefly what someone used to the rough conditions and frightful medical challenges of the frontier worlds would make of the comparatively sedate nature of starship duty. He had little time to think of anything else, as he noticed that he was being looked over as well. Sharp hazel eyes in a calm face glanced down the length of him and paused, rather annoyingly, to consider his midriff and the two extra kilos that had lodged themselves there while Jim was waiting for word to come in about the drive. Then those eyes flicked up to meet his again, and there was a laugh in them as their owner read both Jim's mild chagrin, and his resolution to do something about the two kilos. "Sir," the nurse said, taking the hand Jim offered her. "Lieutenant Commander Lia Burke. I'm very pleased to meet you."

"Yes," Jim said. "Welcome aboard. Did you have time to make your goodbyes on Terra? You were pulled off leave on rather short notice, I understand."

"There were no goodbyes to make, sir; I'm Earth-human by derivation, but home for me is Sa-na 'Mdeihein. I was just taking a couple weeks' vacation."

Jim considered that anyone who would choose to live with the na'mdeihei, surrounded by semi-extradimensional creatures made primarily of stone, probably deserved her vacations. Bones was making I-need-to-see-you-*now* motions with his eyes, though; Jim let the rest of his questions go for the moment. "Well, enjoy your stay with us, Commander. Bones, what have you got for me?"

McCoy led Jim into his inner office, and before answering, not only shut the door but opaqued the walls. "The damndest assortment of fairy tales, weird stories and oddball visions you ever heard, Jim. And other problems. Whose good idea was *she??!*"

"I noticed a certain talent for, ah, getting to the point," Jim said dryly as he sat down in front of Bones' desk. "But looked at another way, she was doing her job—you've been twigging me about my weight for a month now."

"That's not the point."

"What is?"

McCoy reached over to his desk, picked up a cassette and dropped it into a slot. The screen embedded in the desktop came alive and started reading out the new crewman's service record. BURKE, LIA T., LT. CMDR, RN, ND, MA, EXMT, FICN . . ."Look at that!" Bones said, waving his hands in the air in exasperation. "I sent for a nurse!—not alphabet soup!"

Jim shrugged. "So she's good at her job . . ." He glanced up. "She *is* good at her job?"

"That's the problem, Jim. She's very, *very* good. She's *too* good. Nurses like that start wanting to be doctors. Or start acting like them. Why can't I just once get a nurse that knows how to be one? All I—"

"Bones," Jim said, tapping the table and blacking it out, "what happened to *you* during transit?"

McCoy stopped dead, and favored Jim with a long, annoyed, rueful look. "You should have gone into psych . . ." He sat down behind the desk. "Jim," he said, very slowly, "I've been sick a few times in my life, sick enough to have hallucinations. I know what they feel like. But never, never have I had an experience so vivid that it makes *this—*" and he pounded his fist on the tabletop—"feel like the hallucination instead of the reality." He stared moodily at the fist and the table. "Ever since we came out, I keep expecting to walk through things like a ghost—because I was somewhere so much more real and solid than physical reality that I could see through my hands, couldn't touch or move anything." His voice dropped. "The—country—I don't know where it was. It burned my eyes. The edges on everything were sharp as shadows in space. Colors—were almost a torment. Stars would have looked pastel by comparison. It was a terrible place." He looked up at Jim, then, wonder and fear in his face. "And I'd give anything I can think of to get back there again."

Very slowly, Jim nodded. To his own surprise and dismay, the same thought about his own experience had occurred to him. "The rest of the crew?" he said.

"Similar." McCoy picked up another tape, dropped it in the slot. Readout flowed across the table. "Leaving out details—as much for confidentiality as anything else, Jim; some of these visions, experiences, whatever, were pretty private—the vast majority of the crew had hypersensory experiences of events or places they had never seen before. The surprise was that some of those are identifiable—planetary environments, envisioned in such detail that it seems impossible for the person not to have physically been in that place. Some are of places we're unable to presently identify. Some people seemed to see things that happened in the past—events we've been able to confirm via the computer, that the people involved knew nothing about. I checked a random sampling with neuroscan, by the way," Bones said, as Jim opened his mouth to say something about unconscious memory of events heard about, or studied, and forgotten. "Pattern search revealed no neurons imprinted with relevant references except the ones involved in the experience itself—the people really hadn't heard of these events. The common factors among all the reported experiences are initial discomfort—secondary, I think, to everyone's perception of loss of duration—and extreme vividness of experience, to the point where physical reality seems insufficient, or temporarily ephemeral, on recovery.

Oh, and one other. A perception of the experience as desirable—even if it wasn't exactly pleasant at the time—and a desire to return to it. A few people made the distinction that it wasn't the experience specifically they desired to reenter, but the background—the context—and the emotions it inspired in them." He touched a spot on the desk, and a recorded voice spoke: Uhura's. "The whole thing," she said, her voice quiet and pensive, "would have broken your heart." "Why?" said Lia Burke's voice, equally quiet. "Was it so sad?" "Sad? *No!*" said Uhura—and the joy and longing in her voice were astonishing to hear.

"Evaluation," Jim said. "Are these 'experiences' going to impair the crew's ability to function?"

McCoy shook his head. "I have no idea, Jim. I see no such impairment at present. But some of them might be covering. How are *you* doing?"

"Well enough. You might as well add mine to the assortment—" Jim told McCoy about what it was like to be a starship. Bones sat quite still, nodding occasionally, until Jim was done. "So what do you prescribe, Doctor?"

"Work," McCoy said sourly. "*I'm* finding it very effective. When are we jumping again?"

"Half a day or so."

"Well enough. Warn them first—well, you would anyway, I know. Maybe it'll be easier the second time . . ." Bones sighed. "We're working with an unknown here, Jim. I don't see any dangerous trends yet—I'll let you know if I do. Meanwhile I'm trapped in a Sickbay full of killer nurses . . ."

"Christine's training Burke, isn't she?"

"Supposedly," Bones said, sounding weary. "But sometimes I wonder who's training who in what . . ."

"Such syntax."

"I'm a surgeon, dammit, not a grammarian." They

got up and headed for the door together. It hissed open to reveal Mayri Sagady talking to Lia Burke, while Ensign d'Hennish stood by. "What's wrong with *you,* then?" McCoy said to the Sadrao.

"Nothing, sir."

"Nothing??"

"No sir. I'm just here to hold Lieutenant Sagady's paw. During transit, she's having one of those experiences." That was as close as a Sadrao could get to past tense.

"And you *didn't?"*

"No, sir . . ."

D'Hennish trailed off in apprehension as McCoy advanced on him. "Come this way, my boy. You come right this way. I have a machine that would love to meet you. Several machines."

"It's not hurting, is it?" d'Hennish said, rather plaintively, as Bones led him away. The Sadrao looked over his shoulder at Jim and threw him a look like that of a small child asking to be rescued from a mad dentist. Jim shrugged at him, not without sympathy. "Let me know what happens, Bones," he said, and turned to leave Sick Bay.

"I will, Captain. —Right over here, son. Now you tell the nice computer *all* about it. Christine, show Lia how to set up the synapse synchronization metafile—"

"Thanks, Chris, I know how. —Doesn't he ever say 'please'?—"

Jim went quietly away to snatch a few hours' sleep before the next jump.

The ship was on red alert when he woke up. That was no surprise—he had ordered it. The ship's complement would have rearranged itself with the addition of epsilon shift to alpha, beta, gamma and delta; watches would be shorter—one-in-five rather than one-in-four —and the crew would be sharp and ready for whatever inversion might bring. He got up and dressed in a hurry, and made for the Bridge.

Spock was there, as might have been expected, pacing around the railed circle and inspecting everything with his usual cool thoroughness. As the lift doors opened he stepped up toward them and met Jim near the science station.

"Everything all right?"

"Yes, sir. We're ready to leave orbit around zeta-10 Scorpii as soon as you give the word. Which—if I may say so—I would be gratified if you do quickly. The star's spectrum is not showing any sign I can clearly diagnose, but there are again irregularities that have disturbing implications."

"All right, we'll be out of here shortly. Did you check the computers?"

"I did, Captain. According to all our standard diagnostics—and some nonstandard ones of my own devising—the Damage Control computers are working perfectly. I am at a loss to explain their failure as regards the flaw Mr. Scott found in the port nacelle."

"Damn," Jim said, making his way down to the command chair. Chekov was at the helm, but Sulu was not; this was his offshift, and his apprentice navigator Lieutenant Heming was handling navigations. Absently Jim nodded to them both and sat down. "Spock," he said as he did so, "if we have to do hands-on checks of everything, it's going to slow us down quite a bit."

"Captain, I concur. Yet it seems the only way to proceed safely until I can determine the cause for the failure of the diagnostics."

Jim grimaced. "All right." He hit the 'com button on

the command chair as Spock went back to his station. "Engineering—"

"K't'lk here, Captain."

"Where's Scotty?"

"Making final checks, sir. More out of nerves than anything else, I think—he pronounced both warp drive and impulse engines 'clean' hours ago. The reweave of the injured hull section was completed two shifts back."

"Is the inversion apparatus up?"

"On line and ready, Captain. Course laid in is for the 'midway hang point,' halfway between the outer boundaries of the Galaxy and of the Lesser Magellanic—'x' minus-forty-five degrees Gal-latitude, 'y' two hundred ninety-nine degrees Gal-longitude, 'z' one hundred one thousand two hundred thirty-seven lightyears from the Arbitrary Galactic Core. Navigations, please confirm."

Jim smiled. She was taking no chances this time, and making sure he knew it. "Navcomp confirms, Captain," Mr. Heming said in a crisp Oxonian accent.

"Good enough, K't'lk. Have Scotty get back on post; we're about to jump."

"Aye, sir. Engineering out."

"Sickbay—"

"McCoy here."

"Ready, Bones?"

"If you mean are we prepared for jump, yes. If you mean am I happy about it . . ." He didn't finish the sentence, but his tone of voice made it quite plain how he felt. *"I finished with the scans on d'Hennish, by the way."*

"And?"

"The machine confirms it—he's the only crewmember other than K't'lk to sustain no inversion experience. I've got him hooked up to the neuroscan so we can get live

data on what happens in inversion. Lia's hooked up too. I just wish we had another Sadrao."

"I have a few wishes of my own—most of them having to do with nonfunctioning computers. Keep an eye on your machinery, Bones. Bridge out." He turned to Lieutenant Mahásë, who was holding down Uhura's post. "We'll count it down, Mr. Mahásë. Five minutes from now—mark."

"Counting, sir."

"Confirm red alert status on all duty stations—personnel presence and readiness."

It took a few moments. "Confirmed, Captain."

"Good. Give me allcall." Mahásë touched a light, nodded at Jim. "All hands, this is the Captain," he said. "At four minutes, forty seconds from—now—we will go into inversion mode. Grab hold of whatever you need to grab hold of, and hang on—we're going to come out a long way from home. Kirk out."

He sat back in the chair, breathed in and out and looked at his Bridge crew. There had been times before that had seemed to justify the old cliché about tension in a bridge being thick enough to cut with a phaser. This was another; just raising a hand to scratch an itch cost Jim more effort than was natural—the air seemed stiff. "Three minutes, thirty seconds," Mahásë said. Jim wanted to swear, to jump up and walk around, to do something. His crew sat quietly around him and did their jobs, making it look easy in a murmur of calm voices.

"Solid cameras rolling."

"Holos up."

"Shields—"

"Shields positive."

"One minute, thirty seconds—"

The screen burned with the violent and lovely image of zeta-10 Scorpii, nested deep in its eye-searing indigo and violet shells. Jim looked at it long and hard by way of distraction, shifting his eyes away only when they began to hurt.

"Defense departments—"

"Phasers hot."

"Photon torpedoes—"

"Tubes loaded."

"Forty-five seconds—"

The star was broiling and bubbling with sunspots; Jim wondered if those were a symptom of the irregularities Spock had mentioned. Certainly the star had a rather active photosphere, but that could be expected with a sun that blew off the upper layers of its atmosphere every now and then—

"Log entries—"

"Complete and transmitted."

"Fifteen seconds. Fourteen. Thirteen—"

"Warp drive—"

"Temporarily disabled."

"Impulse engines—"

"At point one-five cee."

"Nine. Eight. Seven—"

"Inversion drive—"

"On line, double confirm."

"Four. Three. Two. One—"

"Inversion implement—"

—and the world started to go away. *Amazing,* Jim thought—and the thought didn't feel at all normal—*you can actually feel it coming a little, like anaesthesia.* That was almost the only true thought he had time for; next "moment" the lack of duration choked him again, and it was harder to bear this time, not easier. But the last thing he saw while still able to think and see made him want to start right out of his seat, except he couldn't move. The surface of zeta-10 Scorpii heaved and writhed like liquid that's had a weight dropped into it; then lost its shape and spread out and out and out, in a frightful, splendid, deadly flower of fire, pursuing them in incandescent rage as 109 Piscium had. *Oh no,* Jim managed to think before time stopped and held everything still, even his thoughts. *Not again. And not* this *star. I think when we get home, I'm going to get yelled at . . .*

And *Enterprise* and the universe were gone again.

Seven

Time was gone again too. That being the case, it seemed impossible to say that the experience took longer than the first one. But it seemed to—or else, as Jim put it to himself later, when he could think again, the experience wasn't exactly longer, but *deeper* somehow, more real. The last time, there had been the very slightest sense that the real Jim Kirk was somewhere else. That sense was gone now—replaced by the knowledge, both bizarre and commonplace as in a dream, that he was some*one* else. . . .

—the light of Sol glared down white on the snow, making him squint as he looked across the Square at the Kremlin. At this early hour, the great towers of Novy Moskva to the west cast no shadow on the Red Fort and the parklands about it. He wondered what it was like, two hundred years ago when there was a city all about this spot, with city dirt and noises. Now there were only the gold-glittering onion towers of Saint Basil's, facing the red towers of the Citadel across the Square. High in the fiercely blue sky of winter, a hawk sailed over, calling. He shivered.

He had not been here since he was a very small child. Before he could read, Luna had become his home—craterbases like Bianchini under the shadow of the great Jura Range, or maria bases like Flamsteed and Herigonius. That was when he had begun to read the great old stories, of the ancient tsars and the voyaging knights, the *boyars;* of evergreen forests that seemed to cover the world from horizon to horizon, and green plains that went on forever, from the polar ice to the Euxine—promising freedom, and room to voyage, and along the way of the voyaging, mighty battles and adventures. When he read those tales, it was like waking up from a dream; he knew at last where his true home was.

It had been bad, then, going out on the surface in his pressure suit in dark-lunar, and looking up at the blazing blue-green jewel—so close, and so very far away, out of his reach forever—or until he grew up, anyway. "Moist-Mother-Earth," they called her in the old stories of the *bogatyri,* the godling-lords. He looked up at her with terrible longing from the cold dark aridity of the dusty Moon and swore great oaths in Bog's name that he would find a way to those green fields. He would walk the wild country, and the noble cities where free-handed lords reigned in splendor; he would ride the lonely steppes and find some adventure for himself—the glory of matching himself against danger and great odds, and finding himself their equal.

He looked back on those longings now and found them, not childish, but deeper and truer than ever. His parents had shown no desire to move back home from the Moon; his simplest way back was through Starfleet. Once in Academy, though, he had discovered adventure and danger and bold journeys enough in the spaces between the stars—more than enough to last him for the rest of his life. His love for the spirit of this land had led him out into a life richer than he had ever imagined.

But this was still the heart of all his loves. And there was no more time to spend here—he was expected offplanet within the hour. He looked across at the silent walls of the Kremlin, where heroes lay buried, and men who had been mighty, or become that way. He looked past them, to ancient kings and old lost glories, to dreams that failed and dreams that succeeded, and praised them one and all for daring to dream, to be. And then there was nothing more to do but go back to the work this land had sent him to—to his own personal dreams and glories: the stars.

He turned around to walk back to the flitter, noticing as he did so another figure standing in the snow far away, looking in his direction. Some brother, some child of the Motherland. He waved at the man as he popped the roof of the flit open, slightly preoccupied. He had to get back to the Fleet field at Kazalkum in a hurry; if his shuttle left without him, Captain Kirk wouldn't be interested in his explanation that he was late because he'd stopped to sightsee. Funny, though, now that he thought about it. The watcher in the snow was wearing Command/Flag uniform. And there was something about the stance, the build—He laughed at himself as he brought the iondrivers up and lifted the little craft off the ground. He had Kirk on the brain this morning. . . .

Jim stood silent in the snow, watching the little silver ship leap up into the bitter-cold air as if a bomb had blown it off the ground. *If I'd given any thought to how he'd fly, I could have anticipated this,* he thought, his breath going out white in front of him as he laughed. *It matches him. The knight spurring his charger. Meanwhile, how am I able to be him and me at the same time?*

And is everybody else walking into other people's experiences too?

Are any of us going to be sane after this? . . .

And it all changed—

—home, oh God, home! —it had been too long. She was in her own workroom again at the base on aia'Hnnrihstei; and the worldwindows were on, revealing the great thousand-ringed globe of Sa-na'Mdeihein hanging in green-golden splendor over the snow-dusted, cratered stone of its satellite, in a sky that burned with stars. Everything was as she had left it the last time she'd gone away—the big goldstone desk hovering on its pressors in the middle of the room, the ranks of bookshelves dustless but undisturbed, her work pad up and running as usual where it lay on the desk. Her pressure suit was in its clamps and charged. "Been gone a while, Lee!" the computer said to her.

It was too good to be true. She hurried out from behind the desk, laid a hand on Mikelle's console. "That's for sure, cherie. Orual, Vulcan, Andor, Vercingetorix IV, Terra . . . Any messages? Oh, God, I have a million things to tell you. I missed you!"

"I missed you too, m'cher. Dithra's been asking for you."

Dithra too! Was there any joy that wasn't going to happen? "Open the door," she said, "I'm on my way. Do I need to take anything with?"

"Just you, from the sound of her."

The doorway on the left side of the room, beyond the inset cupboards and closets, shimmered with transporter effect. She practically ran through it, bursting out onto the beach—golden sand, and emerald sea, and fierce green sky piled with citron-colored fair-weather clouds so bright they burnt the eyes. Her delight at homecoming was so acute, it was almost a pain. "*Ae' sta-mdeihei, ae' hhnsmaa tirh desdiriie!*" she shouted for the sheer delight of loudness, looking hurriedly around her as she ran—and then immediately skidded to a stop. The beach wasn't empty, as it usually was. She was surrounded.

Terrible dark shapes of stone stood all about her: huge as monoliths or statues of old monstrous gods, but faceless, featureless, weather-worn and age-blunted—and alive. For a long few breaths they looked eyelessly down on her in silent, implacable regard. Then slowly they began to bend down over her with a frightening sound of stone grinding and rasping massively on stone. She looked up at them, shaking, unable to move as they bent closer and closer and shut the light away—a hand of stone closing with her in its fist. From the great rough shapes came a scent of scorched rock, and a rumbling that vibrated in the bones like the speech of the moving earth. Their shadow closed about her. It became quite dark.

Most of the inward-leaning shapes stopped still, though their rumbling continued. Only one bent lower, closer, till it hung right above her head, less seen than sensed—a hot smell of burning, a promise of crushing weight. She stood still until she couldn't bear own her stillness any more—then reached up and dared one more time to try what had always been impossible before. She threw her arms as far as she could around that low-bending shape, and her heart nearly burst with shock and joy as she *felt* it, pulled herself to it, held it tight. The rumble of the great voice entered her and shook her, blotting out the world until only she and it remained. /Air-daughter, flesh-daughter, how is it that you come to us in truth and not in dream? It was never your wont to be so solid when you were among us./

She shook her head, not knowing the answer, not caring. This was impossible and she knew it, for to the na'mdeihei, the physical world in which the humanities moved was a dream they could not touch; and when she tried to touch their warm stone in companionship, her hands went through them as if they were ghosts. Often enough she had longed to be able to touch, just once, the strange creatures whose wisdom and slow-spoken hearts and inner beauty had long since turned one more liaison job into first friendship, then love. And now the wish had come true. "Dithra," she said in the Speech—finding to her great amazement that for the first time she spoke it, not haltingly, but with their own leisurely certainty—"all I well know is that some great marvel is on me, and I wish it not to end. And I have been long between the stars, and have seen much death and much life and many wonders; yet all my desire has been to return here, for my heart was sore without you my people."

/We also have been sorrowful for lack of the Untouched who had gone from us. Now you are gone no more, and neither are you untouched any longer; and if you will dwell with us again, that is well. But the truth says you will not; the truth has an end, for you./

Her eyes burned, and though that ashamed her—for she had seen hundreds die and had worked on dry-eyed in their midst—there was no stopping the tears here and now. "This much I feared," she said. "Yet though I 'dream' all the rest of my life, this 'truth' cannot be taken from me. For this little while, we touched—"

/Air-daughter, we have touched always. And we will touch again, though you must break your bonds first. That is a light thing; you will do that, some day, in an instant. But go now. Your dream calls you back into it. We will always be here, as we always have been—/

She nodded, letting her hands lie for one last sweet moment against the hot stone of her companion. Dithra straightened up, then, followed by the other na'mdeihei; sunlight fell once more on the sand in the circle. She glanced down at it, noticing something interesting. Though the sun fell untroubled on her head, she still stood in shadow—as if some great bulk yet hung over her.

/As always,/ Dithra said. She nodded, sorry to leave but too joyous really to be sad, and walked back toward the door. There was a lot of work to do—

Jim stood on the beach, behind the na'mdeihei, watching her go. "Fascinating," someone said beside him, in a whisper that was almost lost in surfcrash. Jim glanced to his left. Spock was standing there, gazing at what Jim had been watching: a lone woman walking down the beach toward a dark opening in the empty air. She stepped through it, was gone; the doorway vanished.

Spock glanced at Jim, then in another direction. Jim looked where Spock did. The na'mdeihei, like an interested Stonehenge, had turned toward the two of them—and eyeless, faceless, were staring at them. That calm, boneshaking rumble started again—

"Mr. Spock," Jim said, "if you are indeed real, and not an inversion hallucination, I think it would be a very good idea if we got out of here. . . ."

"Sir, I was having the same thought—on both counts. If you have any suggestions—"

"*Emergence confirmed,*" said K't'lk's voice, a little shakily. "*Inversion complete, targeting accurate. Navigations, confirm.*"

Faces were pale all over the Bridge, Mr. Heming's no exception. But his fingers danced with their usual speed over his console. "Positive lock on DG Magellanis Minoris," he said, less crisply than usual. "Distance—one hundred one thousand one hundred twenty lightyears. Retrolock on Rigel—one hundred thousand, eight hundred lightyears. On course as plotted, coordinates—"

He trailed off. He might as well have, for no one was really listening. They were all staring at the viewscreen. "We're here," Mr. Heming said.

They were. The intelligent screen had widened its angle to enclose the most prominent object in sensor range. As a result, it held utter darkness, and at the heart of that darkness a great fiery whirlpool of stars—the whole Galaxy at once.

Ragged whooping and cheering started, both on the Bridge and down in Engineering. Jim let it go on for as long as it took him to swallow hard twice. "All right, as you were!" he said then, and the Bridge quieted. "K't'lk, report."

"The apparatus functioned without fault, Captain."

"I'm not so sure," Jim said, rubbing his head. It ached. The shock of finding himself in a woman's body wasn't too difficult to bear—Jim having been in such a situation once before—and the mindset that came with it had been peculiar, but congenial. Being Chekov hadn't been too bad, either. The headache, Jim thought, probably came from being suddenly forced to think in Russian. *No language should have that many cases—!* "What about you?"

"I, ah, I think I shall have to see Dr. McCoy myself, Captain. Evidently my species is resistant to inversion effect only to a certain point—which I passed." Her chiming had a thoughtful sound to it. Jim immediately had a second thought about his own experience—that he had been lucky to experience only the thoughts of other humans. *Her headache's probably worse than mine. . . .*

"Have Scotty relieve you when you've got things cleaned up down there, K't'lk. And tell him I'll be seeing the department heads in Main Briefing, this date point seven. Kirk out." He looked over his shoulder. "Pass that on to the Heads, Mr. Mahásë. And get me Sickbay."

When he came on, McCoy sounded concerned. *"We've got a few collapses among the crew, Captain."*

"Diagnosis?"

"Emotional overload. Similar to stress syndrome, but the overloads seem due to 'positive' emotions rather than to anxiety or fear."

"How're your two guinea pigs?"

"They both had inversion experiences. I got a scan on Lia's—damned if I know what to make of it." Jim said nothing for the moment—*he* knew what to make of it, and would let Bones know later. He glanced at Spock; the Vulcan met his eyes and nodded very slightly, then went back to what he was doing at his station. *"But d'Hennish's is even more interesting than hers. While he had inversion effect, he* didn't *have the problem with duration that everybody else has been having. It's something to do with that Sadrao timesense, I think. Or lack of timesense, rather. In any case, his profile'll be complete in a few hours. We need a briefing—"*

"Point seven."

"Good, it'll give everyone a chance to recover. Anything else, Jim?"

"No, Bones. Keep up the good work. Out."

And there was nothing else to do for a while. Jim looked around at his Bridge crew—who all seemed to be doing their jobs as usual—and felt uneasy. There was something slightly off. It took him a moment to pinpoint it. He noticed that they were having difficulty looking at each other, as if they all knew uncomfortable secrets of one another's, and didn't want to let on—

Jim thought uneasily of the disasters that had attended the *Enterprise*'s earlier attempts to leave the Galaxy. What was likely to happen, he wondered, when crew people suddenly found themselves wandering through one another's innermost visions and dreams? *I'm not sure that I wouldn't prefer good old-fashioned insanity to this—this* whatever *this is,* Jim thought. *I can't even talk to Starfleet—not that they could give me any useful advice if I did. . . .* "Mr. Spock," he said, getting up, "run whatever checks on the ship you think appropriate to the circumstances—special attention to the engines, and also to the information systems this time. This would be a poor place to have something go wrong with the sensors. Crew in need of seeing Dr. McCoy are to do so as quickly as possible—have them make arrangements with Sickbay. That goes for Bridge crew as well," he said, looking around the circle. Various strained-looking faces glanced up from their work, and there were mutters of acquiescence.

"Acknowledged," Spock said, stepping down to take the command chair. "Where will you be if you're needed, Captain?"

"My quarters. Then observation deck."

Officially, of course, it was Recreation Deck Level One; that was the name on the plate by the doors, and the one that appeared in the *Enterprise*'s plans. But the crew never called it that, even though the deck truly was located directly above Recreation proper, and connected to it by stairs and lifts. Much more significant to the crew was the fact that Observation was the only part of the ship (except for scuttle ports and such) not armored in proof with the monocrystalline iridium-rhodium alloy so resistant to phaser blasts and shock. Even though the huge windows were clearsteel two feet thick, triply reinforced and failsafed by both the skinfield and their own redoubtable bracing, they were still the *Enterprise*'s most vulnerable spot. The crew, who wouldn't have given up the windows for anything, nonetheless usually referred to the observation deck by any number of joking names, most of which had to do with various physical orifices up which an assailant could shove something if you weren't very careful. There were other names—the second most popular being "Deck Double-A-Zee": "Almost-Absolute-Zero." Though they were field-insulated, the windows were unfailingly chill. Touching them, you could always get a taste of the terrible cold outside, a black winter that no outpouring of suns' light would ever break.

The casualness of the names, though, masked the chief attraction of the deck—the stars. Jim had noticed a long time back that when the *Enterprise* was in realspace, the observation deck was rarely empty on any shift. Evidently his people liked to see where they'd been, or where they were going, or what their jobs were about; and for all their fidelity of reproduction, the viewscreens didn't seem to satisfy that need somehow. Often, too, there was more involved than mere sight, for many of his people didn't so much look at anything, as simply gaze *out.* "The hugeness," one of the Andorian crew had said quietly one day, while she leaned near him on the railing of the upper level. "The immensity . . ." She had trailed off. Jim hadn't been sure whether she'd been speaking to him or not, but after a few moments he answered her. "Yes, Ensign," he'd said. "The hugeness, the trillions of miles . . . and moving in it, the smallness of planets—of us—It awes me."

She'd glanced over at him, then, with gentle surprise that he'd mistaken her meaning. "Oh, I didn't mean *that* hugeness, sir," she'd said. Momentarily just as surprised, Jim had put up an eyebrow at her, by way of inviting her to continue. "That's just the universe," she'd said offhandedly, looking back out at the night. "It's just bigness, a physical symbol for another kind of magnitude, that's all. It's worth praising for its magnificence, certainly. But being awed by that without also thinking of what's—beyond it—would be like . . . I don't know. Like praising a wonderful menu and then not eating the meal it was about." Then she'd remembered who she was talking to, and had blushed azure and fallen silent, unable or unwilling to talk about what hugeness she perceived beyond the physical one. But Jim had leaned beside her and contemplated the question for a long time before going back to duty.

That was the way the observation deck usually was, though. People went there alone, or gathered in quiet twos and threes and larger groups, talking or being silent as it pleased them. And one could say all kinds of astonishing things there and not hear a sound of surprise from anyone, nor hear a comment spoken of in amusement or derision afterwards. It was chiefly on the observation deck that Jim realized the term 'humanities' was no euphemism, no non-discriminatory fiction—though he rarely put the statement to himself just that way.

That was what the deck was like in normal space, with the stars all about them. But here, in the great darkness between the galaxies, things were a bit different. There were more people on deck at any given time, and the groups seemed larger than usual; and they were all much quieter. The quiet, too, had more than the usual considerateness about it. *There's a reverence,* Jim thought as he leaned alone on the railing. *I don't think I've felt anything like this even in the chapel. And I'm not surprised. . . .*

He leaned further forward on the railing, feeling the slight breath of chill from the clearsteel against his face and hands. He knew ship's sensors and the incomparable solid cameras were recording the vista, but he still felt sorry for all the people who couldn't be here, now, seeing this. Despite all the stars he'd seen, all the blazing skyscapes, he was amazed again. Away beyond *Enterprise* the Galaxy hung, its spiral structure clearly visible for the first time in the history of the humanities—a spiral even more complex in the subtleties of its structure than the astrophysicists had suspected. But the sober structural details were themselves defined by and composed of a dust of silver-golden light so delicate that only the most remarkable stars could be made out as discrete entities. Others melted together in a tantalizing shimmer that defeated human eyes entirely, and, from conversation Jim heard here and there, left even Ielerids and Mneh'tso squinting. Yet all the delicacy did not prevent the home of the humanities from burning fiercely in the dark; a still, relentless, profligate fire that left its prints on the eyes when they turned to the utter cool dark beyond it.

Close to the Galaxy, that dark wasn't quite so complete. There was also the "halo" of globular clusters that surrounded the Milky Way, bright silver-blue spatters against the night. Out beyond the halo, the most isolated of the globular clusters, NGC 2419, the "Far-Wanderer," sailed along on its solitary course like one bright and independent angel parted from the rest of the heavenly host. But elsewhere was nothing. Not even a wandering star had come out this far, and the blackness was total. Suspended in it, huge, majestic, unmoving, the great whirlpool of suns hung and burned in silence; and the clearsteel wall breathed the ancient cold in which it hung.

Jim leaned on the railing and watched the Galaxy as steadfastly as if it might be stolen should he turn his back. He stayed that way for a long time. The administrative parts of his mind got bored in a hurry and insisted that he get back to work, that he'd been here long enough by now to know what this looked like. But he didn't move. At one point he looked over to one side and noticed that Uhura had come from somewhere or other to stand beside him in the same silent reverie. For a long time he didn't say anything, though they traded glances when he first noticed her. Finally, "Offshift?" he asked.

"Department head's privilege," she said, easing her elbows down onto the railing to match his pose. Jim nodded. His heads could rotate their active shifts any-way that pleased them, as long as they spent enough time on each to adequately supervise each of the four shifts in their department, over a given two-month period. "This would normally be morning for me. But I wanted to be here at 'night.' So do a lot of my people, evidently. . . ."

Jim nodded, smiling slightly; the computer, somewhat bemused, had told him that such shift-trading and shuffling was going on all over the ship. "Some 'dawn' for you," he said.

"Well . . . it is. It is." Uhura didn't take her eyes away from the great silent pool of light. "First time any of us have seen this light, after all. . . ."

"I would hardly say that, Lieutenant," said the quiet voice on Jim's left hand. Jim didn't even have to move; he just let out a small breath of amusement and gazed out into the dark, listening to the old familiar game among his officers begin. "This light has rarely left *Enterprise's* hull since her keel was flown. For an expert in communications, you exhibit a shocking imprecision of expression. Were you instead to say that you have never seen the Galaxy in this particular fashion—"

"Mr. Spock," Uhura said with great affection, "you are incorrigible."

"Only impermeable, Lieutenant," Spock said. His voice was calm as usual, and revealed nothing; but Jim stole a sideways glance and saw that shadow of a smile that Spock occasionally wore. The Vulcan did not lean on the railing. He stood straight, but his stance had comfort about it, and his eyes were lifted up to the great darkness as if inviting it to appreciate his humor—though not to do anything so gauche as laugh out loud. It cooperated.

Jim bent his head a bit, speaking only for Spock to hear. "I was going to congratulate you on your timing, by the way."

"Sir?"

"Getting us out of there. —We *were* there?"

"Surely I was. And I perceived you to be."

"Mindlink?"

"Again, I think not, sir. Though stress on either member of a . . . team . . . that has mindmelded in the past, will sometimes reactivate the linkage, this experience did not have the same 'flavor.' Also, I was unable to break it, as I would have been able to do were it a true link—so I must decline the congratulations with regrets. We must look for another solution—and, I suspect, a more complex one."

"You want something complex," Jim said, glancing toward the stairs, "here it comes."

"No, no," came a chiming voice that was slowly making its way up to the level where they stood. "Try it with another set of names for the 'relatedness' aspects. Call them 'change, transformation and source'—"

"But change and transformation are the same thing . . . aren't they, lass?"

"No, change is one-dimensional alteration, alteration of form alone—say, smashing a rock with a hammer and breaking it. Transformation is two-dimensional alteration, alteration of substance —turning the nonliving rock into a live flower. Source is three-dimensional, an alteration of essence—producing a state in which rocks not only turn *themselves* into flowers, but are enabled to have *other* rocks turn into flowers—"

"Oh, come now, lass, that *is* magic ye're talkin'!"

"Possibly. The Anglish term I always associated with it was 'miracle,' though, because there's a paraphysical context to the 'source' concept. Religious, you would say. Can you use 'magic' as a religious word in this context?"

"Uhh—"

"Scotty," Jim said in greeting as the Scot and the Hamalki came up the stairs together and joined the group at the rail. "K't'lk—"

"Captain," the two of them said. K't'lk "sat" down just under the rail, tucking her legs in; and Scotty, standing beside her on Uhura's far side, looked up and got his first good look at the view outside. "Oh my," he said, and leaned on the rail, saying nothing more for a while.

"Mr. Spock," Jim said, "I meant to ask you. Do you understand this physics of K't'lk's?"

"I believe I understand some of its premises," the Vulcan said. "Though I hope the Commander will correct me if I err." He inclined his head to K't'lk; she shook herself in windchime acquiescence. "The concepts tend to be quite novel. Probably the most novel is the assertion that not only all classical and modern physics, but all other affiliated and nonaffiliated phenomena of physical existence, are both aspects and direct creations-by-'enactment' of the minds that move through them. In other words, in this scholium, one may say that the Laws of Motion are the way they are specifically *because* (among infinite other 'causes', and 'causality' itself has some novel definitions and operations in this system)—because Newton was an accurate enough observer of the Universe around him to correctly deduce and declare the nature of those laws. And—so a Hamalki physicist would say—it was that accuracy, that truth of declaration, that itself set those laws into the Universe, from its very beginning. He 'created' or ordained those laws; the only sense in which he discovered them, by the criteria of this school of physics, would be that sense in which a sculptor might turn on the lights in his workroom and 'discover' one of his own statues there. Thus the popular name, 'creative physics.'"

There was an amiable snort from a ways down the railing, to Spock's left. Jim glanced in that direction and noticed that McCoy had joined them, and Harb Tanzer was leaning on the railing on Bones's far side. "How do you 'discover' a statue you have yet to sculpt?" McCoy said in good-natured derision.

"Because you *have* sculpted it, even before you pick up your first chisel. This time scheme discards both succession—'cause and effect'—and simultaneity, as fragmented and incomplete glimpses of the larger continuum in which both coexist. In such a scheme, the rude comment you will make in a moment has existed complete since the beginning of time—it 'was, and is, and shall be,' to borrow a phrase, 'forever and ever.'"

McCoy glared at him and said nothing. Harb laughed. "But Mr. Spock, he didn't say it!"

"That is entirely like the Doctor," Spock said with an expression of mild annoyance. "He cheerfully flouts the natural course of a whole Universe to prove me wrong."

There was laughter about that. "We would say that he simply created it otherwise than Sp'ck did," K't'lk chimed, merry-voiced. "Just as more complex structures like scholia of physics can be expanded by later scientists—and their creations are no less true than those of their predecessors."

Spock nodded, keeping his face very neutral. Jim noticed that. "And what do you think about this school of physics, Mr. Spock?"

"I think," Spock said gravely, "that there may at last be some things that Vulcans were not meant to know."

"But with this school of thought in mind, there's one thing about the inversion drive that's disturbed me," K't'lk said, musing. "I'm troubled by the constant attendance of difficulty on the testing. The drive does, after all, involve the breaking of natural law—a number of natural laws—every time we use it. Such breaches can't be without consequences—"

"You're saying that the universe is giving us fines for moving violations?" McCoy drawled. Jim chuckled.

"Why L'nrd, you surprise me," K't'lk said. "One of your own Terrene philosophers says otherwise. Small his name was, or Short, something like that. 'The universe doesn't give first warnings.' Except in a most circumstantial fashion, and never as a favor. I'm beginning to suspect these incidents are something of the sort, that's all."

"I must admit," Spock said slowly, "that I also have been disturbed about the drive, but for different reasons. There was no reason for zeta-10 Scorpii to have gone nova when we left its neighborhood . . . except one. There is a possibility that it was our bending or breaking of natural law in the neighborhood that caused that star to explode. The consequences lie within the parameters for what such an 'integrity-breach backlash' might look like . . ."

Doctor McCoy looked from Spock to K't'lk and shook his head. "It sounds like superstition to me. That natural law is breakable, I can just barely accept. But the idea that breaking it might make bad things happen to you—"

K't'lk shook herself, chiming. "Many Earth-human physicists might agree with you about how it sounds, while also agreeing with me about the soundness of my hypothesis. For centuries, since your postatomic times at least, some prominent Terran theorists have been noticing what seem to be linkages between old traditions of your world about the way life works—the 'Tao,' I think the term is—and classical physics, especially the scholia that deal with subatomic particle interactions. Most specifically, if you force a particle to do something it can't ordinarily do, then somewhere else a particle will do something slightly catastrophic or chaotic to even the balance—inches away, or miles. Evidently, though physical law may be altered, it's not to be flouted with impunity while in operation. When our meddling ceases, sooner or later the Universe will snap back and remind us of the rules. Even in the commonest branches of physics this is true—equations must balance, nothing be created or destroyed. I'm becoming disturbed by the things that are happening coincidental with our use of the inversion apparatus. I don't suggest that we sit on it and do nothing—but I do suggest that we be prepared to deal responsibly with the consequences we produce by using it."

Jim turned that one over in his mind once or twice, watching with some interest the thoughtful expressions on the others' faces. Spock in particular interested him—the Vulcan was wearing an impassivity even deeper than usual. He wanted to see that stillness move a bit, or find out what was underneath it. "Could it be, then," he said, by way of starting the process, "that there are literally things man, or Vulcan, isn't meant to know, or do?"

"I wouldn't say 'meant,'" K't'lk said. "Meaning implies sentience; you would have to tell me who was doing the meaning. The physical Universe lacks sentience—"

"If you asked one of the Thinking Planets about that," McCoy said drily, "it might give you an argument. DD Tauri V is specially touchy on the subject, if I remember right. Keeps throwing planetquakes at the research colony when the subject comes up in conversation."

"There are exceptions to everything, L'nrd," K't'lk said affably, "and as Mr. Spock has noted, you usually make sure of where they are so you can throw a simian wrench into the conversation—" Eyes crinkled with amusement all up and down the line. "I say again, 'meant' is an inaccuracy. Rather, the occurrence of consequences to actions performed in the Universe's domain is simply part of its basic structure. We may act as we wish in regards to, say, gravity, or lightspeed in normal space; but we'd best be prepared for the falls and time dilation effects that come of playing with them. In the case of the inversion drive, I suspect the consequence might be that one breach of integrity would be paid for with another . . . the way lies are eventually paid for in painful truth, or more conventional lawbreaking with enforcement."

"A breach in psychic integrity, for example?" Harb said. "Is that what these 'inversion experiences' are?"

"Very likely. Or the backlash could as easily involve an 'attack' on our physical integrity—it may have, if the damage to the port nacelle was an example of the backlash too."

"I knew you were a physicist," Jim said. "But it's beginning to sound like you're an ethicist too."

"For my people, there's no difference," K't'lk said, sounding somber for the first time since Jim had met her. "I have to admit, I've never understood how your physics neglects to include the ethical mode—as if only one part of life were mathematics, rather than all of it. The physical universe, after all, is what determines the nature of the bodies and brains we're hooked into—"

"Ah," Scotty said, "the old 'human-soul-as-software' line of reasoning, eh lass?"

"That it's lasted as long as it has in both our cultures might make you suspect there's something there worth investigating, Mt'gm'ry. From my people's standpoint, the major design limitation of matter—specifically, that it's subject to physical law, time and space, mathematics and so forth—can't help but dictate, to a certain extent, the way the Self inhabits a body. For your lifetime, that Self is bound into a condition mostly subject to the dictates of the laws that bind matter and energy. How then should you be surprised that your lives have a certain logic, a certain mathematics about them—that service is sooner or later repaid with service, and violence with violence—death with death, and life with life?"

"'Do unto others,'" Spock said quietly, "'as you would have others do unto you.'"

Heads turned to look at him. He gazed back, unruffled. "Or as the Vulcans would say," K't'lk said, "'the spear in the Other's heart is the spear in your own: you are he.' Common sense. So many species have noticed this—that if you assist others, you'll eventually be assisted yourself. You can't put energy into a system and not get it back again, sooner or later. It may come back so late that you don't see a connection between deed and result. But there *is* one, unfailingly. Action and emotion are both energy, and energy is conserved."

K't'lk chimed softly for a moment, not words but a reflective little sound. "There are deeper implications involved here than the mere desirability of mutual assistance, of course." She looked up at Spock. "Just as it wasn't only survival of your species Surak had in mind, when he first began to teach them the mastery of emotion. There was something else. *M'hektath.*"

Spock lowered his eyes. Kirk looked from him to K't'lk. "Vulcans are so private," she said, chiming more softly than before, "that they can barely agree among themselves on how to translate their language . . . and they don't presume to correct others' translations. Look how the lexicons have been mistranslating *arie'mnu,* 'passion's-mastery,' as 'suppression of emotion' all these years. *M'hektath* is even more difficult to render. But it's 'integrity' again; not in any of the new meanings, truthfulness and keeping promises and so forth, but in the old sense of the parent languages of Anglish. *In the same skin with,* the word said. The basic kinship of souls, however diverse; the one thing all species have in common under body shape and the superficial diversities of logics and life-goals, and philosophies, and judgments of 'good' and 'evil.' Their soulness, their selfness . . . and their independence, once and later and now, from the physicality which houses them. In which, for the time being, they've chosen to be housed."

"There, lassie," Scotty said very quietly, "I think we differ a mite. I don't so much see mysel' as having done the choosing, as having been chosen to be here and now. By a Power better equipped than mysel' to do the choosing."

Kirk kept his eyes to himself, wondering slightly. He had never heard Scotty's voice go so gentle except when discussing a particularly beautiful piece of design. *Then again,* Jim thought, *maybe he is* . . .

"I find truth in that, Mt'gm'ry," K't'lk said as gently. "I honor that. And I honor as well our mutual diversity, and your willingness to let the divergence be all right. Your logic and your biochemistry I find peculiar, and to me you seem a bit short of limbs. Yet we're in the same skin, you and I, and we can celebrate that undistressed by our belief systems and differences. Certainly our differences, as two people, and on a wider scale as a Galaxy full of peoples, are infinite, and worthy of celebration. And our likeness, at all our trillions of cores, transcends and informs those differences. We *are.* We know ourselves to *be.* The duration or nature of that being doesn't much matter. Our areness is the heart of our kinship. The spear in your heart *is* the spear in mine. We're one. . . ."

The communicator whistled in the middle of K't'lk's last few words, so stridently that some of the others started at the shattering of the tranquil mood. Jim started less violently than the others; he had learned better than most that a starship was for either excitement or boredom, rarely for tranquility. *"Astrocartography to Mr. Spock."*

"Spock here, Lieutenant Sagady."

"Sir," Mayri Sagady's voice came back in great excitement, *"would you please come down here? We have a problem."*

"If you would describe its nature, Lieutenant—"

Mayri sounded as if she were perplexed, and frightened, and wanting very much to laugh, all at once. *"Sir, we have data from the Lesser Magellanic that would seem to indicate that the Universe in this neighborhood is either blowing up, or stuck. Would you come and tell us which?"*

"On my way. Spock out." Jim turned and saw that, indeed, the Vulcan was already down the stairs and halfway out of Recreation entirely. "Posts as appropriate, everybody," he said, and took off after.

Eight

Jim got to the turbolift and found that Spock had already caught one, losing him. *I'll never understand how he always manages to get a lift so fast. Maybe he has an understanding with the computer. . . .*

The next lift arrived after what seemed several hours. When Jim stepped out of it onto Deck Four, down the hall from Astrocartography, he could hear excited voices already. He followed them into the big Astrocartography lab, and found Spock and Mayri Sagady and d'Hennish all bent over a huge worktable covered with live readouts and hard copy.

"Look at that light curve, Mr. Spock. It's flat!"

"Instrument failure."

"Sir, give me a break! You know very well I would triple-check the instrumentation before calling you in. It's clean. Besides, look at the other stars in the cluster. There are all shades of curve, from bare fluctuation to near-normal—"

"What asymptotic relative efficiency?"

"Point, uh, three three five so far—"

"Have you determined an average of curve orders—"

"Will someone please—" Jim began. The jangling down the hall alerted him; he had just enough time to move out of the doorway before K't'lk came charging through it—an effect like being almost run over by a xylophone. "Someone tell me what's going on!" Jim said.

The three at the table looked up at him with mild surprise. "I'm telling you, sir," d'Hennish said, and left the group. K't'lk replaced him, climbing up onto a chair to look down at the data, and the polite wrangling began again.

Jim let d'Hennish lead him over to another readout console. "This is something really extraordinary, Captain," the Sadrao said, sitting down at the console and bringing up a graph on the wall screen. "What I'm showing you is the way we get a sense of how any given star behaves over a length of time. We plot the star's absolute magnitude—that's its brightness on a standard scale—on the vertical line of the graph. Then the period of time over which we're observing it goes on the horizontal line. The method's being used in the past mostly for variables, but now we use it for all kinds of stars to forecast stellar weather. There's always a little fluctuation in the curve, even with the steadiest stars." D'Hennish patted the console, brought up a sample curve. "Sadr, my homestar. See the curve? A very very slight fluctuation, but regular. But look at one of the stars from the Lesser Magellanic." Another graph came up—and the star's magnitude line ran as straight across it as a flat EKG.

Jim shuddered. Even knowing as little as he did about the subject, he was disturbed. "Implications?"

D'Hennish looked disturbed too. "Sir, I'm not sure. The most obvious one is impossible."

"What is it?"

"That entropy's not working there."

"Uh . . ." Jim nodded. "Thank you, Ensign." He turned away from the console and stepped back over to the table.

"—uncomfortably like 'symbiotic' stars—"

"—prolonged 'reverse novae'?—"

"—tachyar artifact—"

"—unsupported theories about temporospatial 'soluency'—"

"Pardon me," Jim said, a bit loudly.

They all looked up at him again. "I get the feeling that this is going to go on awhile," Jim said. "Please don't forget, you have a briefing at point seven. And if you get done squaring the circle before then, I'd appreciate a call."

"Yes, sir," Spock said, and looked back down at the readouts. Beside him, as Jim walked away, he heard K't'lk chime softly, "Sp'ck? I thought you did that last year?"

There was a second's worth of silence. "The Captain is very busy," Spock said. "Doubtless he is behind in his journals.—Now about this pattern—"

Jim passed by Recreation's lower level on his way to the Bridge. The soundproofing wasn't working there either—the sounds of laughter and singing were evident even out in the hall.

For curiosity's sake he stepped in. Harb's forest was back up again. From it came the sounds of smothered chortling, of leaves rustling and footsteps moving softly or running. Phaser-whine and an intolerably bright flash of pink-white light erupted in the forest, then vanished, to be followed by laughter and cheering. From the sound, there were about twenty crewpeople playing hide-and-seek in the forest, with phasers set on "tag."

Jim went in, walked around the fringes of the forest, then passed the line where the holography stopped. On its far side was normal lighting, and more merriment. About thirty people were sitting around in one of the conversation pits. They had appropriated Spock's Vulcan synthesizer/harp, a couple of guitars, a squeezebox, and several other instruments Jim didn't immediately recognize. At the top of their lungs (or other vocalizing apparatus) they were singing one of the choruses from that bawdy ballad about the (improbable) offspring of the marriage between an Altasa and a Vulcan: "Oh, I was the strangest kiddie/That you have ever seen:/My mother, she was orange/And my father, he was green. . . ."

Quietly, so as not to disturb them, Jim made his way along one side of the room and sat down in a small sheltered alcove that was a favorite spot of his. Right across the great room from him, past the singing crewmen, was the display where paintings and pictures and solids of all the past *Enterprise*s were collected—an assortment of sloops and yachts and steamships, wet-navy vessels and early spacecraft. But beside him, spotlit on its pedestal, was something he loved better than all the pictures. It was a wooden figurehead carved in the shape of an embowed, cheerfully grinning dolphin—worn, wormholed, its paint flaking with age; the original figurehead of the schooner *Enterprise,* that Stephen Decatur sailed against the Barbary pirates at Tripoli, four hundred years before. He put out a gentle hand to touch it, then let the hand fall and sat back in the chair, watching the singers. Only ten or so of the group were Earth-human. The others were a wild assortment—Andorians, Shediru, Capelles and Adarrin, a Denebolid, a Tellarite, even a Bellatrig singing a duet with itself and a *mrait* from one of the Diphdani worlds making a mirthful howling like a wolf saluting the Moon. The harmony the group made was an odd one, but it made up in enthusiasm what it lacked in orthodoxy. "Now my mother hated greenery,/my father hated meat;/and neither one would feed me/what the other one would eat—"

"They'll all find their way into the same key eventually," said Harb Tanzer, who with his usual quietness had appeared leaning on the wall to Jim's right.

"What amazes me is that they're singing at all."

"Oh, it's not so odd. Most crews will play more, and enjoy it more, the more stress they're under."

"That always used to seem strange to me," Jim said. "Now it doesn't, so much . . . I guess because I see the response so often. But I still wonder about the reasons for it."

Harb glanced down at Jim as the singers went into the verse about what the halfling's pet *rujj* thought of the whole situation. "So have recreation people, for a lot of years now. All we know for *sure* is that it's nothing so simplistic as tension release . . . or almost never *just* that. Beyond that . . ." Harb shrugged. "There are lots of theories. We have fun fighting over them."

"Any favorites?"

Harb nodded, smiling, and looked out at the singers again. "One . . . that fun is good for the brain. That's not really a theory, though . . . we *know* that fun causes the secretion of endorphins, regenerates the transmitter areas of the neurons or neuron-analogues in most of the known species. Even Klingons have to have fun sometimes. . . ."

"Though definitions of 'fun' differ."

"Of course. . . . There's another theory I like that I ran into a while back. It doesn't satisfy Occam's Razor, but in some moods it definitely satisfies *me*." Jim looked up, curious. "You get to know quite a few people rather well, in my line of work . . . and there's something I've noticed about the most successful of them, a common quality. The people themselves all have different names for it. But from where I'm standing, it looks as if they're *playing* their lives like a game. With energy, delight. Usually not with too much anger—they tend not to be poor losers, either in card games or command." Harb considered Jim for a moment. "I wonder, sometimes, if they know something the rest of us don't. Sir, this is all generalization, there are always exceptions. There's nowhere near enough data to base a genuine hypothesis on. But what if what we call life truly *was* a game? . . . as some of, say, the Terrene religions imply it is?"

"A game with what object?" Jim said, mildly interested.

Harb made a gesture that indicated infinite possibilities. "Redemption. Or union with God. Or purposes that seem less important to us . . . say, whipping up a universe so that you have somewhere to play when you've got an eternity to kill. You could make a case for all kinds of purposes, 'religious' and otherwise. Those don't matter for the purpose of this theory. What I'm leading to is that, if life truly were a game, and it started to get stressful—and you had for the time being forgotten it was a game, as people do even when they're playing something as harmless and remote from 'reality' as a board game—"

"I seem to remember spending a certain amount of time sulking the last time I had to sell somebody Park Place," Jim said. "I had such plans . . . Sorry. Go on."

"—then if you had forgotten you were already playing, what would you do to deal with the stress?"

Jim considered the conclusion for a moment before he said it out loud. "Go off and play. . . ."

He sat there for a while, quiet, while Harb stood beside him. "If anything does surprise me," Harb said eventually, "it's that the crewpeople are as calm as they are. Usually on a dangerous mission, or a really stressful one, a lot of people come down here for contact sports or martial-arts workout. Not this time out, though. . . ."

Jim had a thought. "Who's ship's chaplain this tenday?"

Harb grinned at him. "Funny you should ask. I am."

"How's business?"

"Brisk. A lot of people are coming in to talk about their inversion experiences."

"Trouble?"

"No—"

Laughter at the end of a song drowned Harb out. The singing group plunged directly from the green-and-orange song into a favorite space chantey. "To sail on a dream in the sun-fretted darkness,/to soar through the starlight unfrightened, alone—"

"Save it for the briefing," Jim said. He looked across at the chorusing crewmen, shaking his head. "Sometimes I wish I had your job."

"Sorry," Harb said. "No trade."

"I know." Jim glanced up at the lower level's windows, through which the Galaxy looked. "I wouldn't trade either, really."

"I know," Harb said.

Jim stood and headed for the doors. If he got to the Briefing Room now, he would have half an hour to consider his options before the briefing started. He had a feeling he was going to need that extra time.

No entropy—??!

"*Enterprise,* starship, the places you've been to! / The things that you've shown us, the stories you'd tell! / *Enterprise,* starship, we sing to your spirit, / the beings who've served you so long and so well—"

"Report," Jim said.

There were nine of them around the table in Main Briefing—Spock and Uhura and Scotty and Chekov and Harb, with K't'lk hanging over the edges of one seat between Mr. Matlock, the Security Chief, and Dr. McCoy.

"I will go first, if that is agreeable to everyone," Spock said. "Captain, the inversion apparatus has brought us to the exact position outside the Galaxy that our orders indicated. But not without complications—as all of us have noticed. I will leave the psychological and emotional aspects of inversion to Dr. McCoy and Mr. Tanzer, who are better equipped to deal with them than I.

"Of primary interest to the Science Department is the problem with the stars in several globular clusters on the far side of the Lesser Magellanic. I have repeatedly checked our sensors and information systems and found them to be performing faultlessly. This leaves me with the disturbing but fascinating conclusion that, on the far side of the Lesser Magellanic, the passage of time itself is being inhibited, even halted. The stars in that area, though burning, are doing so most atypically. They are not losing energy."

Spock stopped, as if even he needed a moment to recover after saying something so outrageous. "This single discovery is more important than the most important conceivable occurrence that Starfleet might have sent us to investigate. The data we have so far threaten to affect the whole fabric of physics—not just the 'classical' forms, but even nonhominid scholia such as K't'lk's. She will add more about the problem in a moment. But my recommendation as Science Officer is that we immediately set out for that area on the other side of the Lesser Magellanic and investigate it more closely."

"There's a problem wi' that," Scotty said. "We've been fine in inversion, as might be expected. We don't really exist then. But what happens to a starship's operating systems when the ship *does* exist and you take it into a place where time isn't running at the right rate—or it's frozen, as it seems to be over there? For that matter, what happens to us? What if we get caught there? We could be trapped there forever and never notice—"

"I have a solution for that problem," K't'lk said. "The inversion apparatus is capable of more functions than the mere generation of the point of infinite mass. I won't trouble you with the physics here, but I can generate a protective field, a 'shell' of entropy, if you like, that we can take with us into that troubled area. It would be similar to the double-walled warpfield that keeps the speed of light 'normal' inside the ship while she's running in subspace, where that speed is higher, and protects the ship's devices and crew from having to deal with the higher speed."

"Are you sure it'll work, lass?"

"Mt'gm'ry! Of course. It's just a function of the relatedness of—"

"K't'lk," Jim said, "what was the rest of the problem?"

"Oh. Simply this. We are a long way from the globular clusters in question—too far, even with high-resolution tachyar sensing, to resolve two important questions. First of all, is this phenomenon complete in itself, or does it have a locatable source? Second, there is also a lot of interstellar dust in the way. It is interfering with our spectral readings—several of which have indicated something rather frightening: the appearance of the spectral characteristics that preceded the explosions of 109 Piscium and zeta-10 Scorpii. We must go there—at a safe distance, of course—and have a better look, assemble more data. For at present, we have a fairly high, and unresolved, probability that we are somehow involved in the loss of entropy over there. We may even be its proximate cause. And if we are, it falls to us to examine the situation, and deal with it."

Everyone sat quiet for a few seconds. "Thank you," Jim said, "for not saying 'I told you so.'"

"Architectrix forbid, sir. . . ."

"Yes. Who's next?"

"I am," McCoy said. "Jim, this last inversion experience added a new facet to the one before. Just about all our crewpeople found themselves in other people's memories or experiences. What's surprising is that hardly anyone was really disturbed by the situation, even though some of the experiences were again rather private. I attribute this partly to the superior gestalt that has always characterized this ship—*Enterprise* people stick together, they support each other and aren't upset by one another's company in crisis situations. Also, once again, most of the experiences were joyous, or at least very interesting. But I don't know how long that will continue.

"The other thing I'd suggest is that the experiences seem to get more profound with longer jumps. How long would this next one be?"

"One hundred two thousand lightyears," Spock said.

"Even longer than the last one? Wonderful." McCoy exhaled. "Jim, good luck and your crew have saved your ass, and all of theirs, so far. But I can't guarantee what will happen on that next jump."

"Harb?" Jim said. "How have they been with you?"

"Excited," Harb said. "Eager to get on with it. And as I mentioned to you, there's been a lot of socializing, groups getting together—larger groups than usual. I could see that as being an effect of shared experience during inversion. I don't see it necessarily as a bad one. Nor do I see it affecting the crew's work habits adversely. People are going back onshift on time, as usual, and the computer reports effectiveness levels commensurate with expected stress, or higher."

"I agree," McCoy said.

"If we go to look at these stars," Uhura said, "that'll

mean we'll have to postpone the sowing of the targeting buoys, Captain."

"Agreed. But Starfleet won't mind."

"I just wish there were some way to let them know about it," Uhura said. "Heaven forbid, but if we should get in trouble out there, they should know where we were headed and what we'd found. Unfortunately we've known from the beginning that we were going to be far, far out of subspace radio range—"

"I can do something about that," K't'lk said. "Or at least I think I can. If mass can be put through inversion, there's no reason energy can't be put through too. Compile a message, and I'll send it back attached to an inversion, along with instructions for the people back at Fleet on how to do the same thing. We can have communication as soon as they rig another inversion apparatus for it."

"Do that, then. Meanwhile," Jim said, "I'm determined to make this next jump. I agree with Mr. Spock. Our purpose requires that we investigate such anomalous phenomena wherever we find them, whatever Starfleet had in mind for us initially. And if we're going to be using this drive on a regular basis, anyway, we'll need all the data we can get on how it operates. Any dissenting opinions?"

No one said anything.

"Recommendations?"

"The fervent invocation of deity," McCoy muttered.

"Noted and logged, Bones. Anyone else?"

Harb Tanzer looked at Jim for a moment before saying, "By the Captain's leave—you might stop into Rec and talk to the crew for a little while, sir. They're worried about you."

"Also noted, Mr. Tanzer," Jim said. "Mr. Chekov, Mr. Spock, work out our course for the 'troubled area' and pass it on to K't'lk. Notify me when it's set. We'll jump immediately—I want to get to the bottom of this. Dismissed."

The officers of the *Enterprise* went their various ways. Only Jim remained seated in the empty room, his face very calm, as in his mind he went over the words of the filthiest spacers' song he knew—the one about The Weird-Looking Thing With All The Eyes And The Asteroid-Miner's Daughter.

He got up and went out, humming.

Nine

"Is our course confirmed, Mr. Spock?"

"It is, sir."

"Uhura, is the message away to Starfleet?"

"Set into the inversion apparatus, Captain. It will go when we do."

"Is the crew ready?"

"Yes, sir."

"Mr. Sulu, give us—no, never mind the countdown. Uhura, notify the crew we're going.—All set? Very well. Engineering, implement!"

They jumped.

—the evening wind blew and she lifted her head to it, catching strange scents with the familiar ones. Pine was there, but so was raiwasku; she smelled sage and cypress, but also bluestar and talastima. From far away, toward the rose and opal sunset, a sound came floating —a low, coughing grumble that made the hair stand up on the back of her neck. There was no mistaking *that*.

Lion. She lifted her eyes to the darkening sky and saw two white moons, one unmarred, one stained and scarred with maria, drifting toward the burning horizon. A third, tiny and hasty and rose-red, leapt up from under the opposite horizon as she watched, and chased after the other two.

This was Serengeti, then—the fifth planet of Procyon A, where the once-endangered creatures of the Terrene plains roamed free and untroubled by hunters. She had never had the time to come here, though the place had been her idea of Heaven when she was a little girl. Serengeti was just being founded when she was five or six; and some story her mother told her about it got mixed in with all the other stories, about animals that were able to talk to each other and sometimes even to people. She decided then and there that she would be a Serengeti ranger when she grew up, and go talk to the animals.

What she found out as she got older was that it wasn't so much the animals that fascinated her, as the *talking* —communicating with another kind of life, finding out what it was thinking, sharing her thoughts in turn. And Starfleet was the place where they taught you to do that. She plunged into Academy, graduated, and forgot all about Serengeti, beckoned outward by the wonders and strangeness of Vulcan and Tel and the Cetians, Orion and Aus Qao and the Aldebaran worlds. Now she stood in the crimson grass of the Serengeti equatorial high veldt, looking up at Mount Meritaja in his snowcapped majesty, and laughed softly, a small, glad sound in the huge windy silence. This was where what she now was had begun. It was high time she acknowledged it.

She glanced down at herself and found herself suitably attired—jumpsuit, bugbelt, slogging boots; and at her side, not the familiar, minimally-powered Federation phaser, but a blaster worthy of the name, that could vaporize half a hill. Out here it might come in handy. Not for the animals, of course—but there were rumors of poachers.

Heaven help them if they run into me*!* she thought, starting to walk (for lack of a better goal) toward the sunset. The ecology of Serengeti was one of the most delicately balanced in the Federation, the more so because it was contrived. Computers had spent years on it—constructing a careful, complex interleaving of alien species with species, preserving the native Serenget food chains, slipping the once-endangered Terran species in among them, one by one. Poachers, drawn by furs and hides that would command astonishing prices in the far spaces, were the chief danger to the precarious balance. There were other dangers too; the computers hadn't been able to anticipate everything. Plagues, accidents—

The terrible, outraged squall of dismay and defiance that echoed across the grassland from the direction of the Mountain brought her up short. It was repeated, and she was running toward the sound before she clearly knew what she was doing—the blaster out of its sheath, its safety off, its status circuits singing the high-pitched triad that told her it was at full charge. *Reflex,* she thought with grim humor. But this was no rescue of a beleaguered landing party. There was no telling what awaited her in that stand of nrara trees up ahead. Leaving the tricorder back at the lodge was a dumb idea. *At least I've got the blaster, though—*

She thought she would slow down before getting to the copse of nrara, then circle around and reconnoiter. She never had a chance. Something bigger than a lion, much bigger, erupted out of the tall grass in front of her, leaping straight at her face. Reflex saved her, whipped the blaster up into line and smoked the thing in mid-leap. She thought she recognized the shape before she vaporized it, but it was too late to be sure now. *Whoops!*—for it wasn't too late: two more huge shapes, attracted by the shrill of the blaster, came leaping along after the first.

Landsharks, some part of her observed with great calm. Other parts of her, frantic, concentrated on blasting them before they made dinner of her. She found herself looking right down the roaring throat of the second one, past all the rows of teeth and into the reeking gullet half a meter away, before the blast effect engulfed it and struck her to the ground in an explosion of scorching, stinking gas.

She scrambled up and ran again, heading for the copse of nrara at full speed—stealth was no use now. The terrible, raging beast-cry was closer, louder, and more urgent. Another landshark came plunging out of the trees at her. She had more of a view of it, this time, in the uncertain twilight, and her blaster lit it more brightly still as it killed: the four-meter long body, the vivid vermilion-and-white fur, the eight legs, the blank, blind white "eyes" of a heatseeker. She dodged around the hot smoke that was all the blaster left of it, and ran into the copse.

More of the landsharks saw her, but not before she saw what they were after. There was a tarpit at the heart of the stand of nrara, slicked over with water from an earlier rainfall. Trapped in it, one terribly torn flank turned toward the shore, was the biggest elephant she had ever seen—the only one she'd ever seen in the flesh, anyway. It saw her, slashed sidewise with its tusks at one of the landsharks that was trying to get at it, and then raised its trunk and trumpeted in savage salute.

She had her work cut out for her. There were too many landsharks, and they were fast. The only chance she had was to get her back up against something so that she couldn't be attacked from behind. Reflex took over for her again. She blasted a landshark coming at her from one side, rolled, twisted, and came up with her back to the tarpit and the screaming bull. And the hunting pack's tactics changed. They gathered together and began attacking cunningly from one side, then another, testing the new alliance. She heard the bull squealing in rage, striking; a bright-patched body thumped to the grass by her feet as she smoked one of its packmates. The landsharks were snarling now. The sound first surprised and frightened, then heartened her. *They hunted silent when they thought they had the advantage*—Two more leaped at her from opposite sides. She blasted one of them and was about to do the same to the other, but never had the chance; a huge trunk plucked the landshark out of the air in mid-leap and smashed it with a thick, wet sound to the earth.

Eight left, now. No, seven. But that was still too many. The chord her blaster sang had dropped four tones in pitch—it was losing power, and a crisis light on one side told her she'd been stuck with a defective charge pack. If the ship didn't send her some help pretty soon, she was going to be dinner despite all her intention otherwise.

—and there was the shimmer of transporter effect a hundred yards away. Ears among the watchers twitched at the soft singing whine. Several of them turned to leap away toward it. "No!" she screamed, and the suddenness of the sound confused two of them enough for her to smoke one and burn a leg off another. It screamed too, and went hobbling off into the tall grass at terrible speed. She had bad thoughts about wounded beasts as the light of the transporter faded out. *Oh, let them be armed.* "Look out!" she cried as loudly as she could. "Look out, they're coming!" And then two more of them were coming for *her* and there was no more time for shouting—

Breathe, damn you! Breathe! Breathe!

It was his worst nightmare come true. He damned for

the thousandth time the idiot courage that let this man throw himself among wild beasts and into blaster crossfire for his crew's sake. Luckily it was just a graze he'd taken. But things were bad enough. His hand on the chest found no respiration, no heartbeat. He peeled back an eyelid, found the pupil reactive even in this fitful light—it contracted immediately. *Thank God!* Still no pulse at the carotid, though. *No problem.* He felt the sternum, made sure of the location of the cartilaginous xiphoid process at the sternum's end, so as not to bruise the liver or spring the ribs loose—then let him have it, the "precordial thump" on the sternum that starts the heart going six times out of ten: WHAM!!

The fingers on the carotid still felt no pulse. *Goddammit! You couldn't make it easy for me, could you?!* He started cardiopulmonary resuscitation. "Cris! Lia!" he yelled. "Some one of you get over here and breathe for him, damn it all!" *Keep the pressures sharp, now. Don't lean on your fingers and lessen the force. Don't you dare. Don't you dare. Oh, Jim, don't you dare!!*

—blaster fire erupted too close by in the strange-smelling night, followed by the thick sound of a corpse slamming into the ground some yards away. He saw the glitter of a phaser being tossed to someone else, and Christine fell down beside him and right on top of the unbreathing form. He didn't have to say a word; she grabbed the patient's head, pried his jaws apart, made sure the airway was patent, and began artificial respiration—great gasping breaths probably high in CO_2 due to her own terror. *That's all right—it'll start his chemoreceptors working faster, he'll breathe.* "Lia!!" he hollered.

Another phaser went off, right above his head. The body that fell did so practically on top of the three of them this time—stinking of singed fur, its ruined face sagging slowly out of a rictus of shock, staring at him reproachfully from where it lay. He knelt there on burning knees, with sweat rolling down into his eyes, and noticed in that odd timelessness of crisis that Lia had needle-burned the monster right between its milky eyes. *Probably waited until it was close enough for that shot, goddamned little showoff,* he thought. *She is good, though. And you have to say this for Christine, whatever else you might say about her—she's got great lungs.* "Take it for me," he gasped, and Lia thumped down to her knees beside him, hesitated a second to get the rhythm, knocked his hands aside, positioned her own and thrust down, not missing a beat. *Not bad at all, maybe there's something to be said after all for nurses who act like doctors—*

He fumbled for his kit. *Cordrazine. Hell no, he's shocky, kill him for sure. Cyclohexan—No. Enverasol—no! No! Who packed this kit, anyway?! Goddamned supply computers, if he dies I'll take an axe to them—!!* The roar right in front of him brought his head up just in time for him to see the landshark's leap, and say goodbye to life. Prematurely: K't'lk flashed glittering overhead, leaping right over him to clutch the landshark eleven-legged in midair—simultaneously knocking its leap sideways and using the twelfth leg to slit its throat with a cool precision that made him shudder. Dead landshark and live Hamalki hit the ground together, several meters away. He turned his attention back to the kit. *Rofenisin, Unifactor, Suspenar—Ardrosam-G,* yes*!!* He slapped the ampule into his spray hypo, didn't even bother hitting the pre-sterilize cycle—*he's got bigger worries right now than germs!* "A-V," he said to Lia, and she slipped out of his way to let him fist the hypo into the space between two ribs to the left of the sternum. The body under all their hands spasmed as the drug violently stimulated the heart's A-V node and the cardiac muscle started working again—

"Watch him," he said, hoarse-voiced, shaking all over at the disaster that had been averted one more time. "Dee-five concentrate till we can get him topside. Don't bolus it, Lia—he's got enough problems. Neonor if he flutters, Christine. Or Caledax, whichever you think better as the blood pressure requires. What the hell's the goddamn ship doing??! . . ."

The Klingon phasers hit their screens, and this time there wasn't the whole power of a warp drive behind them: they were failing. He had never wanted to see screens really begin to radiate into the ultraviolet, as in the old stories, but the *Enterprise*'s screens were doing it now. He hoped it hurt the Klingons' eyes. It sure hurt his.

"Scotty!" he shouted at the intercom. No answer came back. *This is awful,* he thought. *Where* is *every-body? We can't do anything about the landing party, not with the damn Klingers hammering at us like this—*

The ship lurched after one particularly nasty hit. A bad sign; it told him that the skinfield was failing to protect the *Enterprise*'s sensitive electronics, and the particularly sensitive guidance and artificial gravity systems were going. *Oh God, what do I do?* he thought, as for lack of a better idea he started tying all the major Bridge functions into the helm—including Engineering, which he scrutinized carefully.

The ship was in orbit on impulse, as usual. *Scotty'll kill me if he finds out about this. And he'll find out about it. That's the idea, though—to leave everyone alive, so they can be mad—*

The last time they had supercharged the screens from the warp engines, the *Enterprise* had escaped being blown to plasma only because she was travelling so close to *c* already. He didn't have the leisure to bring her up to that speed now, even if the Klingons would allow it. Yet the shields had to be strengthened, and he knew how to do it—or thought he did. He didn't pretend to understand the inversion apparatus in the slightest, but he knew from his boards that it put out a tremendous amount of power when operating—which it was now.

Are we in inversion, then? Must be. Doesn't feel like it—not that I miss choking. Never mind that now. He spoke hurriedly to the Engineering computers, making sure of the connections he should have the inversion apparatus's power feeders make to the screens. The Engineering computers, programmed by Scotty, confirmed that the connection was possible, and with Scotty's own conservatism urged that it not be made. "The hell with that," he said—even as he himself hesitated for a moment in terror—"triple override, implement!"

The ship began howling with imminent-overload alarms as the illimitable power inherent in de Sitter space poured itself through the tight little funnel of *Enterprise*'s control systems and out into the screens. The screens backed down out of the high violet, through indigo and blue and green, then began to glow brighter and brighter till they were searing white. None of the Klingon fire made the slightest difference to them now. *So much for that. . . .*

He slumped back a little in his seat—then straightened up again, horrified, fascinated. *What did I do??!* he thought—for the screens began to *grow,* swelling outward. Several of the attacking Klingons backed away. One did not, just kept firing—then stopped abruptly when the *Enterprise*'s screen hit his, and both the Klingon screen and the Klingon ship simply winked out of existence as if someone had turned them off. *Good Lord, what've I discovered?* he thought, watching with frightened satisfaction as the other Klingons backed off even farther. *Hope this doesn't do the same thing to the planet!*

As if they heard him, the screens' expansion began to slow, until finally they stabilized at several kilometers' distance from her. *Thank heaven! But there are other problems. . . .* He bent to his boards again. With this new power source, there was a way to get the landing party back even with screens up. Connect the transporter system to the inversion too, so that the signal would be strong enough to pierce the screens and not pick up interference. Just to be sure, tighten the bandwidth of the transporter signal to near-coherence at the ship end, allow it to fan out again onplanet—a neat trick, that, one that Uhura had suggested to him for more mundane signals. He spoke to the computer again, told it what to do with the transporter beam—and soon was hearing by remote that satisfying musical whine that told him everyone was back—

"RED ALERT! RED ALERT!" the ship was shouting—so that Sulu had to shout, too, to make himself heard over the din of sirens and other alarms. "Emergence confirmed, sir!"

"I'll say! Shields—" but a glance at the writhing, distorted image on the front screen told Jim they were already up. *That writhing, though!* "What in the—" He started to get up, then sat down again. He felt terribly weak and dizzy; a bar of pain like a phaser burn lay across his chest, and his ribcage felt like somebody had been using it for a trampoline. The communicator whistled, and it was all he could do to punch the button, he was in such pain and confusion. "Bridge—"

"Jim, don't you move! How does your chest feel?"

"Uh—" Memory came back. "I jumped in front of Spock, there was this wild animal—" He stopped. At least it felt like memory. Confused, he hooked a finger in the collar of his uniform tunic and peered down inside. Then he wished he hadn't. "I did it again, huh Bones?"

"I'll be right up with a stretcher."

"Bones, this is no time—!"

"You be quiet. You'll only be on your back for an hour or two, long enough for me to regenerate any heart tissue that got damaged. Argue the point and go into shock, and you'll be down here for two days."

"But Bones, it wasn't real!!"

There was a very brief pause. *"You look at the front of you again and tell me that, Jim. Out."*

Jim hit the toggle hard in annoyance and bewilderment. "What the devil's the matter with the screen?" he said. "Ship's status—"

"The problem is not with the screen, Captain," Spock said, stepping down beside the command chair, "but with the sensors, which are giving us data that makes very little sense. Or very little conventional sense. If I take the present readings at face value—and there is no reason not to at this point—we would seem to be in a place where the fabric of space itself is being terribly deranged by repeated intermittent loss of entropy. Something acted to augment the ship's screens during inversion—"

"I did that, Mr. Spock," Sulu said, sounding pleased, and confused, and worried, all at the same time.

Spock put one eyebrow up. "Then it's well that you did, Mr. Sulu.—He somehow tied the screens into the inversion apparatus, Captain. Despite the fact that he could not have; neither we nor the ship 'exist,' or should be capable of physical motion or even mental action during the inversion state." Spock made an expression of patient resignation. "At any rate, what Mr. Sulu did probably saved all our lives. K't'lk's 'portable entropy,' if I might call it that, was keyed into the screens—their failure would have entailed the failure of our protection as well. And had that happened, there are thousands of fatal errors that could have occurred in the most vital operational systems of this ship—fatal not only to the systems, but to us."

"Good work, Mr. Sulu," Jim said. "So, Spock, what are all these damn alarms about?"

"Well, Captain, as I said, the conditions the sensors are picking up from outside are mostly unlikely, and occasionally impossible. There is a great deal of radiation of all kinds out there, including Hawking radiation —a very distressing finding, for Hawking radiation is typical of the close neighborhood of black holes. Yet the sensors also insist there are no black holes hereabouts—or not for long, at any rate—"

"Not for long??"

Spock actually shrugged. "The readouts are most illogical. Mass and energy seem to be coming and going at unpredictable intervals. Stars appear and vanish—or go nova and then reappear unchanged—in complete defiance of conservation of energy. Not surprising; the laws of thermodynamics all require the flow of time to function—"

Jim stared at the screen. Someone had turned it off. "Get me a visual."

"I would not recommend it, sir."

"Why not?"

"Medical reasons." Jim opened his mouth to get tough with Spock, then felt the cough waiting down in the bottom of his chest; if he tried to get loud now, it would completely ruin the effect. "Precisely, Captain," Spock said. "Sir, you know I am the only member of the crew who cares to be on the observation deck in otherspace. The view outside the *Enterprise* right now is one I will have to look at in the pursuit of my duties. But I will not inflict it on myself more than necessary.

Vulcans are prone to a number of behaviors the other humanities find difficult to fathom, but masochism is not one of them."

The doors to the Bridge hissed open then. Jim had just time enough to glance around the Bridge and see how uneasy everyone looked, before McCoy came in, with a tall handsome blond-bearded man pushing a floater in front of him. "I'll want a report in a couple of hours, when McCoy's done," Jim said. "You, Scotty and K't'lk, whoever else can cast light on this mess—down in Sickbay."

"Shut up, Jim. Don, tilt that thing up, will you? About eighty degrees. Good. Step onto here, Jim. All right, Don, level him out. Come on, Captain Hero—"

"Take the conn, Spock," Jim said. "And keep her safe."

The doors closed on him.

Ten

"The data are in," K't'lk chimed. "And the only good thing about them is that you can't possibly be as disturbed by them as *I* am."

"Try me," Jim said, sitting up on the diagnostic bed and stretching. Bones had pumped him as full of pharmaceuticals as a drugstore; he felt much better, and wondered how long it was going to last.

Gathered about the bed were Scotty and Spock and K't'lk; McCoy leaned on the wall at its head. "Let me go first, Kit," McCoy said. "Jim, I've had opportunity to go over quite a number of the crew while you've been down here. There were a lot of minor injuries during this past inversion—injuries like yours, sustained in the experience itself, when it was impossible for anyone to move or even breathe—much less be in the places they report having been. None of the injuries were very serious. I still have a few people to check; you were something of a priority for me."

"Bones, I still don't understand. How could these things have actually *happened* to us? They weren't *real*—"

Bones folded his arms and leaned back, shaking his head. "Jim, you're heading for trouble. A lot of problems—wars, for example—get started when we point at one reality and claim that it's 'realer' than another. A lot of years in xenopsychology have convinced me that *anything* you experience is a reality—and that's not a difficulty, since realities naturally include one another. For example, my reality includes an *Enterprise,* and a Jim Kirk, and a Spock—God knows why—" Spock put up an eyebrow. "—and yours include not only all those things, but a McCoy too. There's also another kind of inclusion. For example, you might dream that a monster's after you and *know* it's real—then wake up, and know you'd been dreaming, and also know that you're in a more inclusive or 'senior' reality now. There are 'waking' realities apparently senior to ours; Lia's na'mdeihei would be an example, by their standards."

McCoy sighed. "What I'm suggesting is that all our personal realities are becoming far more inclusive, more 'senior,' than usual. Our inversion experiences seem to have started out with an inward emphasis—and have since been turning slowly outward, to include not only other people, but other people's perceptions."

"Could this have something to do with the increasing 'length' of the inversions?" Scotty said.

Bones shrugged. "Might be. The barriers living minds erect between their own realities and others' could very well be a function of entropy—and we've been spending more and more 'time' away from it. Something else interests me more, however, and I wonder if the space we're in has something to do with it. There was a common factor among all of the experiences the crew had this last time out. Every one of them perceived some kind of danger to the *Enterprise,* and acted to stop it. This is going to sound a little peculiar, and I have no proof for it whatever—but I'm not sure it was Mr. Sulu alone who saved the ship. I think the entire crew sensed something the matter, and it was the intention and concentration of the whole group that did the trick."

Jim nodded. "All right. Spock?"

Spock had been gazing at the table. He raised his eyes now, looking very grave. "Sir, Science Department's assessment of the situation in the space around us is extremely distressing. We have succeeded in determining that the time-space turbulence in this area does indeed have a locus of origin. That locus is far from here, even in terms of use of the inversion drive—nearly two million two hundred thousand light-years beyond the borders of the Lesser Magellanic, almost out of the Local Group of galaxies itself. Our sensors have been able to detect it primarily by indirect methods—not that they are able to actually sense anything in that spot—but, when pointed in that direction, that is where all their functions fail most catastrophically. That fact in itself joins with the presence of staggering amounts of Hawking radiation to suggest the nature of the locus. What we are seeing—or more accurately, not seeing—is a place where another universe has breached ours."

Scotty looked at Spock, surprised, but not very worried. "We've seen that before, man; what's the problem?"

"This other universe," K't'lk said, "appears not to have entropy at all. It is leaking non-entropy, 'anentropia,' into ours. And the breach through which it does so is widening."

"How fast?" Jim said.

"At a huge hyperlight velocity," Spock said. "The effect is able to propagate with no regard to the speed limit of light in this universe, since it is actually a function of the other universe's expansion. Within a month at most, it will have affected all of the Lesser Magellanic Cloud. Within two months, three maximum, it will encompass our own Galaxy. And within a year, or perhaps two, it could not only have encompassed the entire Local Group, but the whole 'megagalactic group' of which the Locals are an insignificant part."

Scotty went white. McCoy stood absolutely still beside him. Even K't'lk wasn't chiming. "What will happen?" Jim said.

"To the inhabited planets, you mean?" Spock looked at Jim, and no Vulcan calm could hide his distress. "Without entropy, there can be no life as we know it. Existence as such will simply cease, without time to pass through; as that other universe intrudes into, or rather around, ours, and finally contains it, anentropia will everywhere abolish life. And it will not happen quickly, or easily. Entropic space will first mix slowly with anentropic, like two fluids. As it is doing in the space around us."

Spock stepped over to the Sickbay wall screen. "On," he said. "Outside visual."

The screen came on, revealing a vista of blackness and stars that for the first fraction of a second looked like any other scene at the edge of a large globular cluster; a scattering of stars, thicker toward one side, thinning toward the cluster's fringes. But immediately the illusion of normality and tranquillity was destroyed. The stars would not be still. And this was no healthy fluctuation like that in the skies of faraway Lórien. These stars glittered feverishly, as if seen from the bottom of a dirty, turbulent atmosphere. Some of them exploded, and did so not cleanly, but hesitantly, by fits and starts—then contracted sluggishly to dim, diseased-looking globes. The stars flickered and guttered like failing candles in a bitter wind, as entropy and the lack of it washed over them in waves lightyears long, and time ran forwards, backwards, every which way. This was no pure, fierce burning into slow collapse and oblivion. This was protracted suffering, lingering death. Not even the darkness of empty space seemed clean. It *crawled.*

Jim looked away.

"Some of those stars have planets, Captain," Spock said. "Some of those planets have life. If you can call it that. It is a life in which nothing can be depended upon, where the laws of nature may be abruptly suspended at the whim of whatever eddy of time or not-time a world is caught in. I dare say the inhabitants would welcome death, if they could completely achieve it—for many of them will have been in the process of dying for what subjectively would feel like ages. Such a fate awaits all the known worlds. The Klingons, the Federation, all the hundreds of kinds of humanity we know, all the myriads we do not, in our Galaxy and in every other."

Jim looked at the screen again in fascinated horror, looked away again as the horror outweighed every other feeling. "There must be something we can do for them," he said in a whisper.

"Deal with the problem at its source," K't'lk said. "Indeed we *must* do so, Captain. We caused it."

Her chiming was pained, somber-sounding, a dirge for dying worlds. Jim looked at her, then up at Spock. Spock nodded. "Probability approaches one hundred percent very closely, Captain," he said. "The presence of the 'symbiotic' spectral lines in the stars here, the same lines as in 109 Piscium and zeta-10 Scorpii, confirms it—a breach of physical integrity on a massive scale, just considered locally. And out there, past the Local Group, a place where the physicality of our own universe's very fabric has been compromised. The topological process going on out there is fascinating—

but that is all there is to be said for it. It is a multi-dimensional analogue to the old topological puzzle in which one torus linked through another may completely 'swallow' its companion. Our universe will wind up contained within that other—and time, becoming impossible, will cease. All existence will go with it. I theorize, and K't'lk agrees with me, that every time we have used the inversion apparatus, the strain on the universe itself has become worse. Finally, on the jump before last, it tore. The jump we just made, as far as our measurements can tell us, aggravated the situation considerably. Should we go to the locus of this anomalous effect, the extreme length of the jump will aggravate it even more, accelerating the process. Yet so, to a lesser degree, would any attempt to return home and warn the humanities."

"Recommendations," Jim said.

"Attempt penetration of the Anomaly," Spock said.

"Allowing that we do—what can we do there?"

"There's a strong possibility that this breach can be healed," K't'lk said. "Captain, you and Mt'gm'ry have been pleased to joke about what my physics is good for besides confusing you. But we are alive and talking now partly because of it—"

"We're in the problem we're in *because* of it too," McCoy muttered.

K't'lk jangled at him, an annoyed sound. "Please, L'nrd. I don't disclaim my direct responsibility for the imminent destruction of life as we know it and as we don't, everywhere. But with that in mind, I don't have the time for thorax-thumping—"

"'Breast-beating,'" Scotty said gently.

"Right, thank you.—I don't have time for that, and you don't have time to stand around and watch me indulge in it. I need to *do* something about this mess. Starfleet can courtmartial me later, if I live. Captain, I can maintain and manipulate entropy on a local level. I can tailor the 'entropy shell' that has so far been protecting the ship so that it also protects each individual crewperson; nothing that generates a life-field will be in danger of facing anentropia unshielded, in the ship or out of it. Also, I am very sure I can work out a way to use the inversion drive itself to add enough power to my equations so that I can blanket that whole rift with entropy and weave space together again. Once that's done, we can return to this area—using short hops rather than the long ones that strain space so—and I can undo all the damage possible here."

"And if you can't?"

"Then, since we will be so close to the effect, we will, as the story says, 'go out—bang!—just like a candle.'" Spock looked down at K't'lk. "However, I ran another estimate of the probability of your success. It is much higher than we thought at first."

"Oh? How much?"

"Forty-eight percent."

"It's gone *up* to fifty-fifty, is that it, Spock? And this is an improvement?" McCoy said, exasperated.

"Bones," Jim said as calmly as he could, "do you have a recommendation?"

"Yes! One that worked real well for me when I was younger. I'm going to get in bed and pull the covers up over my ears so that all this will go away. I recommend you all do the same." He looked at Spock. *"You're* going to need more covers—"

"Bones—!"

"All right, all right. Jim, with each jump, the crew's individual mental integrity has broken down further—so that they're perceiving external realities as—well, no, that's not accurate. All experience is internal when you get down to it—"

"Doctor, this is no time for a lecture on ego-positivism—"

"When the theory fits, Spock, wear it or freeze in the

wind. Jim, I submit that a longer jump is going to break down those walls between people even more completely. There's no guarantee that we'll still be able to function as individuals. We may wind up as some kind of weird group mind. Also, any nightmare or dangerous vision that one of us may come up with might be able to affect some or all the others—with fatal effects. You'd better instruct the ship to run itself as completely as possible when we pop out, and to refuse override orders from anyone but department heads. Not that they'll be any more resistant than anyone else—it just seems it would cut down on the possibility of accidents. And for Heaven's sake, warn the crew about what might happen."

"I haven't yet chosen a course of action," Jim said. "However, all that is noted. Anybody else?"

No one said anything.

"Very well. Mr. Spock, I'm going to step out for a few minutes. You have the conn while I'm gone. Bones, will it be all right? Just a quick walk outside the ship; I won't go far."

"Don't overdo it. And stay on the opposite side of the ship from that." McCoy gestured at the deactivated screen.

"No argument." Jim swung down off the table and headed out.

He made his way down to Maintenance, surprising the Sulamid lieutenant there, who was cleaning off consoles with antistat spray and five or six cloths in as many tentacles. "Break me out a suit, Mr. Athendë," Jim said. "Not a work rig; just a routine maintenance pack with a full-angle helm."

"Sir affirmative, pleased," the Sulamid said, putting down the wipes and spray. It whirled over to the measurement console while Jim stepped up on the sensor plate to let the computer read his mass and size and metabolic rate. Mr. Athendë's tentacles slipped expertly along the surface of the console for a second. "Bay twelve, sir," he said, "helm fetch one moment."

Jim went to the suit bay that hissed open for him, and backed into the suit held by the grapples. They did up the lower seals for him, and by the time he'd detached himself and was sealing the top of the suit, Athendë came waltzing along the suiting floor in a whirl of tentacles, some of which were holding an observer's helm, clear all around. The Sulamid put the helmet on Jim, touching its seals into place and then checking the readouts on the front of the suit. "Heat pressure astrionics positive up running," Athendë said. "Sir exit preference? Captain's gig in shuttle bay?"

"Too long evacuate," Jim said, falling into holophrasis mostly for the fun of it. "Maintenance lock."

"Scuttle chute aye," Athendë said, flushing mauve with the old pun, and whirling away to the console again to start the little "scuttling" lock cycling. It chimed green-and-ready within a few seconds.

"Gratitude, Mr. Athendë," Jim said, stepping stiffly into the lock.

"Service pleasant, Captain," the Sulamid said over Kirk's helm intercom as the door slid shut between them. "Nice communication."

?? Jim thought, not quite getting the syntax on that last statement, as little by little air and sound hissed out of the lock around him. *Oh well.* He was left little time to wonder; the door into space opened as he turned to it. Jim took hold of one side of the lock and jumped out, pushing himself free of the lock's light gravity and out into the cold dark.

No sounds now but his own breathing and the gentle creaking of the suit as it made the best compromise it could between the near-absolute-zero of outside and the 24° C within. *We can fly out of the Galaxy,* he thought to himself, *but we can't build a suit that won't creak like old bones and make you look like a gorilla. What's Fleet coming to these days, anyway?* He laughed at himself, and at the silly cavil, as he punched the controls for the propulsion pack. Thrust pushed him strongly in the lower back, away from the great dim wall he hung beside.

On purpose he restrained himself from looking around on the way out, wanting to save the view for just the right moment. This proved difficult, for something was missing: the stars. The million familiar eyes that had always stared at him before were gone, leaving a darkness that unnerved him, and drew his eyes. But he refused to be drawn.

Jim turned up the heat—it was getting chill in the suit—and applied reverse thrust about a hundred meters from *Enterprise,* bringing himself around to look at her. Silhouetting her from far behind, the Lesser Magellanic was a bright spill of blue gems falling together through the empty night. The ship herself lay becalmed with only minimal running lights up, so that except for a red gleam here and there she was mostly a great shadowy shape floating in the void, with only a thin skin of faint starlight defining her hull on this side.

She looked mysterious, numinous, huger than ever. She made Jim think of that time he'd been night diving off the coast of northern California, and had been surprised in moonlit water by the whale. The humpback had hung beside him, singing-saying something in that incredibly complex language the scientists said bore the same resemblance to human speech that a Beethoven symphony does to a kazoo solo. Then, uncomprehending and uncomprehended, the whale had cruised off about its lawful occasions, leaving Jim to feel he had been examined, accepted, and left to his own devices. He felt that way now. The *Enterprise* of his vision, "alive" and familiar and solicitous of her children, was gone—replaced by a remote, unconcerned entity, more an absence than a presence. She floated untroubled in the freezing dark, in her element. She belonged here. *He* was the stranger.

Deliberately, then, as if turning away from even her slight safety, Jim brought himself about to look at what cast the starlight on her hull. And the view was very different from the vista available on the observation deck, where one was snug inside a ship.

There it hung above him. A galaxy, *the* Galaxy, not shut safely outside a clearsteel window, not even nearby any longer, but more distant than the Magellanic; a bright-shored island hanging grand and silent in the airless wastes, displaying all of its starry majesty at once. Jim just drifted there, letting himself see. Sol was lost in the sweep of stars in the leftward arm, an utterly insignificant 24th-magnitude spark that not even the great ten-meter Artemis/Luna reflector could have made out at this range. The whole Federation, from the Orionis worlds to the Vela Congeries, was a patch of sparkle that an upraised finger could cover. The Klingon and Romulan empires were lost entirely—

Awe grew in him again, and a muted joy; but also an increasingly powerful disquiet, so strong that inside the suit Jim simply shook for a moment. The world that all his life had been around him, was suddenly outside him—and he was outside *it*, way out in the coldest deeps where no star shone. Jim gazed in uneasy wonder at the little spiral-shaped home of life, with all its lights left burning in the dark. It finally sank in, as it hadn't even after the first jump, what he'd done to himself and the people he commanded. He'd gone too far, this time. He and four hundred thirty-eight souls were truly where no man had gone before, alone as no one in history had ever been. It delighted him. It terrified him. His voice sounded loud in the helm as, meaning it, he whispered that old phrase he'd read first in Anglish: "O Lord, Thy sea is so great, and my vessel so small. . . ."

And the shaking and the awe went away, for that brought him to the matter he had come out here to resolve.

It wasn't his crew's feelings about the danger of this situation that concerned Jim. The great starships' crews were selected with the danger of their missions in mind. No one made it onto a starship who didn't have one very important trait—an insatiable hunger and love for strange new worlds and "impossible" occurrences; a hunger so powerful that even the fear of death could be set aside for its sake when necessary. *Enterprise* and her sister starships were crewed by raving xenophiles.

What *was* on Jim's mind was potential loss of life—or in this case, the permanent discontinuation of it. As usual, he had to get past that issue so that he could choose what to do. It wasn't easy. All the other times that he'd almost lost the *Enterprise* came back to haunt him now, neatly summed up in the thought of his whole ship "going out—bang!—just like a candle." Once again Jim faced his responsibility for four hundred thirty-eight beings, some of whom he'd come to love dearly. This time, though, there was also the small matter of the whole Galaxy he was looking at, and all other Galaxies everywhere, "going out" in the same way he feared the *Enterprise* would—ceasing to be, forever.

Jim's first thought, after the loathing that instantly followed the idea of risking the lives of his officers and friends for *anything,* was that their lives were a small price to pay for the continued wellbeing of every other life in the Universe. But (whether they would agree with him or not) that was a kneejerk reaction, a position as potentially immoral as its opposite—that all a Universe's lives could or should be sacrificed for the sake of four hundred. It didn't necessarily follow that the needs of the many outweighed the needs of the few, or the one; that was a choice that could be ethically made only if the "one" was your own self. What proof was there, after all, that four hundred souls outweighed four trillion—or the other way around? Trying to equate numbers with value was a blind alley—nothing but one more way to avoid making a responsible choice.

Once when he was younger, he had seriously considered sacrificing a whole universe-to-be for the love of another human being. He wasn't that person any more. Another question occupied Jim today. When he and his crew signed aboard the *Enterprise,* they had all sworn to serve her purpose—the defense and preservation of life, and the expansion of life's quality by exploration and discovery. The question was simply, how could they serve that purpose best? By hurrying home with word of the breach in their universe, and letting Starfleet find an answer—one that might be better than any *Enterprise* could come up with unassisted? Or by attempting to deal with the situation on their own, and sending back word of how they did?

Are you kidding? Don't you ever learn? They'll treat the results of the drive the same way they did the drive itself. They'll give it to a committee. The Universe'll have been eaten by anentropia before they even manage to pick who the committee chairman will be. Besides, K't'lk is the expert on this stuff, and we've got her right here. And the Federation would just send out for some Vulcans, anyway. If you want Vulcans, you've got one, and he seems to know what's going on—

More reasons and rationalizations of that sort kept coming up. After a minute or two Jim put a stop to them and pushed them all aside. Totaling up the arguments on either side of a situation to see what outnumbered what was no way to choose, either; if you tried to treat the universe as a sum, no matter how carefully you added it up, the answer was always an irrational number. Nor was the cool guidance of logic a reliable refuge. "Logical alternatives" had been the death of many a starship captain and crew before.

Jim held still and spent a moment just looking at the whole problem, in the form of the bright-burning home that hung before him—symbol of all the uncountable lives that lay in his hands, symbol of his responsibility to them. Then he put all the reasons aside, all the hopes, all the fears, and chose.

He glanced at his chrono. It had taken him seven minutes.

Jim touched the communicator toggle on one sleeve. "Kirk to *Enterprise.*"

"Bridge," said Uhura.

"I thought you were offshift."

"You went for a walk," she said, as if that should have been explanation enough.

"I did that. Have Sulu and Chekov work out that course for the anomaly with Spock," Jim said. "And tell McCoy to speak to the department heads so each of you can warn your crew. This next step is going to be a doozie."

"Coming in now, sir?"

"Just a few more minutes, mother. Kirk out." He switched off to the sound of her decorously stifled laughter.

He drifted in the dark and the silence awhile longer, gazing at the mighty spiral, now so small, and then at the *Enterprise,* seemingly huger, but just as still. He began to get a glimpse of what that Andorian crew-woman had meant so long ago; that apparent size was indeed a symbol, as irrelevant to the essentials it contained as someone's height—McCoy's, say—was to the quality of his soul. It was the inner nature that counted—the meaning, not the matter; and even then, as K't'lk had said, what mattered was who was doing the meaning. Everything was the same size, really, until consciousness endowed that size with affect. If the "sea" seemed huge, and his vessel small, and the radiant Galaxy infinitely beautiful, it was because he saw them, and loved them, that way—

Jim snorted at himself in mockery. (Getting sentimental in your old age,) he thought, and turned himself with care, aiming himself back at the *Enterprise.*

But he stole a last long look over his shoulder before he cut in his jets.

"Is the crew ready?—Good. Then take us out, Mr. Sulu."

"Yes, sir. Engineering—implement inversion."

"And God have mercy on our souls," McCoy muttered from behind the command chair.

Eleven

Jim was beyond surprise. It was simply interesting, now, to find himself not in his command chair, but standing on a scrubby hillside that ran down on one side to a little gullied dry wash, and up on the other to a crest standing against blue sky. The sky was clear, and from the shade of blue, and the particular soft shadowless light that lay over everything, the time seemed to be just after sunset. *Well, let's get on with this,* he thought, and began to climb.

He passed manzanita bushes on the way up, and stands of featherduster grass, and a yucca plant with its tall flower-spike just beginning to break out in creamy white bells. *This could be anywhere in the southwest of N.A. Spring, or early summer; the air's a bit cool*—Jim made the hillcrest, puffing. *Should I be exerting myself so soon after cardiac arrest? Bones was right behind me, but I don't see him now, can't ask him—Oh well.* He looked down.

The hillside fell away from him in broad curved

ridges for a thousand feet or so. At its feet, spreading far ahead and to left and right for miles, lay a broad flat valley, thick with trees and crisscrossed with a webwork of golden lights in the dusk. Far across it, streetlamps dotted the foothills of the Santa Monicas like a fall of stars; and the scream of a commercial iondriver lifting from the suborbital port at Van Nuys drifted to him through the still air. On the far side of the Santa Monicas, a faint warm glow in the sky went up from the ten million lights of Los Angeles. Jim shook his head and smiled; this was a vista he hadn't seen since he took up climbing while in high school. It would have been pleasant to sit down on the hilltop, as he'd done so many times before, and watch the stars come out one by one through the haze. But he wanted to find his people. *Downhill will probably work as well as anything else,* he thought, and took a step—

—and the suit creaked around him as Jim half slid, half bounced down through the red dust and gravel of the slope inside the crater's rim to where the other suited figure stood, hands on hips, gazing upward. The other's suit was Fleet issue too, with commander's stripes on the sleeves, and the pierced-barrier-and-arrow of the Starfleet Corps of Engineers. Jim bounced over to Scotty's side, tapped his own faceplate as a signal for Scotty to unpolarize his.

"Half a moment, Jim," Scotty said over Jim's helm intercom, pointing upwards. Jim looked up and saw the reason. They were lowering the crater dome into place, a tremendous Fuller-ribbed clearsteel shell that blocked out more and more of the hard black-violet sky as the tractors of the *Thermopylae* and *T'Laea* let it down.

"Lord, Scotty, that thing must be ten kilometers wide!"

"Eleven point four five eight eight," Scotty said, almost absently. His mind was very much elsewhere,

Jim knew, for he could feel his old friend's concern as if it were coming from within himself, not from outside. The computers had said the thing wouldn't collapse under its own weight this time, but then they'd said that the last two times, before Scotty had come on the job and suddenly gotten the hunch about the distribution equations for the bracing. Now they would find out the truth in the only way any engineer ever really trusted, no matter what the paperwork said.

Scotty gestured at Jim, and together they bounced a little further down inside the crater wall. The dome shut out nearly all the sky above them now, and the small, ferociously white Sun low down in the sky was briefly cut off, then shone again less blindingly as the clearsteel polarized it. *"Mind the balance, Jennifer,"* he said over the 'com to the engineer-captain of *Thermopylae.*

"Stop worrying and enjoy the show, Scotty."

Scotty snorted. He was sweating. The dome dropped lower and lower, now hanging right above the vast, double-walled support rim that had been built for it, circling the crater. It was meters above the rim, feet above it, inches. The light of the sky winked out, and still Scotty stood as still as if frozen—

Even in this light gravity, the ground boomed and shuddered for seconds as the tremendous mass of the dome nested and settled into the rim. And as it did, as all its power contacts went home, up and down the dome's bracing struts the lights came on, glowing red, dull orange, yellow, brilliant white—

People on *T'Laea* and *Thermopylae* were cheering. Scotty let out a long breath and turned to face Jim, his helm unpolarized now. Jim leaned over to touch helmets with Scotty, and as he did so was surprised. This was Montgomery Scott, all right—but where was the grey hair, where were the wrinkles? Where had this younger man come from? "Scotty, you didn't tell me you'd done this big a job on Mars—"

"I haven't, yet," Scotty said. "This project was still on the drawing board when my orders came in to leave for the *Enterprise*. I just wanted to see how it was going to come out. But I guess we'd best be looking for the others—"

"I suppose so," Jim said. Together, under the dazzling lights of the dome, they headed down the slope of the crater wall—

They found Uhura singing in a little downstairs nightclub on Antares II; and Sulu leaning over the rail of one of the terraces of the Ten-Thousand-Step Stair on the third moon of Mirfak XI, admiring the view of the methane glacier; and Janice Rand standing in a pine forest with a covered picnic basket over one arm, and a bemused look on her face, while a wolf she'd been talking to when they arrived slipped off into the shadows. Every few steps Jim and his little escort would find another crewman or three, and then walk on a little way more, and the environment would melt away into another one more marvelous or strange than the last. Wide plains of waist-high blue grass, cinnamon-scented and blindingly jeweled with dew under a white-hot sun, became a summer evening roofed over with a single burning spiral arm of the Galaxy, floored with an endless waste of black sand and echoing with the roars of unknown beasts. A road of white glass, stretching toward a distant desolation of barren peaks, turned into a greensward rolling down in gentle hills to the sea; gulls wheeled and cried about the pinnacles of a great many-towered castle that rose on a little peninsula there, the castle's crystal windows reflecting the sunset at their backs and shining like a star. Dusty golden afternoons, pale days that held the silver sun captive in cloud above alien trees, seven-starred mornings without a shadow, glowing green dawns—they replaced one another in never-repeating procession. Not sure what else to do, Jim walked onward through them, and his people followed him. After a time—if it could be called that, for even moments past felt like now, and Jim knew that time was not really passing—he was walking along with about half the complement of the *Enterprise,* and picking up more every few minutes.

Jim was as fascinated by the people themselves as by the places where he found them. Many looked younger than they had when the mission started, or else simply *better*—healthier, more powerful, more alive. Also, each time the environment changed and more crewpeople turned up, Jim found himself experiencing the newfound world, not just from his own viewpoint, with his own emotions and reactions, but from the perspective of one or more of the people he found there. The effect was like double vision, but non-visual, and for quite a while Jim found it profoundly disturbing. *Is this what Spock has to put up with when he's aboard ship? No wonder he has to withdraw sometimes—*

There were other matters, though, also demanding attention. Jim noticed that no matter how the landscapes shifted, they tended to find themselves going either uphill or down; level stretches there were, but they were rare. He mentioned this to Scotty as they made their way up one more hillside, this one with what appeared to be a walled garden at the top of it.

"Oh aye," Scotty said, "I'd noticed that myself. I suspect it might have to do with the changes in the entropy gradient hereabouts—so that we're perceivin' the waves of entropy and anentropia as 'ups' and 'downs.'"

"Then maybe if we find ourselves going uphill more and more—"

"—it should mean we're gettin' closer to the core of

the Anomaly, the source of the anentropia, aye. Then K't'lk can do her bit. Whatever that may be."

"I haven't seen her."

"Ha," Scotty said with a grin, and pointed up the hill. The garden wall had a gate in it, and out through the gate came K't'lk, along with several crewpeople who were munching on fruit from the trees whose branches overhung the garden wall. "So, lass," Scotty said as she came down toward him and Jim and the great crowd of *Enterprise* crew, "where to now?"

She glanced up the hillside. "Farther up," she chimed, "though we may have to go farther down to get there. Captain, are you well? Is the lack of time distressing you, or all this climbing? You look troubled."

Jim shook his head. "No problem with the time—I've had a lot of practice getting used to that lately. And the climbing—no. Not even slightly, which is odd. If you can call anything here more odd than anything else." He looked around him and kept on walking. "I'd like to find Spock, though. And I haven't seen Bones either—"

He didn't even have time to take the expected few steps down the slope of the garden hill before things shifted again. The landscape this time was fierce, harsh, craggy, all stones and sand and cracked crimson earth. A hot wind laden with strange scents, rich and aromatic and sharp all at once, blew across rising land from a red-dun sky; while a huge orange moon, terrifyingly close, swam up from beneath the high horizon, gibbous under a furious blue-white sun.

Vulcan, Jim thought, and wasn't surprised at the sight of the tall form walking up the slope toward them. For one thing, as soon as this place had appeared, he'd caught the distinctive tenor of Spock's thoughts—the silent love and longing the half-Vulcan felt for this savage and desolate beauty, interwoven with the incessant activity of the man's mind as it worked to analyze the present situation. For another, Jim thought of how quickly K't'lk had appeared when Scotty said he wanted to see her, and suspected strongly that, despite Spock's disclaimer, the things you wished for *did* happen in this space. What Jim *hadn't* expected was McCoy, walking up the slope alongside Spock and looking around him with such a still, reserved look, he seemed Vulcan himself.

They came up to him and the group walking in the lead of the *Enterprise* crew. Experimentally, Jim groped around for the "feel" of McCoy's mind. It was more difficult to pin down, subtler, though no less complex; geared to receiving, in contrast to Spock's orientation toward giving; as if Spock was a light source, but McCoy was a mirror. *Well, that's not quite it. But you can see other people in him.* The mirror reflected Spock's bright cool fire, and the curiosity and perplexity and delight of the crewmen all around; it even reflected Jim's own feelings, his desire to get to the heart of this mystery, his own fascination with what was going on. The perceptions were peculiar, but considering what Jim knew about Bones, they made perfect sense. *Is this telepathy? No wonder Spock has so much trouble explaining it to us . . . comparisons, regular words, can't, don't adequately describe it—*

"Yes, Captain," Spock said. "It's a supremely subjective experience. Are you well?"

"Quite. Gentlemen, I am glad to see you. I think we're just about all here now. The only question being, where is it we are?"

They began to walk again. Spock fell in on Jim's right side, McCoy at his left. "We are in the ship, Captain," Spock said. "How should we have left it, after all?"

"Spock," Jim said, "if this is the *Enterprise,* Harb

Tanzer's been putting a *lot* of extra equipment in the Rec room that he hasn't told me about."

"Nonetheless, we are aboard the *Enterprise,* Captain," Spock said. "What has shifted is the way in which we are perceiving her. And in those shifted perceptions, there is room for anything—just as you can imagine the whole Galaxy, without having to be physically large enough to contain it."

"We've reached the Anomaly, then?"

"Its outermost fringes, I would say. My tricorder—or the artifact of thought that is presently manifesting as my tricorder—indicates the entropy gradient increasing toward the high ground. That is the way we must keep going."

"As usual," Bones muttered.

"Which brings me to another question. Bones, people are looking a lot—better—"

McCoy nodded. "So I see. The answer's straightforward enough, if the way we're going really is toward an area of decreased entropy. Aging, trauma, physical death, are all functions of heat death, ultimate energy loss. So's trauma of the mind—and if that's being halted or reversed, it's no wonder people look better. The mind affects the body, it can't be otherwise. What I'm not sure of is how far the effect will go. But I suspect it'll continue to accelerate as we approach the heart of all this. I tell you, it worries me a little."

"No need, Doctor," Spock said. "Indeed, you will not be worrying about it much longer, if my theory is correct. As we head further into the region of anentropia, entropic aspects of behavior—anger, fear and so forth—will rapidly decrease, even disappear."

"Are you saying we're going to become less human than we are—?!"

Spock sighed and looked at McCoy with nearly unalloyed affection. "Leonard, please stop disagreeing just to have something to say." McCoy's mouth fell open. "If you are truly going to sorrow to see your fellow crewpeople lose greed, rage, terror, anguish, and the other 'darker' emotions that beset most of the humanities, you are not who I thought you were. And I suspect we must make our peace with who we are as quickly as we can. In this place where nothing else remains stable, that is information we will probably need to succeed in this mission."

"Let's get on with it, then. Uphill?"

"Uphill, Captain."

They went. Despite the strangeness of it all, Jim found the going pleasant; especially since the one sensation that frequently got lost for him, during a mission, was the feeling that it wasn't just him acting alone at the center of the Bridge, but a whole crew doing so in concert. Having the four hundred thirty-eight actually physically around him (if any of this was either actual, or physical) was a joy. If there was a problem, it was that the changes of environment began to become irregular, unpredictable. Worlds began to shift, not with the melting grace he'd become used to, but spasmodically; images tore, whirled, jumbled together.

He glanced to his right. "Trouble, Spock?"

Spock lifted his tricorder, studied it. "Very likely. We are entering an area of turbulence in the entropy mix. The tricorder readings are chaotic, but I suspect that beyond the turbulence lies an area in which the gradient of anentropia increases very sharply indeed. We are coming close to the core of the Anomaly, Captain."

"All right," Jim said, and turned to face the four hundred who followed. "We're almost where we're going, but we're in for some rough stuff," he said—and then had to stop talking for a moment. He hadn't looked back at his crew for a while. This place, however, had not stopped working on them; they looked so young, so strong, so capable and powerful, that he wondered for a moment why he was bothering to warn them about anything. It was strange to have said, for all these years, "I have the best crew in the Fleet!"—and to suddenly not just know, but *see*, that that was true. Jim was in fact a little abashed to be standing in front of them, they were so splendid. But they looked at him with their usual calm acceptance of whatever he had to say, so Jim found his nerve again and went on. "Stay together, keep an eye on the people around you—don't lose anyone. Mr. Spock tells me we're going to have some pretty steep ground ahead."

He didn't even need their murmur of acquiescence; the wave of their thought—agreement, support, a willingness to follow wherever he led—hit Jim so hard he thought he would fall down. "Let's go, then," he said, and turned to rejoin his Bridge crew and lead the way.

For the first time, climbing started to become difficult —as if gravity had reasserted itself, then had become stronger and stronger, building to several times Earth-normal. Jim struggled up through it, while around him the scenery changed more and more swiftly, swirling around him in an increasingly disorienting storm of instability. It was as if the world were coming apart. His body felt as if it was being torn and tugged in many directions. "Jim—!" someone gasped by his side.

He looked over at McCoy. "The kids in back—" Bones said.

Jim looked over his shoulder. The storm of imagery almost hid his crew, most of whom were walking heads down, struggling into the tempest. "The air's—a little clearer here," Jim said.

"That's what I meant. They need us—their officers—

to be with them. They're worried about us, and it's making the going harder for them."

"We'll split up, then." He glanced around him at the Bridge crew, many of whom were close by. "Everybody find a group to take care of. Bones, send some of the kids in the middle up to be with me—"

McCoy patted Jim on the shoulder, vanished into the howling maelstrom.

Jim gathered his group of thirty or forty about him, took a few steps to determine which way uphill was—sight was almost no use now—and headed up the steep slope, through the whirling, tattering landscape. He was in increasing pain. His slow-growing telepathy had begun bringing him the distress of the crewpeople around him as their own minds and bodies were torn at, shaken. If the tearing had been merely physical, he could have borne theirs and his without too much trouble. Spock had long since taught him the simpler of the Vulcan disciplines for handling pain, by which one accepts and accepts the pain till it becomes part of one, and vanishes. *But this is beyond accepting,* Jim thought in his own terror, as again and again his thoughts seemed to slip out from under him, becoming someone else's, and Jim Kirk got lost. *What if I can't find myself again afterward?—Never mind that. Just keep going—*

—can't hear myself think, what are all these people doing in my head? Dear lady Mother, just help me keep moving, I can't burden my crewmates with me—

—Robbie, you've got to keep up—

—no fearing in the past is anything like this fear; I wish I'm lying down and dying here, but I can't, I'm needed. Mayri needs me. He *needs me, alone there leading as I'm not alone even in this following. Keep walking, sir, I'm here. Dying, but here—*

—terror-terror-concern for another-rage-defiance!-denial!-defiance!-intention to follow!-follow!-anguish-negation-rejection-follow!-follow!-follow!—

It got worse. It couldn't get worse, and it got worse. His people's frenzied thoughts hit him and hurt him like hail, and Jim didn't dare shut them away; he knew that if he did, they would lose him. *Just keep going. It has to end.* The going became precipitous; the surface he walked on seemed to try to drop away from beneath his feet with every step he took; and the terror, the others' terror, filled him until he couldn't tell where his own fears left off and theirs began. *Lost, I'm lost, we'll wander here forever—No. No. Feel how steep this incline is. There has to be an up somewhere on the other side of this down. Keep going, they depend on you, keep going—*

—aye, lass, mind Ensign Dabach over there, she's having a hard time/don't know, I haven't seen him, let's look—

—hang on, Jim, this can't last much longer or get much worse. I think. /Oh God, get that thing off Susanne! Jerry, you take her arms— /No, Tasha, don't look at that. Just keep going—

—Lieutenant, you must keep your eyes open to walk. Stay behind me—/where she went, but she can take care of herself if anyone can, what about/Christine! Christine! Get up, it can't hurt you, let me/don't let it, oh Master of Everything, it's all in my/sweet Architectrix, where do you suppose that *came from, and how can I keep it* away—

/I won't, I won't, he's *not and* he/*I will not collapse in front of all these/doctor, not an exterminator/pain, there is no pain, there/courage! courage! the worst/it can't get/never drink* that *again as long as I/don't give up, Jim! keep going! keep/we're here, we're behind/if you don't give up, we won't, keep/can't get worse, they're all watching, keep/on, just a little/rrhn'meieisae tamnusiaierue ien'toa/die, won't die, won't/te morituri saluta/must, keep, going, one/morituri/must! keep! going! Must/can't/dare/will/will/ will! not! give! up!, will*

not!willnot!giveup!onemore!step!onemore!onemore!one more!justonemoreonemoreonemore—

—and without warning the terrible downward slope was all gone, and Jim opened his eyes and looked around him, astonished to find himself walking uphill again, but (again) with greater ease than on any downhill side he had ever walked before. Jim paused a moment, squinting in the great light, to wipe the chilly sweat off his face. His people were all around him—shaken, pale or flushed or contracted or vibrating as their species dictated, but otherwise whole—and looking much better than he would have expected for people who had just been through the same repeated almost-death he had experienced. A few of them—Mr. Athendë from Maintenance, Janice Kerasus from Linguistics, Larry Aledort from NavComp—reached out to touch him with hands or tentacles. He suffered the touch without complaint, grateful for one thing that he still had a body; considerate of their need, for another —they seemed to be reassuring themselves of their own existence by virtue of his. "Ladies and gentlemen," he said, to them and to the other crewpeople standing around them, "this place *can't* offer anything worse than *that.*"

There were murmurs of agreement. "If you're all well," he said, "let's go, then. Pass the word back that we're starting up. Anyone unable to continue should find Dr. McCoy and make arrangements to wait. Ready?"

They were, he knew; as he knew, without even having to look, that no one was remaining behind. He began walking again—then slowed almost immediately as he had a chance to look around him. Partly it was the blinding brilliance of the landscape that stopped him—though it seemed to get less blinding as he peered into it. But what he saw through the light—the actual features of the land, that now held still though its details shifted and melted as whole landscapes had before—distressed him more than any mere brightness could.

"Dear God," he said to the crewpeople surrounding him, "what have we gotten ourselves into?!"

Twelve

The gates didn't last long, and that was just as well. Jim didn't know whether he would have laughed at them, or started shaking, if they'd proved permanent. Great golden gates they were, ornate, resplendent, set in walls that looked like brick and shimmered like pearl, and went on and on in either direction, forever. Jim glanced to his left, where Mr. Matlock stood, his mouth open; and to his right, where Amekentra from Dietary stood shaking her emerald-scaled head and twitching her gill slits. "Do you see what I see?" said Jim.

"Sweet Queen of Life, I hope not," Amekentra said. "Ups! there it goes—" and the gates vanished. But the three of them kept staring, feeling no relief, and behind them the rest of the crew did the same. In place of the gates, a wall of stone appeared, low enough to step over, with a terrible stillness of black sky behind it; and in place of the wall, a river so cold that it smoked and the stones among which it ran were rimed with ice; and in place of the river, a lintelless doorway that reached up and up out of sight, and was full of stars; and in place of that, a great sheer flat cliff, surely one of the legendary walls of the world, with some message written on it in letters so huge that no one could read them. The whole crew had to back up many paces before the words could be made out. A whoop of wild laughter broke out then, from somewhere way back in the ranks—*Lieutenant Freeman, from Life Sciences,* Jim thought; *his laugh stands out even in a crowd.* Freeman had even more reason for it now than usual. In red block letters, very neat, the writing on the wall said THIS SIDE UP. Unfortunately, the arrow painted beside the words pointed at the ground. The sign was upside down.

"I always *knew* there was something fundamentally wrong with the universe," someone female said from behind Jim. "No," another voice replied as the sign vanished, "that's just paranoia; everybody has *that* . . ."

The barrier changed and changed, while about it the landscape remained the same; barren, pale stone underfoot, and a clear sourceless brilliance all around, as if the air itself burned. *We're seeing symbols,* Jim thought. *Boundary lines. Our minds are trying to warn us that we've come to the end of the World as we know it—the end of physicality, the beginning of the paraphysical. Past this line, anything can happen—*

Jim found himself looking at a little brook, not cold like the other one, but floored with waving weed and half choked with the sedges that climbed up its banks. He recognized it. While he was still a midshipman stationed on Terra he had hunted for this spot—so that he could stand where Caesar had once stood with the Tenth Legion at his back, gazing across at Rubicon's far bank, and past it toward the angry might of Rome. Two steps would take Jim across the creek. He thought of turning to those nearest and saying something about the die being cast—then thought better of it. Caesar had been grandstanding for his nervous legion's benefit. He had no need of such tactics with *this* crew. "Let's go," Jim said, and stepped down into the cold water, slipping once on the mossy stones before making the far side. His people followed him.

The landscape stayed still, now—barren, featureless, and level, so that Jim wasn't sure in which direction to go. On a hunch he said to the crewpeople with him, "Fan out in standard search pattern and see if this light seems to get brighter in any one direction."

They did, twelve of them casting about with tricorders or just with eyes. "Sir," one of the Ielerids sang back to him from twenty or thirty meters to left and forward, "there is a difference here. The air seems clearer."

Looking at hir, Jim could see a difference too. Despite the fact that s/he was farther away than the other crewmen, Ensign Niliet's sable-furred shape looked somehow closer and more distinct than the rest of them did; hir green eyes glittered as if reflecting a brighter light than surrounded Jim or any of the others. "Good work, Ensign," he said, and saw hir throat-pouch swell with pleasure. Not that he needed to see it; he could feel hir pleasure as if it were his own. "That way, everybody."

On they all went; Jim more or less at point with a few of the crew scouting ahead of him in the direction he'd indicated, more of them flanking him on either side. The air got swiftly clearer as they went along. At least that was the least inaccurate way the effect could be described. What one saw grew sharper; colors grew more vivid, and detail richer, finer, more complex. The air itself became sharper to breathe, even a little painful at first—then a growing pleasure, as one became more sensitive to a clean crispness like that on a mountain height. But this wasn't cold. It was a delight just to walk, to breathe, to look at other people as their vividness increased. Jim did a lot of looking, and began to notice something new.

The crewpeople about him were beginning to change. The changes weren't always immediately obvious, and there was nothing terrible about them; it was as if the things Jim saw had always been latent in his people somehow, waiting to come out. But the transformations were no less strange for that. Some of the crewpeople abruptly lost all resemblance to their usual selves. Some kept their bodies, but there was something bizarre or new or wonderful about them that Jim had never noticed before. Some seemed completely unchanged in form, but picked up odd companions.

Jim let his own pace slow a little, out of sheer amazement. There was Lieutenant Brand, a slender little dark-haired woman with a pert, pretty face, one of the designer-engineers from down in Phaser Tech—walking alertly along with one hand on her sidearm, and her other hand held by a giant rabbit that was walking on its hind legs beside her. There was Mr. Mosley from down in Stores; one moment he was fine, but a breath later Jim found himself looking at an Andorian alicorne that paced calmly along on six delicate hooves, and paused once to polish its indigo horn against the creamy pelt of one flank. Janice Kerasus from Linguistics went by, arguing and laughing in many tongues with the crowd of hominid and nonhominid sentients surrounding her—proud-faced people with indigo skins, and big lithe felinids, and fierce-eyed, black-robed folk with veiled faces. Tall, stoop-shouldered Lieutenant Freeman from Bio, walking to one side, noticed Kirk looking toward him, and waggled a small, grave salute at him to let his Captain know he was being taken care of. But in the middle of the gesture things became otherwise, and Freeman's Life Sciences white was changed for the dark somber splendor of old twentieth-century dress. He was suddenly taller, slimmer, and inhumanly handsome; in the hand that had held his tricorder, Freeman now bore a rose that burned silver as a sun.

That kind of thing by itself would have been enough to make Jim glance away. He felt sure that this vision, like the others he was seeing, was a physical expression of some profound personal truth, something very private. However, there were also mildly disturbing aspects to some of the images he saw. For instance, Jim had never been completely comfortable with furry things since the problem with the tribbles; so maybe that was why the great shaggy-pelted pink caterpillar-alien flowing along behind Freeman, tugging at his clothes with cruelly clawed arms and begging him for "dessert," made Jim so uneasy.

Unnerved, he turned his eyes to McCoy's little contingent for reassurance. Most of them looked normal. Uhura was walking with that group; she seemed unchanged, but she was accompanied by a huge crowd of animals from many planets that went striding, thundering, hopping and slithering along with her while she held earnest conversations with one or another of them. Lia Burke was there too, near the front of the group, herself unchanged—though there *was* a darkness about her, as if some huge creature Jim couldn't see was following Lia closely, and she walked in its shadow. And McCoy—

The doctor saw Jim's stunned look, spoke a word or two to a couple of the people who were keeping him company, and left them behind to see to Kirk. Jim literally had to squeeze his eyes shut as Bones approached. McCoy blazed, not with light, but with an intense compassion that could be felt on the skin, even from a distance, like sun in a desert. Jim had always known Bones cared deeply about people, but he was unprepared for the full truth of the matter—this passionate allegiance to life, this fierce charity that wished health and joy to everything that lived. Jim felt all the death in him, all the entropy, screaming and cowering away; it knew its enemy. It tried to drag Jim away with it, but he stood his ground, wondering whether he would survive McCoy's touch, or be able to stand the burning life it promised if he did. "Jim? You all right?" the familiar voice said, as a hand took him by the arm—the fingers surreptitiously on the inside of the arm, to find the brachial artery for the pulse.

"Never better," Jim said, and gasped, too shocked to say anything else for a moment or open his eyes. Strangely, it was true. The casual touch of McCoy's hand had staggered him like a graze from a phaser set on kill, but now he was feeling almost more alive than he could bear—and moment by moment the aliveness became more bearable. He tried to hide his need to gulp for air, then gave it up and just gulped, hoping his friend would simply think he was winded from the long walk. *Hidden natures are getting loose,* Jim thought. *What we conceal doesn't stay that way, here. It may be this isn't going to be a good place to stay for very long. Or, well, good, but not* safe—

"Just let yourself breathe, it'll pass," McCoy said, sounding slightly abashed. "Sorry. I keep forgetting, and that keeps happening." Jim opened his eyes and found McCoy easier to look at, though no less bright with compassion. Bones let Jim go, then glanced down with wry amusement at the hand that had both steadied and unsteadied his Captain. "I want people to be better," he said with some wonder, "and they get that way. Dangerous stuff. —That armor getting heavy?" Bones said, sounding a bit tentative now. Jim shook his head, thinking What armor, what's he seeing? . . . "No problem," he said. "Bones, have you been noticing people?"

McCoy looked away, nodding. "More than people,"

he said. "If this crew wasn't comfortable with itself before, it will be now! But Jim, have you seen—"

"Captain," the other familiar voice said on his other side, "are you well?" And Jim turned to look at Spock, and was dazzled again, but this time he couldn't look away. Spock hadn't changed; but here his spirit showed as it never had before, even in the harrowing intimacy of mindmeld. From the meld, Jim was already familiar with the incessant activity of that cool, curious mind as it tirelessly hunted answers. But now he saw where the activity came from—Spock's utter certainty that there was no higher purpose for his life than to burn it away in search of truth, and to give that truth away when he found it. More, Jim saw what fueled and underlay the certainty: a profound vulnerability paired with a great, unreasonable joy—the deepest-hidden parts of Spock's Earth-human heritage, both of them sheer terror to a Vulcan mind. Even when Spock had been trying to suppress or deny those hidden legacies, they had managed again and again to escape and express themselves as valor, and wry humor, and the endless good-natured fencing with McCoy. But Spock wasn't denying the inheritance so vehemently any more, and the power of the older, wiser man was a joy to behold, and a terror. *This great mind has been standing behind me and quietly obeying my orders for all these years? Why?? He could be so much more*—But in this place, the answer was plain to read. Loyalty was frequently unreasonable and illogical—and Spock had long since decided that this one aspect of his life could do without logic.

"Spock," Jim said—and ran out of words. He was deeply moved, and didn't know how to adequately express it—until he abruptly felt Spock feeling the emotion with him, and knew there was nothing more that needed saying on the subject. "I'm fine, Spock," he said then, and glanced over at McCoy. Bones was gazing at Spock in a curious, almost grudging calm.

"Leonard," Spock said, "you are not seeing anything now that you have not long suspected was already there. Nor am I." The shadow-smile, the flash of humor, pierced Spock's outer and inner sobrieties once more. "And you need not be concerned about your 'dark' places revolting me. I have seen them before, in meld, and may yet see them there again. More apparent here is that neither of us is quite the hopeless case the other has sometimes considered him to be."

"It'd help if I understood why it's apparent," McCoy said, grumbling—though it was obvious to Jim that his heart wasn't in the grumble.

"I'm sure you've already come to suspect part of what is happening here, Doctor. True natures are becoming evident, and latent talents are being enhanced, due to the increasing anentropic nature of this space—so I infer. Already I need not touch for mindmeld. Nor need you . . . as you just found. And probabilities are high that we shall see stranger things yet."

"Speculate," Kirk said, doubting Spock would care to.

"On the contrary, Captain. The boundaries between separate minds are thinning, as the Doctor suggested they might. But the result seems to be that people are becoming *more* themselves as a result, rather than less. The exact cause for this, I cannot state with certainty. It may be a function of the nature of mind, hitherto unsuspected; or a function of this particular space. But we must do what we can to find out, for that too is data we may need where we are going."

There was something about the phrasing that made Jim hold still and look around him at his people, who moment by moment were becoming more real, burning with surpassing selfness as McCoy did with compassion and Spock did with knowing. "Which is, I take it," Jim said very slowly, "to 'the side of the angels'?"

"Idiomatic, but precise in mood if not in particulars," Spock said, as they began to walk again. "Jim, consider it. A truly anentropic space—a place where energy is not lost, where time may not exist, or may be perceived as a whole rather than a sequence of events. A place where the emotions sprung from mortality and the fear of it have no foundation, no reason to exist. Where is that?"

McCoy looked at Spock with an expression compounded of unease and awe and delight. "Where 'there shall be no more death,'" he said slowly, "'neither sorrow, nor crying, neither shall there be any pain, for the former things are passed away. . . .'"

Spock nodded. "The question becomes who, or what, we will find there. And what will be required of us—for I am becoming increasingly sure there is a need for us, something we have to do. In neither the Vulcan mythologies nor the Terran ones do mortals walk the realms of the gods without reason. There is always a task to be performed—one to which gods are unequal, and for which mortals must therefore be enlisted. So we must be ready. We must make our peace with what we find in ourselves here, and in others—"—he looked at McCoy with his own version of the doctor's curious wondering calm—"—so that we are prepared for the stranger truths ahead." He glanced at Jim. "And the sooner we manage it, the better. We must not overstay our welcome. If we remain here so long that this space begins to remove the mind-scars that we call our memories, we are undone. And sooner or later, even K't'lk's shielding will yield and leave us frozen and unconscious for eternity . . . if eternity can be properly said to exist in a place without time."

They walked on. The laughter of the crewpeople following them became less frequent, but that was not to say the crew was becoming any less merry or excited than before. Jim could feel his people's delight settling down into a kind of sober joy and expectation that found words and noises an inadequate expression. Thought worked better, and Jim could feel them exploring one another's minds with a shy and childlike excitement, beginning to weave themselves into a great whole of which their old "crew morale" had been a pale foreshadowing. Some of the exploration Jim found rather familiar, except that it now sounded strangely like the ruminations of a single mind instead of a discussion between two—

"I'd been thinking that the system shouldn't just stop with 'cause'—"

"And it doesn't. There's a higher level of responsibility still, with more power attendant on it. When you're ignorant of cause, of your personal responsibility for the way the Universe is, no matter how much you try to change things, they stay the same—because down at the bottom of your mind you're believing it's someone or something else's fault that things are the way they are. But the acceptance of cause enables you to bring about true alteration—making things *other*—without the persistence associated with change. That acceptance makes possible the 'archonic' functions—the ability to ordain energy states for entire universes—"

"Lass, it still seems impossible. To alter a universe's whole operating system just by sayin' you *want* to—"

"But Mt'gm'ry, there was at least one person I know of on your planet who used to do such things rather routinely. He codified one of the basic rules for the art: 'Ask, and it shall be given unto you.' An inspired creative physicist, way ahead of his time. Anyway, the rest of the system is simple. Extropy, entropy, and anthotropy are the three energy-states in this paradigm —there are probably more, in higher 'dimensions,' as with all the other relationships. Entropic universes you know about; they start out with a fixed amount of energy and lose it. Extropic systems can be generated by ordinance, but generally no one bothers. They're 'sterile'—sealed systems that don't lose energy and therefore rarely produce life unless something 'punctures' them. And anthotropic systems are eternal and undying—universes capable of 'reproducing' themselves by generating new energy to replace the old—"

"By taking it from somewhere else?"

"By creating it out of nothing."

"Magic again. Or 'steady state'—"

"Aye, lad. See, though; once you've ordained an energy state for it to exist in, matter *can* exist—as bound energy—rather than mere dead ylem floating in a sterile void. And it all starts again with length and width and depth . . . and around we go."

"It seems so simple, on the surface—"

"It's simple all the way down. You're just used to things being confusing, that's all. . . ."

Jim sighed, considered that he must be used to that too, and kept walking with his crew. As they all went, the surroundings were becoming increasingly featureless; it might have been a smooth white floor they all walked on. And the burning in the air grew brighter until every feature of every crewman showed with terrible and splendid distinctness. Uniforms blazed and glittered like royal raiment, and faces were so bright they seared the eyes.

"You're *glowing,*" Bones said to Jim, almost accusingly.

"I am *not,*" Jim said, more because he didn't want to be than because he wasn't. "*That* is, though." He pointed ahead.

Perhaps a hundred meters in front of them—the distance was difficult to judge without reference points—everything, even the "floor," vanished in a brilliance the eyes could not pierce, a place where the burning of the air increased by many orders of magnitude. It was not precisely light, but it was hard to think what else to call it. The zone of brilliance reached off to both sides, and upward and downward, beyond the limits of sight. Jim stood still just looking at it for a moment, and the hair stood up on the back of his neck; he couldn't tell why. "Spock," he said.

Spock glanced down at his tricorder and shook his head. "Total instrument failure," he said, and then was very surprised indeed to see the tricorder quietly reduce itself to grey plastic ash and screws and bits of wire, all of which slipped through his fingers and fell to the "floor," through it, and out of sight.

"*Now* ask me why I don't like working with machines," McCoy said.

"Doctor, please." Spock looked up, dusting his hands off. "One simply must be careful what one says in this space. It is likely to come literally true. This is the core of the Anomaly—and apparently a very malleable place."

"Good," Jim said. "Maybe we won't have too much trouble patching the rift between the spaces. Where are K't'lk and Scotty?"

"Here, sir," K't'lk said from Jim's other side, where she and Scotty had not been a second before. "But Captain, we have a problem—"

"Captain," said another voice from behind him. He turned to see Amekentra there, blinking her great wet eyes at him. All her thoracic scales were pale with distress. It was the first pain Jim had seen in some time, and it came as a shock. "Ensign, what's the matter?"

"Captain," she said, "I almost died once—when the Klingons attacked the *Yorktown*, years back. This—" she gestured with her iridescent scalp membrane at the brilliance—"was what I saw when I died on the table—before they brought me back. Before I was *sent* back. But this isn't—" She broke off, searching for words.

"Sir, what I saw, saw *me*. Talked to me, asked me whether I was finished with life. But this . . . this has its back turned. It won't answer."

Jim thought of that quick chill up his neck. He turned to the crew, who had moved up to surround him in a great semicircle. "Anyone else notice something like that?" he said.

The answer didn't come back in words, which was just as well, for it would have taken too long. People on starship duty frequently got into deadly situations, and many of Jim's crew had had "out-of-body" or "paradeath" experiences. Not all of them were alike; the nonhominid species, especially those to whom sight was not their most important sense, reported apotheoses of smell or sound, or assaults of flavor or physical sensation as dazzling as the traditional "white light" was to a hominid. But all the crewpeople who poured their answers into Jim's mind agreed that what they now saw or felt or tasted was like what they had experienced before—except that it was ignoring them.

"Captain," K't'lk said, "what I was about to tell you was that this brightness is the most 'physical' manifestation of a great life-source. Which complicates matters. We can't just start tampering with this space without at least establishing communication and warning the being, or beings, of what we're about to do, so it or they can do what's necessary for protection."

Jim nodded. "How?"

K't'lk laughed at him, a sound like a musicbox telling a joke. "Captain, the way I'm speaking to you may work very well. I haven't had to speak Basic since we all came into this place—the mere intention to communicate seems to overcome the barriers of language and species. If we tell *that* what we're about, it should hear us." She turned toward the great brilliance, and in a clear quick arpeggio sang out, "We're friends, will you talk with us?"

Jim wasn't sure what he was expecting, but he was disappointed when nothing happened at all. "Maybe you weren't loud enough?" he said.

K't'lk jangled. "I doubt that's the problem," she said. "Maybe someone else is needed. Or more people."

They tried both those options. They tried Spock's grave calm speech in both Basic and Vulcan, and Scotty's brogue, and Chekov's melodic, tense-ridden Russian. Uhura tried a couple of sentences in Hestv and Ieleru, and then quit, looking dubious; Janice Kerasus tried Vercingetorig and Shaulast and Ddaisekedeh, with no more success. After McCoy lost his patience and shouted at the brightness in amiable annoyance, many other crewpeople tried shouting, and waving their arms. Then they tried speaking in groups. Then Scotty suggested that the whole crew give up vocal speech and try thinking, very hard, all in concert. The resultant thundering chorus of thought nearly deafened Jim inside, but the brilliance didn't waver as much as a candleflame's worth.

Annoyed, Jim turned around to find Uhura looking at the great brightness with a smile that was a little amused, a little rueful. "Well," he said to her, "any ideas?"

She glanced over at him. "You feel an existence there, don't you? A life?"

"Certainly." His neck hair stood up again as he said it, and this time Jim knew why. There might be no weighing lives one against another—but he could feel to the core of him that this life was somehow immeasurably *bigger* than his. "So?"

"I'm not sure. But we may be erring in our presupposition that this—" —she gestured at the light—"is at as complex a stage of development as we are—at least as far as communication goes. We may be far ahead of it in some ways."

"I don't see how. The—the *power* coming from that—"

"Power isn't everything. Captain, what do you need to communicate?"

"Mmm. A common language—no, we seem to be doing without that, don't we? The desire to communicate, then—"

"True enough. But you need it on both sides."

"Are you saying that this doesn't *want* to communicate with us?"

"It might not even be anything that complex. Say that you're going to start from scratch and invent communication. What do you need first?"

Jim looked at her, thinking. "Not just the ability, or the desire . . ." And it occurred to him. "The concept of communication itself?"

Uhura grinned at him, delighted with the aptness of her pupil. "You do need that, sir. But remember, though, you're inventing communication. There's one thing that precedes inventing the concept."

Jim thought for a while, then shook his head. "Tell me."

"It's easy to miss—the way a fish misses water. To invent something—you have to have invented *inventing* first. Otherwise you're stuck." Uhura grinned more broadly at Jim's puzzled look. "If you think it's impossible to do something about a situation, you never do it, do you? The possibility literally never occurs to you—so neither does a solution. Captain, what if this 'existence' in front of us has not only never invented the notion of communication—but it's never invented inventing either? What if it doesn't communicate with us because it not only doesn't know that there's such a thing as communication—but it doesn't know that there's anything, or anyone, else to communicate with? What if it doesn't even know *it's* there?"

Jim took a long breath, for it made a kind of peculiar

sense. He glanced over at Spock, who nodded and spoke to Uhura. "You are suggesting, then, that the only way to communicate with it is to first teach it 'inventing'—creation—so that it becomes able to grasp its own presence—and then ours."

"That's right."

McCoy, standing beside Spock, looked uneasy again. "You're talking about teaching it self-awareness. That's dangerous business! Remember what happened with the first holographic-analogue computers before the designers got them to generate their own senses of purpose, of fulfillment—"

"Destructive behavior is just as likely in fully human minds, Doctor, even after thousands of years of thinking about the subject," Spock said. "It is always a being's own choice what it will do with its mind once it discovers it has one. Be mastered by it, and become a tool of entropy—or master it, and turn away from destruction. We have some skill in that art among various members of this crew—yourself certainly included." He looked at Uhura again. "Physical communication, as far as that phrase has meaning in this space, does not seem to be working. I am willing to contribute the mindmeld part of this experiment, Lieutenant, if you desire it."

She looked at Jim. "With the Captain's permission, I do."

Jim nodded, not seeing any clearer solution.

"There's another problem, Spock," McCoy said. "There's no time here, no succession, no duration. You need that for thought. How are you going to get through to this big bright whatever with time-based thought concepts?"

"Maybe through me, sir," said a throaty voice from behind McCoy. Ensign d'Hennish stepped out, his fur shining silken and blazing silvery-gold in reflection of the nearby brilliance. "I'm used to living in 'now.' I don't have 'was' or 'will be.'" He said the words as if they were from some strange foreign language. "But neither does this, if I understand Lieutenant Uhura." D'Hennish flicked his ears toward the brightness. "And I do have 'then'—which it needs to understand us, or timebinding, at all. I think I'm the bridge Mr. Spock and Mz. Uhura will need."

Jim looked at the Sadrao, then at McCoy. "Bones?"

McCoy nodded, though reluctantly. "Captain, he's probably right. But this whole thing is dangerous; it could cost all three of them their minds." He made a helpless gesture. "Not that we have any choice—we can't very well just take the chance of killing off this poor trillion-watt whatsit in the name of saving the Universe. It has a right to live too—"

"Go," Jim said to d'Hennish. The ailurin went to join Spock and Uhura, who were already talking quietly together, preparing for the meld. Spock said a word or two to d'Hennish, and the three of them drew close. Jim waited for the conventional touching of nerve pressure points on the face that Spock usually used with the meld—but it seemed that here Spock didn't consider it necessary. He simply gathered the other two in with his eyes. "Nyota," he said. "Ri'niwa. Be with me—"

A great stillness spread outward from them to the crew, until it seemed all four hundred people were holding their breaths at once. Uhura lifted up her head, eyes closed, and whispered something; Spock's lips, d'Hennish's jaw, mirrored the movement. The air began to prickle with an unbearable sense of something about to happen, like lightning about to strike. The anticipation built and built, became as fierce a burning as the sourceless fire in the air. Jim wanted to move, to shout, anything to break the tension. But he was frozen still, caught in the sudden power of the meld with all the rest of the crew—trapped in d'Hennish's eternal now; in Uhura's insistence that whatever heard her create not only time and existence, but creation itself; in Spock's relentless embrace of mind that gathered everything in and made it one. The tension built, the power grew and grew—

Uhura's eyes snapped open in terror. Three cries shattered the stillness in anguished unison—hers, Spock's, a terrible screaming yowl from d'Hennish. The three of them fell sprawling together, as if the same hand struck them down. The unwavering brilliance rippled—then streamed and buckled like a stormblown curtain—then tore.

And all hell broke loose.

Thirteen

The clear fire of the air had been blinding, but it hadn't hurt the eyes; it had burned the flesh, but painlessly. Now what Jim perceived as the source of the burning lashed out at the *Enterprise* crew, so that the bright air writhed and pressed smothering in on them like a weighted wind, carrying with it a wordless expression of awful rage and terror. Reality tattered—not that of the landscape, this time, but of the crew's own selves. Jim looked through the terrible brilliance at his people and saw their images distorting, their *selves* horribly pulled and torn, twisted from unearthly fairness to charnel horrors of bone and wet gristle and naked spilled-out organs. *K't'lk's shielding,* he thought. *Will it hold through this—?*

"Captain!" a hoarse voice shouted at him. With difficulty Jim turned—the air fought him, and there was something happening to his own body that he didn't care to contemplate too closely, lest his attention help it along. Not far from him Spock was doing his best to lever himself up off the ground. Jim looked at the Vulcan, or what remained of him, and his gorge fought frantically with the lower reaches of his throat. Jim wanted desperately to look away, and refused to, knowing who lived inside the illusory horror he was seeing. "The ship!" Spock said, loudly, so his voice would carry over the wicked wind and the increasingly distressed cries of the crew. "Under attack—and if we do not—re-establish our reality—"

"It'll shatter," Jim called back. "And the ship with it. Understood."

What Jim didn't understand in the slightest was how to re-establish a whole ship's worth of reality. He was having enough problems with his own. His flesh had started to crawl with a discomfort growing toward pain . . . as if the things he'd glimpsed happening to him were beginning to happen physically. Worse, by the now-familiar group-mind rapport, Jim could feel the same thing starting to happen in his crew, and also sense their abortive and ineffectual attempts to stave off the effect. *It'll never work, they're flailing around in all directions at once, not dealing with the source—*

That's it, he thought, and braced himself physically as best he could—a difficult feat; the increasing ache in his bones made Jim want to roll on the ground and moan. He looked around. Spock was on his knees now, his face contorted with agony as he dragged Uhura to a more-or-less sitting position. D'Hennish was still crumpled from the blow the three of them had taken. *No help from them,* Jim thought frantically. *Who, then? Who'll be best at protecting the ship's reality till we can get a grip on our own?* "Scotty!!"

"Comin', Captain," the answer came from a short distance away.

"Sir," someone else said, and Jim turned around with difficulty and found Chekov standing there, staggering, but refusing to reach out for support. *You get what you wish for!* Jim thought. He reached out, took Chekov by the arm and shook him slightly—a wake-up gesture.

"Pull it together, Pavel Andreievitch," he said. "Spock and the others kicked that whatever-it-is in the side, and it's kicking the *Enterprise* back—"

"No!!" Chekov said, straightening so abruptly he pulled Jim a little straighter as well. "Sir, what can we—"

"Wait—" Scotty was with them, taking Jim's arm from the other side, supporting him. "Your engines, Scotty," Jim said in a gasp—the inimical pressure of the air was making speech and thought more and more difficult. "This keeps up much longer, they won't be able to toast bread—"

"Not if I have anything to say about it!"

"There," Jim said, staring straight into the frightfully blazing rent in the air. "That's the source. Tell that what you won't let it do. Make it be that what you want to happen, *is* happening. *Do it!*"

He glanced from one to the other, saw Scotty's eyes narrow, saw Chekov's jaw clench—then faced ahead again. The violent brightness made zeta-10 Scorpii look pallid by comparison; Jim feared that, physical reality or no physical reality, he might burn out his optic nerves as he'd once feared Spock had. Not even squeezing his eyes shut would make a difference with light of this brightness. But that was hardly the point. He had a ship to protect. *Not that I know how to do that, either*—His role in most of his telepathic experiences had been passive. That did him no good now, when the best defense was offense. Still, he stared into the white fire, wincing, and denied it the destruction it desired—

Then what McCoy had earlier warned him of happened, and Jim abruptly found his mind fallen together with those of Scotty and Chekov, *into* theirs. He reeled, for the intensity of the joining was no less than what he had experienced with Spock and McCoy. The Scot's and Russian's milder experiences, their joys, Jim had shared in part. Now he shared their passions, both sets at once. It was almost too much. Jim's love for his ship was broad, for all its intensity; an inclusive emotion, extending to those who rode her. But he found now that it was a nonspecific love compared to Scotty's, which was founded in an intimate hands-on knowledge of every circuit, every conduit and shaft and square meter of hull. Because of this, a danger to the *Enterprise* struck Scotty as worse than any threat to his own physical body. Also, his efforts had saved both her and him so many times that survival wasn't survival, as far as Scotty was concerned, unless both of them lived. His utter determination that the *Enterprise* be kept safe and in good working order, along with his demolishing rage at anyone who would have it otherwise, poured out of him and into Jim from one direction—

—and from the other, Chekov's equally fierce anger at an attack on the innocent and helpless came boiling up like a killer storm over the steppes—black, inescapable, licked with lightning. The wild young power that knew no boundaries—the determination to survive anything an adversary could do to him, and then strike one stroke of his own that would stop the fight and prevent others—it all spilled thundering into Jim, melding with Scotty's outrage and anger, seeking an outlet, building, building—

Jim had no idea what to do. He could think of nothing to add to such towering anger. *Maybe I don't need to add anything, though. My art is to be at the center, to direct*—Jim stared into the deadly brightness and thought, as "loudly" as he could, *Will you do us harm? We won't permit it—and this is how we'll stop you!!*

The thought was evidently enough, for instantly Jim

felt Scotty's and Chekov's power go searing through him as McCoy's had. It struck him to his knees in its passing, leaving Jim wondering dazedly whether this was how a gunnery conduit felt when the phaser behind it was fired. He looked up in time to see the bitter brilliance waver. Coming from it, as Chekov bent down to help him up, Jim caught an impression of an immense uncertainty mixed with terror—then the anger again. "No, Pavel," he said, and feeling Scotty's hand on his shoulder, pulled him down too. "Stay down. We're not done, and one fall's enough—"

The great core of white fire lashed out again. There were more screams from the crew, and the sound of them enraged Jim so that he didn't bother thinking anything at the light, loudly or otherwise. He merely struck back, in mind, and behind/inside him Scotty and Chekov were a concentrated force of anger and strength that was frightening for Jim to comprehend. *Has this kind of power been inside them all along? Or is it just this space—* This time Jim felt their united force strike something—though it was something nonphysical; and he felt the stricken essence reel "back," "away" from them, radiating a more virulent terror than before, along with a wordless feeling that the terror was for some reason justified. *Once more,* Chekov said, the words ringing through the wholeness that was the three of them. The brilliance was rippling again, as if for another attack. Pavel and Scotty gave it no chance. Instantly, if such a word applied where there was no time, they gathered Jim in so that he could give them a direction—then reached out and "hit" the brilliance with a mind-blow like the fist of God coming down. And again, harder, till Jim's vision vanished for real from the shock of the "impact" in his mind. *And once more—*

That was when they heard the scream . . . and it came from no one in the crew.

"Enough, you two!" Jim said to the other presences in his mind. "As you were—" His vision was clearing; he looked around him and saw Spock getting d'Hennish up, while various other crew members picked themselves up off the ground. He accepted Scotty's and Chekov's arm-support to get back to his feet again. "Good work," he said to them. "Scotty, you've been taking this lad into too many rough places on shore leave. He's picked up your style in brawling. . . ."

"Ah, na, Captain," Scotty said, as K't'lk came from behind him and chimed at him in concern; he reached down to scratch her longitudinal crest between the top two eyes. "Yon's a natural aptitude, I've naught to teach him. A bit to learn, perhaps.—There you are, then, Mr. Spock. Are you all right?"

Spock and Uhura came up to join the group, followed by McCoy, on whom d'Hennish was leaning. "Mr. Scott," Spock said, "I suspect that I now have a referent for the term 'hangover.' Otherwise, I am well. Captain, our attempt to communicate was a success—"

"If that was success," Jim said, rubbing his own head, "Heaven preserve us from failure. . . . Did that scream come from where I think it did?"

"From that, sir," Uhura said, gesturing at the great brightness. "Yes. We broke through to it. It picked up quite a bit from us, very fast, just as we did from it. It learned existence sooner than I'd have thought possible. Unfortunately, when it fully comprehended there was some *other* existence, that it wasn't alone—it panicked. It was afraid we might hurt it—"

"It can't run, Captain," d'Hennish said. "So it does the only other thing it can think of, with thinking so new to it. It fights, tries to make the strange new somethings go away and leave it safe and secure in the old aloneness. That doesn't work, either. So now it withdraws—"

"Captain," Spock said, "you must understand that

all these communications have been on a most primitive level . . . not precisely 'feelings,' certainly not as complex as thoughts, definitely not words. The word 'being' for once correctly describes what we have contacted. All it is is a 'be'-ing—an experience of existence without event, without other existence of any kind. It has been sealed alone inside this universe for what might as well be eternity—yet also 'not-alone,' for to be alone, there must be other existence to compare the state against. It is of incalculable power—and also powerless, for there has been nothing against which to turn that power until we arrived. Only its inexperience saved us from destruction when it attacked us. We are good at doing; it never even had the concept until it borrowed it from us."

"Then why isn't it doing something *now?*" McCoy said, gazing into the heart of the light.

"We frightened it," Uhura said sadly. "Leonard, we taught it pain . . . not just as an abstract. It knows there's an out, now, but it may never want to *come* out because of the way we slapped it back."

"People," Jim said, staring at the light with everyone else, "we're short of time—"

"Right, sir. So we're seeing what we can do," d'Hennish said, and took Uhura's dark hand in his furry one. Spock put a hand on the young Sadrao's shoulder. The three of them stood silent for a while, and once again Jim felt the power building, building in the air—a wordless plea/demand that whatever heard it must declare who it was, what it was, reach out, *speak!* From back among his crew Jim heard occasional inadvertent cries in response to the command—fragments of words, names, secrets. Jim had to hold his mouth shut, had to clench his fists against the heartshaking entreaty. He dared not allow himself so much as a sound, for fear of distracting the three who sent out the call—or distracting its object. *Speak to us, be known, don't be afraid,* who are you—?!

For a seemingly endless time, there was no response.

Then the air spoke. The reply was soundless thunder; it was a frightened voice like a beaten child's, but immeasurably huge; it was a single thought that held choruses captive in it, and a multitude's power whispering in a trembling unison of uncertainty and fear. Jim felt the shaking begin again. He glanced around as he heard what the voice/s said, concurrently wondering and doubting if the others heard what he did.

We are who are, the brightness said.

"Oh, *no,*" McCoy said in a whisper.

—at least we were. Until you came—

Spock took a step away from Uhura and d'Hennish, then. He lifted his eyes to the brightness and spoke—not in Basic, but in Vulcan, which they all now understood as easily as K't'lk's chiming Hamalki. At the sound of the first sentence or so, Jim understood that Spock didn't dare trust his communication with this terrible, fragile entity to anything but the elegant accuracy of Vulcan, which Jim could now fully appreciate for the first time. "You still are," he said. "We do not threaten that condition, though in your fear you threatened it in us. Do us no more harm. We wish no harm to you. That is why we sought contact with you, so that you might be protected from possible harm."

We—There was no expressing the anguish with which the life in the brightness said the word. Jim found it hard to understand how something so multitudinous, so seemingly *plural,* could be so afraid of mere numbers—especially when the concept by which it referred to itself seemed plural too. He had trouble, in fact, understanding how such a power could be afraid of anything. *How* they *could be afraid,* he corrected himself. Jim stepped up beside Spock. "Beyond this universe in which you live, there's another one. We come from that universe—"

Then that was true, then, that the—the Others told us, the brilliance said. All these concepts, because of their newness, came most tentatively—but none so tentatively as the terrifying concept of Otherness. *And there are—more of what you are—*

"Innumerable more," Jim said, gently, as he might have to a very small child. "Like us, and unlike. Seven hundred kinds of humanity, and even we don't know how many more than that, scattered through our galaxy and a billion others."

The mere act of talking was drawing the great new mind/s into closer and closer union with theirs. Jim got a clearer sense of a power that was truly incalculable—and of an intelligence that would be, given time and experience. He also felt fear turning to wonder and amazement that there should *be* something else to talk to, and a desire that this astonishing thing called talking should continue, feed the wonder, never stop. *Others,* the huge brilliance said. *We, too, then—are Others.*

"Correct," Spock said.

And all of—us—are together—The Others had some experience of time in the abstract from Uhura and Spock, but the form of time they understood best was d'Hennish's, and it was his phrasing they used. —*together now and always!* The wonder grew, built to joy, grew past it—

"No," Spock said. His voice was calm, but even the most Vulcan parts of his personality were distressed at having to shatter this innocent ecstasy—born as it was of what a Vulcan treasured most, the desire to celebrate diversity. As for Spock's Terran parts, Jim felt their pain, too deep for tears, but held his peace. Even here, Spock had his pride.

No?—

"A portal, a doorway, has opened between our two

universes," Spock said. "It must be closed. For the environment in which you live is fatal to us—and ours would be to you."

Vast puzzlement came from the Others. Death, too, was something they only had in abstract from their communication with the three.

"You are who *are,*" McCoy said suddenly, with a terrible gentleness. "Do you want to become 'you who are *not*'?"

The Others' fear came back in an intensity that could crush hearts. Now that they knew what existence was, the thought of its loss was abhorrent. They wanted no return to the permanent peace of their solitude. *Yet,* the great single/multiple thought came back a moment later, *if the portal is closed—*

"We must be on the other side of it," Jim said. "We cannot stay."

But if you are gone—then this is lost, the Others said. What "this" was, was clear; life, communication, the eternal joyous celebration of diversity that had seemed laid out before them. *And without your movingness—* they had no closer equivalent to "entropy"—*if* that *is sealed out with you, then there is nothing for us but what was before.* The thought was a horror. Sterile, silent, utter aloneness, an eternity of it, made worse than ever by the discovery of consciousness—and the knowledge that elsewhere life existed, forever out of reach.

"The portal must be closed," Jim said. "And quickly—"

No, said the Others in a vast unison of grief, as if a whole universe wept for loneliness. And then, with less sorrow and more anger, *No! That you are here—is what* is; *we will not have it otherwise!* The air began to get thick again, the old storm of rage and fear stirring in it, with a riptide of desperation added. *We will not be deprived of what never was before, knowing that it will never be again!* For they had correctly read the context behind Jim's thought—that this doorway must never be reopened once closed. *We will not be shut back into nothingness, where nothing happens, and nothing is, except ourSelf, alone for always—!*

Thunder cracked above the *Enterprise* crew, rumbled in the white stone where they stood. Jim glanced over at Scotty and Chekov, wondering if they'd be able to do anything this time. All through the conversation, Jim had been able to feel how the Others were growing more powerful with every breath, every "moment" they spent conscious. He knew too, as if from inside them, that they were quick students; along with the anger eddying in the air came the sure knowledge that they understood the tactics last used against them very well, and would be quite able to defeat them now. That was hardly enough to cause Jim to give up. He glanced at Pavel and Scotty, a signal for them to drop into union with him again. *Catch some of the others' eyes, you two,* he said silently. *We may need more help this time—*

"No, you won't," McCoy said, and stepped past Jim, waving him aside. He walked up close to the eye-hurting, rippling brightness, so close that the fury of the life inside it tossed his hair like a high wind, and he had to brace himself against its force; so close that even his own brilliance was subdued, and he was only a silhouette. "You were very sure that you didn't want to become 'we who are not,' " he said, and there was more anger than just the Others' in the air now. "Do you want *us* to become 'we who are not'? Not only us, but all the lives there are, on all the worlds we come from, and a billion others? Just because you can't have the 'movingness,' you're going to kill it all, everywhere, is that it?"

Jim watched McCoy with fear, not moving, not daring to. The rage in the air was once again becoming a physical thing, pushing and yanking at those closest.

McCoy staggered in its blast, but would not back down. "Why should we be surprised? The first thing you tried to do was kill us!" His voice cracked whip-sharp. "So go ahead and finish it! And have your first two deeds since you came to consciousness be the attempt at murder, and success at it!"

No one in the crew moved. The ferocity whirling in the air got no less. But it didn't increase, either, and Jim and all the people around him held their breaths. "Kill, then!" McCoy said. "You have the power. But know *what* you're killing—four hundred lives that desire life and the presence of other lives as much as you do!"

He waited, facing the fierce bright wind, not moving. For long moments it held steady, a gale of frustration and pain, and the *Enterprise* crew clutched at one another to stay standing.

Then, very slowly, the anger began to die down. It faded gradually from the air like clearing smoke, and its pressure fell away.

"You are so much more," McCoy said then, in a voice that shook with compassion, and with certainty. "Far more than death and pain. Just let yourself find out—"

For a long while, nothing but silence. Then the Others spoke again.

We can't take this precious thing from you—that we ourSelf would not have had except by your gift. What you say must be done, that we will do.

McCoy had stepped back to stand by Jim and Spock again. Jim glanced silent thanks and praise at Bones, then said again, sorrowfully, "The portal must be closed. Soon."

Then we will be marooned here, by ourSelf—and with no other to stand beside, we *will not be here either,* the Others said in an agreement as bleak as any Jim had ever heard. *That would seem to mean we will not perceive what has happened, once it has. You need not sorrow.*

Enterprise crewmen on all sides turned to one another in pain, feeling the Others' anguish. "I cannot help but sorrow," Jim said. He had rarely meant the words more. The thought of this staggeringly powerful being, shut back in the uneventful, placid, terrible timelessness where they had found it, from which they had freed it—He shook his head. "Spock," he said. "There must be *something* we can do."

The *Enterprise* crewpeople were looking at one another in distress at the Others' anguish as Spock turned to Jim. "Captain," he said quietly, "indeed, there must. And that is not a problematic statement, but an imperative. Once again we must deal with the consequences of our tampering—and with a great irony."

Jim looked at his First Officer quizzically. "You identified part of the situation yourself on the way to this place," Spock said. "'To the side of the angels,' you said. The Doctor identified it more specifically, when the Others named their name. And now all the requisites are here, Captain. Timelessness, being without physicality, potential plurality in oneness, existence without creation and from all time—We have in fact found God. Not one that any of our humanities would recognize as its own God, however. Nor is this some extremely powerful being formerly mistaken for deity, like others the *Enterprise* has met. This—or these, I should say—are a protoGod. They might very well have cracked Their 'shell' in Their own time, invented existence and creation on Their own, and done well enough here by Themselves. But we will never know, now, because of our interference. Our use of the inversion drive caused us to come here and crack Their shell prematurely. And now we have taught Them existence, and consciousness, and the desire for communication—none of which we or any other being may gratify by remaining here. For our self-preservation—for the sake of the Galaxy, and all the 'right' reasons—we are in such violation of the Prime Directive as not even the *Enterprise* has managed before. And ethics would seem to require that we do something to ameliorate this situation—since neither we nor anyone else will ever have another chance."

Jim nodded, feeling numb. The question of what Starfleet would think never occurred to him. He was primarily occupied with the bitter anguish beating in the air like a heart, and the thought of saving one universe while leaving another one maimed behind him. "You taught the Others creation, Mr. Spock—" he said, grasping at the straw.

"We did, sir. But creation, like any other action, requires entropy. And the entropy here is a temporary local phenomenon, due only to our presence—"

Spock stopped, very abruptly, seeing his Captain's eyes widen. Jim looked up at him, a speculative expression on his face. "Mr. Spock," he said. "Are you thinking what I'm thinking?"

For once, the question was rhetorical. They both knew Spock was. "It is no accident," Spock said, with the tight control characteristic of his excitement, "that we have a creative physicist with us."

Jim turned around. "K't'lk!" he called.

"I was wondering when you'd think of me," she said sedately from right behind him. "Best not smile too soon, Captain. The answer's not going to be as simple as you think."

Fourteen

Jim went down on one knee beside K't'lk, to keep the conversation he felt coming up from giving him a literal pain in the neck. "You can do it, can't you?"

"If you mean, can I provide this space with entropy of its own," K't'lk said, "I think I can. I've broken enough laws in our own universe; I certainly should be able to set them up, in this one. It's much simpler—"

Much of the command crew of the *Enterprise* stood gathered about Jim and Spock and K't'lk, and around them stood the rest of the ship's complement. At K't'lk's words, an awed, wondering rustle of words and thoughts went through the group, and McCoy leaned down over Jim. "Captain, isn't this getting a bit dangerous?" he said. "First we teach the Others consciousness. Now you're suggesting we let entropy loose here too. Won't it be as fatal to Them as anentropia would be to us, without protection? And even if it won't, consider what you're doing! Turn entropy loose, and time begins as a result! Start time running, and you've done ninety-nine percent of the work of creating a universe! They"—he waved at the brightness—"may grow into playing God someday, but what makes you think *we're* ready for it?!"

"Oh L'n'rd!" K't'lk said in an annoyed jangle. "This is no time for kindergarten ethics! What do you think *you're* doing every time you save a life? Besides—if it's true what they say, that God created us in Their image, then how should we *not* love creating—and how could it be *wrong* for us to do so, as carefully and ethically as we can, on whatever scale we're capable of?"

"But K't'lk, creation may not be all it's cracked up to be, even for Gods! Look at the state *our* universe is in!!"

"L'n'rd, believe me, I've noticed that large parts of it apparently don't work too well! It's enough to make even a God sit on Their hands after such a first try! And, again, if we're made after such a God's image, no wonder we're chary of 'playing God' ourselves; once fried, twice shy! But the Universe goes on growing and changing every day; evidently the Gods haven't given up creating. Should we?!"

"But doing it on this scale—with a living being at the mercy of what we create—"

"I assure you," K't'lk said, "if I were to insert entropy into this universe, after designing new laws for it—which I would have to do, as you point out, so that entropy won't be fatal for the Others any more—I would be most careful. How could I help it?—being made, after all, in the image of the One Who was burned? But the choice is plain—refuse to create, and refuse to grow; or build, with care and love."

She looked back at Jim. "Captain, subject to your command, I choose to build. I think Mr. Sp'ck is right; there is a reason we find ourselves here. I have no basis for that conclusion, but I might propose a possible other side of the problem Sp'ck mentioned—that perhaps the Others' course of development in this space was somehow arrested, and without our interference, the Others would *never* have 'hatched' into a God." She shrugged, chiming. "A hunch, no more. In any case, it seems no accident that I'm along on this mission. The question before us, though, is what I'm to do on it. What are your orders, Captain?"

Jim took one long breath and let it out, looking around at his command crew. "Seeing no better alternative," he said, and paused, giving them a last chance to interject something if necessary. No one did.

He glanced down at K't'lk. "Go on, then. Found us a universe."

K't'lk shook herself all over, chiming. "Very well, sir. We still have a couple of problems to deal with, though. For one, that of power. This is apparently one of the 'extropic' universes, the sterile ones. I said I *think* I can provide this space with entropy and a set of natural laws that will continue to generate themselves—kicking this universe up a notch, into anthotropy. But to do so I must reach ahead in this universe's time before there *is* time, perceive my solution, and implement it so that it will be the solution I perceived—"

"Ye've been hittin' the graphite again, lass," Scotty said gently.

"No, M't'gmry. I told you, cause doesn't always precede effect. Think of it as dealing a hand from a marked deck, if that helps. In any case, I'm not sure I can do both that, and the 'reweaving' of the rent between our universes—which was already going to take most of the power generated by the inversion apparatus. Only the attempt will prove whether I can pull it off." It seemed to Jim for a moment that K't'lk was regarding Scotty with a gentle regret as she spoke. He looked more closely at her; but she shook herself and went on, sounding as usual again. "—The remaining problem is that the Others—"

She turned a bit sideways, cocking a cluster of eyes at the silent brilliance nearby. "I should not speak of You as if You're not here," she said. "You have no experience of time save what You derived, slightly used, from d'Hennish and Uhura and Spock. Should I give You entropy, time would indeed begin here. If You *had* time, though—what would You do with it?"

There was no response, at first—then a great feeling of confusion and helplessness. *We don't know,* the Others said. *You judge. We will take your word on the matter.*

"Oh, wonderful," McCoy said.

K't'lk turned to Jim, the fires in her eyes swirling blue and hot. "Well, J'm," she said softly, for his hearing alone, "I've heard it said often enough that our own world sometimes seems to have been designed by committee. Here's our chance to do the same, it appears . . . for this is no work of architecture I dare design alone."

"I agree," Jim said as quietly. "But it could also be our chance to create what people dream about. The best of all possible worlds . . ."

"Captain," Spock said, above both of them. "I, too, would like nothing better. And I encourage careful deliberation. But though we seem to have forever, here, time passes outside this zone—and the area of anentropia surrounds more and more of our own universe. We must be swift."

Jim nodded. "Agreed." He stood up. "People," he said to the command crew and to the other *Enterprise* people all around, "we need to find something for the Others to do, some way to spend a period of time that's going to be—" He glanced down at K't'lk.

"A little less than eternity," she said—though there was laughter in her chiming, as if she told a joke. "That's the most I can manage."

"Right. Suggestions, then—remembering that the

Others are going to be stuck with our solution for that long. What approach should we take?"

Jim expected to be deafened by a chorus of voices and union of thoughts. It didn't happen. There was some quiet murmuring, and finally the Chief of Security, Mr. Matlock, said very soberly, "Captain, some of us are feeling—a bit out of our league. What kind of time-structuring device can a mortal safely recommend to a god? Our, uh, attention span isn't quite on the same level."

"He has a point, sir," Uhura said. "The longest-lived of the species we've met have spoken so often of the terrible weariness of their lives. They try everything to divert themselves—and sooner or later just don't care any more. They're driven to all kinds of extremes to try to amuse themselves. Cruelty, tyranny—"

"Or higher levels of development," Spock said.

"That's right enough, Mr. Spock," Scotty said. "But what can you think of that's higher than *this?*" He waved one hand at the Others, and Jim shook his head. The Others' power could still be felt growing greater and greater. Omnipotence, omniscience—They might not have them now, but They soon would. The fact remained, however, that They still had no idea what to do with them, and in an empty universe, neither attribute was much good.

"Captain—" That was Harb Tanzer. "Maybe 'higher' is the wrong place to be looking. And in any case we don't dare experiment with these people, suggesting something we don't know for sure will work; as you say, They'll be stuck with our decision for a very long time. How about something simple, in which They can find Their own complexities, raise them to whatever levels They're capable of?"

"Specify."

"A game, sir."

"Harb," McCoy said, "aside from my initial response to the idea of a god spending eternity playing games—what possible game is big enough to spend all of 'almost-eternity' playing?"

"The one we're playing, Len," Harb said, quietly, and with a sober smile. "The one where you live in a body. You make up issues: good and evil, terror and joy, life and death—"

"Harb, lad," Scotty said, protesting, "life's no' a game to *me!!*"

"And that's just how it *would* seem to you," Mr. Tanzer said, "if you'd forgotten you were playing." Harb turned back to Jim. "Sir, what grander pastime can we recommend to Them than life itself? You leave Them an out, of course . . . a point at which the playing 'piece,' the body, expires. Entropy would see to that, in any case. So that at the end of each round, the players are freed to remember that this *is* a game; to count the chips, and sit the next round out—or change roles and play again."

"What would the object of the game be?" Uhura said.

"For a specific person? For starters, to discover what 'piece' they were. Once that's handled—and how many people find out what they're for while they're still alive?—there's a more advanced form of the game. To find out what the object of the game *is*. . . ."

"But between 'rounds,'" Uhura said, "They would know."

"Certainly. While the game itself is in progress, though—while a particular fragment of the Others is inhabiting a body, inhabiting time—there'd be no memory, or only hints, that it really was a game. That frees it to be played 'for keeps.' All the value of the things that matter because they're essentially transitory —love, success, joy—is maintained. Even pain and loss lose their sting, because they're transcended at the round's end—the player's passed through them and learned from them."

"Or not," McCoy said. "What then?"

"If poker's the only game in town," Harb said, "you learn to play, and win. Or play, and lose—and do it for the sheer delight of playing. Or sit back and kibitz. The player's free to choose. Len, there's a tendency to regard games as not important, not 'serious'—don't be fooled by it! Politics is a game, relationships are games, business and exploration and adventure are games—with rules, and time limits, and restrictions on the players. And there's room inside them all to experience glory, and gladness, and defeat and triumph—grandeur and intimacy and power and joy, sorrow and love. And those are just the four-dimensional games mortals play, inside the boundaries of life. What could a God do, given a chance?"

Yes! the Others said in a great crash of thought, hungry and delighted. *Life, what you have—the being, the knowing, the knowing other lives—the loving, even the hurting—all of it!! Oh, give Us* that, *and teach Us to make more of it ourSelf, and We will need you not at all. All the time We see in the Singer*—They meant K't'lk—*could not use up the possibilities. Give Us that Game, and go with Our love forever. Go quickly, so that We can play—*

K't'lk looked up at Jim. "Sir," she said, "Their approval is making this space very malleable—it will accept new laws even more readily than I'd thought it would. I may very well have enough power to manage everything. So think one last time—then command."

Jim thought, while all around him his crew looked at him with fear and excitement and awe, and the air beat with anticipation. He glanced around at his command crew. Uhura was holding her face dispassionate, and keeping her emotions to herself. McCoy was doubtful, as usual, but there was a suppressed excitement in him, as there was in Chekov and in Sulu. Scotty still stood with one hand resting on K't'lk's dorsal ridge, his eyes on Jim, waiting, ready to follow his Captain's lead. Spock didn't move so much as an eyebrow, but Jim caught very clearly the thought in his mind: *It is logical, Jim. All the same, logic is not everything. Do as you think best.*

"Do it," Jim said to K't'lk. "And if you can—hurry."

Also, if you can—That was the Others, sounding gentle now, and even a bit sheepish, after Their earlier violence. *We would not forget you. Will you leave something of yourselves with Us? Something for Us to remember you by? You have after all been playing this Game longer than We have. We would be glad of some of your triumphs, your—wins—to study between the rounds. And though We see from your minds that We will be mother, father, ruler of this Universe—still you are Our mothers and fathers, in a way. And the only Others We have ever known. Leave Us yourSelves. . . .*

"If you and the crew wish to do that, Captain," K't'lk said, "I can weave the memories you choose right into the fabric of this universe, along with the natural laws, so that the Others will be in no danger of losing them. They'll constitute a sort of 'collective preconscious.'"

"Do that, Commander," Jim said. "One thing, though—"

"Sir."

"You said—'a little less than eternity'. Our 'game' back home is only going to last a hundred trillion years or so, supposedly, before entropy reduces the last star to a cinder. Somehow that doesn't seem like a very long time, for a God—"

"A good point, Captain, but don't worry. After all, who said entropy was a constant? I'll give Them a good long universe, never fear. The Others will remember the *Enterprise* when the galaxies are an old story. . . ."

"And after that much experience in running a universe," Harb said, "They might be prepared to do some modifications on the basic design."

"I will begin, then," K't'lk said.

"Kit," another voice said, and McCoy went down on one knee beside her, looking troubled. "One thing. When you write the equations—do you *have* to give Them death?"

The brilliance about him was dimmed. So was that in K't'lk's eyes—their blue belonged, for the moment, more to twilight than to noon. "L'nrd," she said in somber notes, "you said it yourself. Time is what They need. They can't have that without entropy too. And death will inevitably come along with that—rundowns, breakdowns—"

"You're a creative physicist—couldn't you find a way to leave that part out of it?" McCoy said. There was a wistfulness about his persistence, as if he knew it was hopeless but couldn't bear giving up. "Let time run—but have it leave life alone?"

K't'lk looked at him in silence for a moment. "I could write that into the equations," she said finally. "I could write it into those that govern *your* universe. But I don't know for sure what the result would be—and it would be folly or madness to implement such an option without at least testing it first. There's no opportunity for test here, L'nrd. Once I speak the last Word, the final statement that implements the equations preceeding it, this universe becomes unalterable save by its own types of change, the ones I'll have implanted. I don't dare leave the 'change' equations loose enough to permit easy alteration; natural laws could start coming undone, and the result would be like the chaos we saw at the fringes of the Lesser Magellanic. Nor do I dare experiment on the Others and take the chance of trapping Them in some accidental time-paradox or warped causality loop from which They can never be released."

McCoy, silent, didn't move. "Doctor," Spock said then, gentle-voiced, "you are rarely one for legendry, but this tale I think you know. How did Aesculapius die?"

Leonard's face went bleak. "He was so great a healer," he said, "that finally someone offered him a huge fee to raise a man from the dead. He did it. The death-gods got jealous. They had him struck by lightning."

Spock gazed at McCoy, and said nothing.

Then hope flared in McCoy's face, and the light around him stirred. "*And,*" he said triumphantly, remembering, "afterwards the gods were sorry—and made both Aesculapius and the man he had raised up into gods themselves."

"Yet it required death to bring them both to godhead," Spock said. "Leonard, there is a great potential for tragedy in giving the Others near-eternal time without leaving Them a sure means to transcend it. The equations K't'lk means to implant here as the rules of the game will cause Them to forget what They are—to temporarily misplace Their godhead while alive. How dare we block the only road that we know—or at least have evidence—will lead Them back to that knowledge?" McCoy looked away. After a moment's silence, with great gentleness Spock said, "Leonard, They will do well enough. They are, after all, a God. And even in our own universe—death has its exceptions."

McCoy bowed his head, got to his feet. When he looked up again several moments later, the tears were running down, and he made no attempt to hide them. "Can we at least spare them pain?" he said quietly.

Jim realized fully, then, how good a doctor his friend was; for McCoy wanted nothing more than that there should be at least one place in the worlds where he would forever be out of a job. He reached over and laid a hand on McCoy's arm. "Bones," he said, "with entropy in force, I don't think we'll get away with that one either. We're just the youngest fairy godmothers at this christening. What we give can't remove the curse . . . just soften it."

"If death is truly a curse," Spock said, as soberly as some power pronouncing a hundred years of sleep, but with a glint of private, serene humor in his eyes. "There is little logic in condemning something one has not experienced . . . or does not remember experiencing."

The group grew silent. K't'lk looked from one to another of them, heard no more comment, and finally looked up at Jim again. "Captain?" she said.

"Go ahead," he said. "Is there anything you need?"

"For the time being," she said, "only quiet." And, to the surprise of most of those who listened, she began to sing.

Fifteen

Jim had heard K't'lk sing often enough—in casual conversation, which tended toward inconsequential, merry harmonies; and in deeper, more personal talk, when her melodic lines grew more advanced, strings of dissonances and wry accidentals melting subtly into rich-textured resolutions. But he had never taken time to listen to her singing her work, her physics. He began to regret that omission; for it became plain that however much she delighted in other matters, this was where her greatest virtuosity lay, and where her heart was.

She sang slowly and tentatively, at first, as if she was feeling her way through unfamiliar territory—scattering atonal spatters of notes, delicate chromatic inchings-forward. Jim thought of her description of Hamalki matings, and realized that less emotionally loaded buildings—such as works of Hamalki architecture—must be worked out and proposed in the same way: sequences of notes equalling physical constants, vector qualities, numbers. K't'lk was proposing equations by this singing—reducing them to simplest terms, combining them, using them according to the rules of the bizarre Hamalki physics to find her way, as she'd said, into a future time before there *was* time. Jim saw Scotty watching her with an uncertain, intent expression, as if he was beginning to understand what she was about. But Jim himself had no way to tell how she was doing. Though the air did feel strange. People shifted, twitched. Even the Others' clear brilliance rippled uneasily.

Abruptly, Jim started to suspect that K't'lk was close to what she was looking for. Her chromatic progressions grew swiftly surer, her chiming more complex. And then her vision apparently pierced through into whatever future she needed to see, for K't'lk broke loose and began to spill the music out of her as if she had been saving it up for a long time: a wild, splendid, glittering fall of interlinked melodic lines as syncopated and precise as any Bach sonatina, but (despite the chiming lightness of her voice) somehow trapping a more-than-symphonic weight of complexity and meaning in their net of measures. She sang the equations with precision and delicacy, the way she spoke; but she also sang with passion and joy, and a strange bittersweet regret. *She's building her masterwork,* Jim thought. *The delight, the sense of a great desire fulfilled, is no wonder. How often do you get to start a universe?* But the regret puzzled him—until he caught himself thinking about the kind of commitment and passion and sorrowful joy that a Hamalki might put into the structure she built for her marriage, in preparation for her mate's death, or her own. He also thought of the way K't'lk had glanced from Scotty to him, while discussing whether she would have power to manage this. Then Jim turned his attention away from the idea. Thought was too easy to pick up, here, and he wouldn't have K't'lk distracted by anyone—especially not Scotty

—while setting down the laws that would govern a universe for almost forever.

The sense that the song was taking time was surely an illusion, but one that persisted. *It seems right, though,* Jim thought. *A whole universe's laws to ordain—everything from physical constants on up—it's appropriate that that should take a while. Even God took at least seven days, after all. . . .* He wondered, though, whether God had sung while working—and whether the song could have sounded as glorious as this. K't'lk trembled with the force of her singing, as if the music were something alive that she merely released from her caging self, something that might turn on her if she relaxed her concentration. She showed no signs of relaxing, however. Relentlessly she poured melody out, or it poured itself from her; a torrent of bright music, low-voiced and high—an onslaught of the equations and edicts that she'd perceived in this universe's future, and now turned loose. They crashed outward through the *Enterprise* crew and started to become the operating instructions for a Universe.

As the equations began to 'take,' the air went taut with the unseen weaving of law. No one could move; they were all as immured in K't'lk's swiftly-solidifying matrix of order and command as if in amber. Even breathing was hard at first, and got harder, as they felt her adjusting the equations—knotting up loose ends, weaving the whole cloth of natural law seamless and tight, eliminating the loopholes in this universe-to-be. It seemed a long time before her song slowed, till final harmonies resolved and final chords stretched themselves into silence on the still air. But an end came at last, and everyone breathed out together in a sound of release and relief.

K't'lk looked up at her taller companions with a rustle of weary satisfaction. "The basic matrix is laid down," she said, sounding tired but utterly satisfied.

"People, look inside yourselves; then give them your gifts. . . ."

In the bright timelessness, the crew of *Enterprise* did so. In that place so malleable to thought and the given word, the moments out of their lives that were their gifts to the Others erupted out of nothing and folded sudden reality about the four hundred thirty-eight as their experiences wound themselves deep into the fabric of that universe. Again and again, when Jim remembered who he was—and sometimes it was difficult, looking out of so many other eyes—he was moved to tears; for the gifts were priceless. Without exception, his people were giving their best. Someone's tentacles touched him in love, as one of the Sulamid crew gave away his life's most cherished moment. He gazed down at the mauve and golden landscape from the great silence of an apricot sky, hearing nothing but the faint rush of the wind on the glider's skin, feeling the summer air buoy him up; and understood, for the first time, the fear that underlies freedom, and the joy on the fear's far side. He was wrestling with his brother, a strong sweaty grappling of sixteen limbs, punctuated by grunts and exclamations of surprise and delight at one another's strength; finally they fell away from one another and collapsed muscle-sore and exhausted on the lavender turf, whistling with Mizarthu laughter, as he silently thanked the Powers for the gift of such companionship. He stood down in the dusty azure warmth of the plain and gazed up in awe and marvel at the height where the ancient towers of as'Toroken brooded in their dark majesty, blunted but defiant of the years and the rains. Slowly he began walking toward them, knowing whom he would meet there, daring the meeting anyway—

—methane snow as fine as mist slid and snaked among the stones, borne on a thin whining wind that bit him to the bone. He stood still and endured the teeth of cold, raising his faceted vision to the black-red sky and the great ruddy gas giant that swam in the dark radiance, gazing at it in silent, irrational approval. The workroom and the world fell away as he hammered at the console, spinning the music out of the computer, wringing its circuits for perfection, wringing himself, until finally night was gone and three-sunned day came 'round again and he staggered away to the rack in exhausted satisfaction to hang until just before the concert. His father reached out a handling tentacle to him and twitched that old immobile face upward into the gentle little gesture of welcome he had never hoped to see, after their long estrangement; his insides spasmed and seized his brain, and his consciousness whited out in crazy joy—

—he read the chart again and again, sweated the case as he prepared for it—and finally went ahead with surgery, sinking forearm-deep into the fragile body that had freely made itself vulnerable to his ministrations. After three days of coma and constant weary maintenance—three days of fear that taught him what Hell would be like if he ever went there—his patient woke up and made a gap-fanged Vercingetorig smile at him. As quickly as looked normal, he went away into the next room, and cried for relief and joy—

—she twisted her throat around the bizarreness of the new language, and her mind around the concepts, wrestling them as if wrestling an angel—the object being not to win but to lose to the other: to surrender into the alternate mind-set and think in the other language, and for the hundredth time become more than she had been before the surrender. Without warning, after days of struggle and effort, in the middle of an uneventful morning at her desk, the enemy rose up inside her, took hold of her and flung her down with stunning force against the bottom of her mind. Her head spun for a second with alien terminologies—and then everything was different. Her office, *that* was what was alien, and all the names in it were changed. Her enemy was changed too; she looked inside her, and found a lover there instead. She whooped out loud for sheer delight at her defeat, her victory. And when people came running in to see what was the matter, she started laughing and couldn't stop—

—the beauty of the physical universe, the way things fitted and worked, the fierce bound energy of matter in all its forms, sang in him like a poem until he literally had to lean on the bulkhead for support. He felt dizzy, felt simultaneously small and huge, powerful and powerless, dwarfed and ennobled by the might and manageableness of *things*. And he had to tell that one about it who was primarily responsible for the experience. With a quick abashed glance around him to see that no one was looking, he reached out and laid a hand against the matter/antimatter mix column. It throbbed with power, it sang with life under its clear metal skin. *Thank you,* he said, unsure who or what he was thanking, and not caring. *Thank you.* And he knew she heard—

—it was his business to help them play. He could think of nothing better to do with his life, for he knew that when they felt free to play, their souls showed; who they *were* came out more clearly than at almost any other time. And the more one got used to letting one's self show, unafraid, the more joy came walking into one's life. And then the Self showed itself still more—and the cycle continued, joy engendering joy, endless. He leaned on the wall, warm with the thought of what his work was freeing those around him to be. Then the matter-gain on the 4D chessboard across the room went out again in a scream of feedback, and he grinned and went off to find the sonic screwdriver, and a brush and dustpan for the pieces that had blown up—

—he was the one who knew the way through the dark. To him, every star was one to steer by. He knew them all by name; their spectra were familiar as flowers in a garden. No world was strange to him, and he could find his way home blindfolded if he were a thousand parsecs away, for all his roaming was tethered safe to that great invisible ring, the path of a fair blue planet around a little yellow sun. Earth's green hills were home, and safety; but he would never choose to stay safe for long. The darkness knew his name, and when it called him, he went, doing what he loved best; finding signposts and markers, leading the way into forever for the ones who would follow—

—the massive vessel was a sword in his hand, bladed with ravening light, shielded with fire. He was the winged defender, knight and angel, with blade raised to defend the bright stars in his shadow. He held no malice for the angry powers that came to try him; he would sooner let them pass by in peace. But he would withstand them without pity when they came—and if they chose death at his hands, that was their business. He would accept the responsibility as part of his greater one, sorrow deeply for the slain, and lift his shield again—

—knowledge burned in his brain, sweet and bitter at once as the gods' fruit was so often said to be. And there was always more to know, and an eternity of things he didn't know and never would. There was no futility in that truth, rather ecstasy; for he would be used up by the universe, not the other way around. The latter way (were it possible) would be futile and bitter indeed. In his search after knowledge, he'd chosen to move among the strange ones, the ones who laughed and wept and speculated with such abandon. Their differences were his joy—for those many differences merely overlay their likenesses to him and to one another; and though the likenesses were few, they were profound. There were other joys. Though most of his knowing was turned outward, yet he was known as well; though he was sometimes silent, others knew his name and were not afraid to call on the soul he secretly was. Two others in particular—the one with whom he shared the secret delight of being commanded, and the commander. To that one he turned now, thanking him in mind, celebrating the crazy unVulcan daring that had brought them all to this place, this wonder—

Moved far past words, Jim gave his gift, the thing sweetest to him. To sit at the heart of four hundred thirty-eight souls, and be truly their heart, and their head; the one they gave their power to—not unquestioningly, either, but after consideration, by choice, and sometimes (though he would never understand it when it happened) by love. To command them, to be (by that command) in service to them. To suffer their pains and joys as they did his. To be companion to them, to delight in what they all did together—explore, dare, adventure, work, play. In all the Universe he could think of nothing better to give, nothing more worth being remembered when he and all the humanities and the Galaxy itself were merely old stories. He gave the memory, the feeling of what he loved, to the Others; and tears fell again as he realized who he was, and how lucky he was to be him.

He opened his eyes, then—with the quick humorous thought that Spock would tell him luck had nothing to do with it—and looked around. A lot of people were doing the same. Some were gazing at the Others. Jim looked in Their direction, wondering. Was that brilliance really a little brighter? Or did the idea come of having had his eyes closed?

The Others looked gravely back at the *Enterprise* crew—it was possible to tell that They were looking, though Jim had no idea how. Slowly, even humbly,

They said, *We did not know We were so poor—to now be so rich . . .*

"Our pleasure," Jim said, and glanced down at K't'lk. "Is that it? Can we go home now?"

She shook herself, chiming. "There's one piece of work to do yet," she said. And there were those odd emotions in her voice again—that regret, strangely coupled with an excitement too big for words. "I'll have to couple the Others' power to the power from the inversion apparatus, for the final implementation. This way, They'll not only be living in this universe, but fueling it from Themselves. An appropriate arrangement, for a God—"

"'Coupling' Their power—how?" Scotty said. "Through the equations?"

"Through me," K't'lk said. "Through my mind."

"Lass, you can't do that!" Scotty said in alarm. "That much power would—"

"—disorganize any mind, or body, or even any paraphysical form," she said—calmly, and with compassion. "Yes. Was that ever in question? You were following the way I was setting up the equations—"

"Aye, but I thought maybe I was mistaken—"

She turned away from him for a moment. "So I do as I said I would," she said to Jim, with a wry humor in her chiming. "I deal with the consequences of my handiwork. Captain, you must make only small jumps back to our home Galaxy—nothing longer than ten thousand lightyears at a time while in extragalactic space, and nothing longer than a thousand when you're within ten thousand lightyears of the arbitrary Galactic border. It's these long jumps that denature the structural integrity of space—and even the smaller ones do so somewhat. I think the effect is not cumulative, but best not to find out by way of disaster. Once home, you must speak to the Admiralty and make sure they understand that the inversion drive must not be used any more. Or at least not until the Hamalki find a way to produce the same result without breaking the laws of our own universe—or being forced to rewrite them."

"I will see to it, Commander," Jim said. "What about the breach between the two universes? And the damaged space on the fringes of the Lesser Magellanic?"

"I can repair both those problems from here," K't'lk said. "I hadn't counted on having the Others' power to support that of the inversion drive and the innate power of the physics. It makes some things simpler." She glanced over at the great still brilliance. "We must move quickly, sir, before the damaged area becomes too large to repair. I'll handle your next transit myself. You and the *Enterprise* will find yourselves near the damaged part of the Lesser Magellanic, so that you can check the repair before moving on—"

"What's this 'you and the *Enterprise*' business?" Scotty said, more quietly. His voice said that he knew—and desperately wanted to be told he was wrong.

K't'lk turned to him, gazing at him for a moment—then spidered over to him and leaned against his legs. "Mt'gm'ry," she said, very gently, "I'm going to miss you. You're the closest thing to a Hamalki on two legs, you know that? Even to playing dumb about our physics, to keep the teacher around." Scotty started to say something; she jangled at him affectionately, a "ssh" noise. "I am primarily responsible for the inversion drive," K't'lk said. "So, as usual, the Tao sees to it that I pay the price for the damage the drive has done; and since the damage done has been to lives, that's the coin I pay in. It's all in the equations, dear heart. You saw it coming."

"You mentioned the possibility," Jim said, having to hold his voice steady, "that you might fail."

"That possibility exists," K't'lk said as steadily.

"Do you mean you might fail to seal the breach?" McCoy said.

"No! That's always been my first priority, L'nrd. Whatever happens, our universe will be safe."

"But you might fail at—founding *this* universe—"

"I might."

"If you do—then presumably the former state of affairs here would reassert itself," Jim said. "Being without event, without existence—"

"Eternal stasis," K't'lk said. "So complete that I would never even know I failed. I would never know anything else, either. Nor would the Others." Then she laughed. "But, Captain, don't be silly! Me? Fail?!"

The laughter was no attempt to conceal anxiety. It was genuine. Jim shook his head, smiling through his sorrow, and got down on one knee again. She came to him, reached out a delicate glassy claw and laid it in the hand he offered. "T'l," he said, "it's been a pleasure serving with you. Whatever happens, I'll remember you—particularly in my cabin."

"And I you, J'm," she said, the merriment muted, gentled. "There, and elsewhere."

She turned toward Scotty again. He sank to one knee, hunched forward a little like a man in great pain. Silently she went to him, and did something Jim had never seen her do before; reared up on six legs, and with the other six climbed more or less into Scotty's lap, and held him. He put his arms around her, avoiding the spines. "Such a builder, you are," she said. And after a moment, she cocked her front cluster of eyes at him and said, "You'd better go over that last set of relationships a few more times: the entropy-extropy-anthotropy group. I think you still may not understand some of the more complex implications."

"Aye," Scotty said. "Lass—"

"Go well, Sc'tt'y," she said, and scrabbled down out of his lap. "I'll see you later."

"*Mehe nakkhet ur-seveh,* K't'lk," Spock said to her, from where he stood beside Jim. She glanced up and described again with two spare legs the circular gesture she'd made the day they'd all met: parts-that-were-one, separating, then becoming one again. "The same to you, Sp'ck," she said. "In my present situation, no matter how things go, I can hardly avoid at least the first part."

She turned from him, to the *Enterprise* crew as a whole. "Notice each other, people," she said. "What you see—is who you are. It may be a while before you see one another this way again."

And she walked away from them, into the brilliance—becoming a dwindling, glittering figure, a clockwork toy that chimed absently, like an abstracted music box—until the brightness wholly veiled her, and she was gone.

Jim looked around him at his command crew—at the whole complement of the *Enterprise*, burning in the reflected glory of the Others and in their own wild splendor of selfness—and drank in the sight of them, taken by the feeling that there wasn't much time to do so. Many of them looked at him with the same feeling. Many were busier looking at one another—at old friends, battle companions, sometimes at people they hardly knew—trying to store the memory of this radiance against the time when flesh would be just flesh again, and the dazzling personages around them would once more seem merely human, the usual too-familiar people who grumbled about starship food, or owed them money. "It is fairly unlikely that we will be able to remember much of the way we seemed to one another here, Captain," Spock said quietly from beside Jim. "We are enabled to perceive so clearly mostly by the low entropy gradient. We will probably retain a few vivid images, remembering the rest of what happened mostly in the abstract. But the experience itself, the intensity of it—" He shook his head. "In a universe where time passes, and the passage of energy through a system wears the system down—the spirit may be willing, but the flesh will be too weak."

Jim looked around him at Spock, and McCoy, and Scotty, and the rest of the old Bridge crew—seeing in them a superb assortment of great desires, noble longings, and virtues—liberally mixed with mortal failings; but the failings did not tarnish the virtues. They exalted them. "It has been nice," Jim said to Spock, and to all of them, "*not* to see, for a while, 'through a glass, darkly.' "

They nodded. And the music began again, so that everyone turned toward the heart of the Others' brilliance, from which it came. Jim wondered, now, how he'd thought the earlier singing such a masterwork. Against this radiant interweaving of harmonies, it seemed simplistic. Then comparisons failed utterly, for to the one crystal voice chiming the melodic lines, others were added; first just a few, then more, and more still, ten, fifty, a hundred, three hundred. The voices sang no words, but poured themselves into melodies that built through wild fugues of unimaginable complexity, into crashing masses of chords poised on the line between dissonance and harmony; and the voices were of all kinds, Ielerid, Andorian, Mizarthu, Tellerite, Terran, Vulcan, Diphdani. They washed over, but could not conceal, the single Hamalki voice that led the progression upward. More and more voices added themselves to the chorus, until nothing could be heard but the great unity of sound, weaving in and out of itself in an ecstasy of terror and wonder and anticipation, and building, always building—

The light grew brighter. Jim squinted at it as it grew, not only in intensity but in size—reaching for him and his crew, washing over them. He covered his eyes; it did no good. The brilliance was too blinding, piercing through and into him as the sound did, till whiteness filled the world and he dimly felt himself thump down to his knees, overcome. What the rest of his crew was doing, Jim had no idea; all he could hear was the rising chorus as multitudes added themselves to multitudes, weaving around the single bell-like voice that showed them the way in endless upward-mounting ascents of song. *Very like her,* Jim thought, while he could still think. *To die like a swan, in music*—If that was what she was doing. It did not sound like death. Up and up the sound scaled, in pitch and power, till it seemed a whole universe's population could not have made such a sound; till the chords, for all their tremendous size and weight of voices, drove into the brain as piercingly as spears. One voice, innumerable voices, drawing closer and closer together; chords resolving, narrowing, into an unbearable single note that would have broken the hardest heart, shattered the walls of the worlds. An infinite number of voices forging and forged into one terrible, ecstatic unison against which nothing could stand. One voice, speaking, singing, crying one note, one word. . . .

Time and space heard the word, and obeyed it—exploding outward, and inward. The blinding light swallowed everything as Life shattered itself into lives. And instantly, when it had done so, darkness fell. Or grew, rather; sprang from the heart of the unrelieved, burning whiteness, and with glad, mad speed, raced outward in all directions, to the edges of the new Universe. And the darkness was not total; the light remained, transformed. Newly created galaxies blazing with young stars were rushing outward with the darkness, along the wavefront of a Big Bang only seconds old.

Only that glimpse, Jim had, before something threw him backwards, hard—

* * *

—into his command chair in the Bridge of a starship floating serenely in space, at the fringes of a Lesser Magellanic Cloud that had nothing wrong with it whatever.

"We may have blown up a couple of stars along the way," McCoy's hushed voice said from behind him, "but we sure as hell replaced them!"

"Report," Jim said to the air, hoping someone would be able to manage it.

It was Spock who stepped down beside his chair, as he'd thought it would be. "The rift between the two universes is sealed, Captain," he said. "And as you can see from the screen, this space is untroubled once again."

"Effects on the planets? The people?"

"They are not species with which we are familiar, so it is difficult to say with much certainty," Spock said. "But there is an eighty percent possibility that K't'lk invoked some sort of closed time-loop to repair the damage here. None of the stars we saw go nova show the slightest sign of spectral irregularities. And the planets are without physical damage."

McCoy was standing beside Jim's chair, with a look of sober wonder on his face. "Bones?" Jim said.

"The crew's all accounted for," he said. "Except one. She was with Scotty, though—"

Jim hit the toggle on his chair. "Engineering. Mr. Scott—"

"Engineering," someone said: not Scotty. *"One moment, sir."* There was a longish pause.

"Scotty—"

"Na, sir," his voice came back, heavy with grief and control. *"She's nae here."*

"Acknowledged," Jim said. "Scotty, I'm sorry."

"Aye, sir. Scott out."

Jim hit the toggle again, shaking his head sadly. He had half believed that she was going to pull something off, pull some rabbit out of the hat—*Damn.* "Log her deceased, Spock," he said. "Note that she gave her life in preservation of two universes—and for the birth of one."

"Yes, sir."

Jim looked up at McCoy. "Bones," he said, just for his friend's ears, "I meant to ask you about something—" He broke off for a moment, then said, "It's strange, having to ask questions and wait for the answers, now—strange not to know what other people are thinking and feeling, just by *wanting* to know. I feel like I've gone deaf somehow—like my head's in a sack—"

"You can be grateful for that sack, Jim," McCoy said. "Where we are now, *isn't* where we were; people's 'dark sides' were reduced almost to nothing. Lucky for us, considering the sensitivity we had. I've really wished sometimes, on *this* side, that I didn't know what other people were thinking . . . even to the limited extent that I know. What was the question?"

"Well—when you were reading the Others the riot act—the one thing you didn't mention, that you might have, was that if They destroyed us, they'd soon enough be destroyed Themselves by the addition of entropy in large quantities to their space."

"I know."

"Why didn't you?"

"Because if They really were a God," Bones said, very quietly, "They would respond to our pain as to Their own. I wanted to see if They really had that much divinity—or what the humanities take for divinity—in Them."

"And if They hadn't?"

"Then," McCoy said, "we would all have died—and so would They. And a good thing, too. What could you let loose on any universe that would be worse than a God that wasn't godly?"

Jim thought about that for a few moments, then ealized that he was going to have to take that question, along with various others, down to the Observation Deck. "One other thing," he said. "That last word I heard—"

Bones raised his eyebrows. "I heard words. Plural. 'Let there be dark.'"

Jim put *his* eyebrows up at that, but said nothing. "Night isn't going to be frightening, in that universe," McCoy said, musing. "And K't'lk always did have a sense of humor. . . . It'd be nice to go there, some day, and see what kinds of gardens she's talked Them into planting."

Jim gazed out at the stars, nodding.

"I bet there won't be snakes in them," Bones said.

"No," Jim agreed. "Spiders, though. . . ."

They did not jump right away. There were reasons enough for that—instruments to be recalibrated, data to sort; it wasn't every day that a starship was present at the birth of a Universe. Ship's systems needed time to recharge themselves for the great leap back to home-space. But mostly *Enterprise* hung becalmed in the emptiness between galaxies because her Captain had one last piece of business to settle there.

He had K't'lk's memorial service held on the Rec deck. Harb Tanzer dressed the room as he had for the briefing at which K't'lk had first spoken to the crew. But no one perched on the pedestal now. It stood empty, and except for the spotlight on it, the only other illumination in the room was that of the Lesser Magellanic Cloud shining in the great ports—the light her efforts had brought them, a blue blaze of Population I starlight that touched upturned faces with a gentle peaceful radiance. The place looked and felt like a cathedral—dim, and silent, and charged with emotion.

Jim stood to one side and toward the front, with the rest of the command crew, missing K't'lk.

Even in his "sack" he could tell he wasn't alone in that. The crew as a whole were as silent as the department heads; and Scotty had spent the past hours in a wincing wordlessness that never looked far from tears. Even Spock had been sufficiently moved to come to Jim and request the honor of conducting the memorial service. Surprised, Jim granted the request—not without wondering quietly to McCoy how Vulcans memorialized the dead. "Probably they read excerpts from the departed's last paper," Bones had muttered. Spock, working at his station, hadn't needed to turn; neither had either of them. They could feel his eyebrow going up halfway across the room.

Spock exercised command privilege and chose the music and the service to be used. Standing on the dais in Vulcan-white command full dress, his hands clasped behind him, he looked out at two full watches of the crew—all in their own formal dress, the barbaric splendors of many worlds—and let the sorrowful sweetness of the end of *Ein Heldenleben* sing its way down into silence. Over the quietly weaving chords, to Jim's surprise, he began to speak not the usual All-Fleet service—which might have been expected when the lost crewperson had not specified one in her will—but the Terran one. A pang went right through Jim as he understood Spock's line of thought: that the living needed comfort more than the dead needed honor. She had achieved honor some time back, and was done with it now. ". . . We are those who visit Time, but belong to Eternity; and to each of us comes a moment when that visit is done. For one of this company, our dear sister K't'lk, the hour of that departure has been fulfilled, and we are met to bid her farewell. In her living and her dying, she has conquered both life and death; and her mortal nature has put on immortality, bringing to pass the ancient words: 'O death, where is thy sting? O grave, where is thy victory?'"

The dry, harsh sob that broke the silence was Scotty's. Jim didn't look at him; his own eyes were burning badly enough, and he concentrated on standing at attention. Spock went on in stately, measured periods, and it amazed Jim how calm that voice could be and still reveal, to him at least, the Vulcan's profound sorrow. ". . . therefore, seeing that our sister K't'lk has taken the Universe unto herself, we commend her spirit to the night, and to the stars from which she came—"—and Jim swallowed hard, for the words were a bit too true—"—knowing that by so doing, the night shall never lack for starlight, or our lives for our beloved sister's memory, till time's end. . . ."

The room was too still for anyone to be breathing. "Honors," Spock said quietly. Uhura, off to one side, touched a console. The ship struck her colors, killing all fields but the skinfield, dousing even the running lights. Sulu moved to the console and spoke to it softly. Out the windows, intergalactic space was briefly bright with phaser blasts—the three shots that prevent evil spirits from entering grieving souls at the funeral of a comrade-at-arms, when the doors of men's hearts stand open. Harb spoke to the console, then, and Moira sang "Taps" in a single, sweet, wordless Earth-human voice. And Sulu had the bo'sun pipe assembly dismissed, and by ones and twos the crew went away, and all the music was done. Except inside many crewpeople's minds, where one music they had heard, in a universe forever sealed away, would never quite be still. . . .

Sixteen

They made Sol system in Jim's offshift. The arrival was not something that required his presence on the Bridge—and in any case he was tired. He sat in low light in his cabin with a glass of old port in one hand and a little spun-glass-looking structure in the other, considering patterns. His triumphs always seemed to find him on the Bridge; but the pains, and those forms of joy deeper than triumph, always seemed to find him here.

Curious, it's all curious. The reading he had done about the non-causal sciences, way back in Academy, had always sounded like something escaped from a fairy tale. These days, however—having walked through many situations that would have made fairy tales seem tame, especially this last business with the Anomaly—Jim was willing to be a little more credulous than he had been as a cadet, and to speculate a little more wildly.

How much power does a protoGod really have? he

wondered. *Even before They're conscious, or aware of other beings? That we should happen to have K't'lk on board . . . and a crew capable of handling the 'places' beyond the Anomaly . . . does seem to be stretching probability a bit.* He paused to sip at the port. *Yet K't'lk said she reached into that Universe's time before it* had *time, to find the laws she was going to insert. If she could do that . . . can I really be sure that the Others, even before consciousness, couldn't have reached into* our *world, our time, and caused K't'lk to invent the inversion apparatus—for the purpose of breaching Their universe and setting Them free to be its God? . . .*

. . . of course, that would mean that she caused Them, by way of the inversion apparatus, before *They caused the apparatus, by way of* her. . . . He stretched, smiling to himself at the "paradox," which was perfectly permissible in a non-causal system. *Maybe I'm old-fashioned,* he thought, *but I really prefer cause and effect. They seem tidier, somehow.*

Then the image and sound of those last few moments with the Others came back to him—fading, as Spock had warned, but glorious still. *Then again,* Jim thought, *tidiness may not be everything. . . .*

The 'com whistled the same note it had an age ago, the day *Enterprise* had received her orders to go to Hamal. This time Jim didn't jump. "Screen on."

It was Sulu, and there was an odd look in his eye. "*Sir? We're coming up on final approach to Earth.*"

"Noted." He would have said, "Screen off," but that look of Sulu's kept him silent a moment. "*Jim,*" Hikaru said very deliberately—not Captain—"*I think you should see this.*"

"On screen, then."

The view changed. They were a ways out in the system as yet—inside and above the zone of the Asteroids' orbit—and dumping down from a leisurely two *c*, doing no more than a couple of trillion kilometers per hour. The stars were bright about them. And more was bright than the stars.

"Good Lord," Kirk said, and put the drink down, and stood to watch the screen.

Enterprise was not alone out there. She had escort. The screen was filled with ships closing in on her, all with screens up. A few of them had already matched velocities and vectors with her and were riding close around, at the fringes of the mandatory five-kilometer traffic boundary. Those closest ships were heavy cruisers of her own class: *Indomitable, Potemkin, Surak, Isshasshte, Tao Feng, John F. Kennedy,* the new *Intrepid.* Their screens flared with the average index-colors of their stars-of-registration—*Surak* and *Intrepid* with Vulcan's fierce blue, *Isshasshte* with Deneb's blue-white, *Tao Feng* and *Potemkin* and *Kennedy* with the tamer yellow-white of Sol. Far out in the dark, and closing, more ships yet came riding in with screens tuned to their stars' colors. Jim swallowed the lump in his throat out of the way of speech. "Answer colors, Mr. Sulu," he said. "We went out there for all of them. Continuous spectrum, infrared to ultraviolet."

He shook his head in wonder. *God,* he thought, *it looks like the center-spread holo-foldout in* Jane's Fighting Starships. . . . Space got full of slender nacelles and primary and secondary hulls, sleek shapes and lumbering ones—all clothed in fiery light to do *Enterprise* honor and bring her home. Some few of the great *Defender*-class battleships were there, God knew how —multi-hulled monsters cruising along like great silent whales through dark water, keeping their own eight-kilometer limit: *Rodger Young* and *Divine Wind, Arizona* and *Bismarck, M'hasien* and *Dataphda* and *Inaieu.* Carriers were there, many-tubed beasts full of scouts and shuttles and fighters—*Queen Christina* and *Valkyr* and *Erinnye, Marya Morevna* and *Hypsipyle.* Every light cruiser in this area seemed to be there—*Constitution* and *Constellation, Resolute* and *Bannockburn, Sadat* and *Malacandra* and *Bonhomme Richard.* Even alien-crewed "visitor" ships of Fleet were there, to his amazement—*Sorithias* and *Mor'anh Merin'hen, Na'i'in* and *Sulam* and *Kamë.* And little cutters by tens and twenties, lean sleek shapes that he knew well, having commanded more than one of them in his younger days: *Lewis* and *Clarke* and *Ferris's Folly; Ransom* and *Armstrong* and *Ewet.*

What a collection, Jim thought. *What's been going on here?*

From the Bridge Uhura's voice said, "Kennedy *is hailing us, Captain.*"

"Put them on."

The vista of ships and stars winked out, to be replaced by a view of the *Kennedy*'s bridge, and Commodore Katha'sat sitting in the center seat with a droll look on its face. "Welcome home, Jim," it said.

"Thank you, Katha . . . believe me, we consider ourselves welcomed. But this—" and Jim waved one hand in a gesture indicating immediate space—"can't all have been just for us."

"Certainly it was, Jim. A few of us were in the neighborhood—"

"Katha!" He laughed. "Give me a break. Starfleet would never let you—"

"Jim," Katha'sat said, leaning back in its command seat and crossing its legs at both sets of knees, "we *are* Starfleet. A fact which sometimes gets lost over at the Admiralty . . . but did not get lost today. When sensors detected you coming in, every ship from theta Carinae to the Cetians told Fleet where it wanted to go. And when Fleet saw which way the ions were blowing, they cut us new orders in a hurry. It wouldn't do to have the Klingons see all of Fleet suddenly mutiny so close to Terra. They might get ideas . . ."

"You old blackmailer," Jim said with great affection.

"I object to that," said Katha'sat, round-mouthed. "I am not old. There's this too. You're back early, if I understand your original schedule. I was hoping that nothing had gone wrong with your testing this time; I don't think Fleet will put up with another demonstration like this, and somehow I doubt they're going to let the *Enterprise* out of the galaxy again."

"Katha," Jim said, "I doubt they will too . . ."

Katha'sat tilted its head slowly to one side in a "nod" of speculative agreement. "You doubtless have a story to tell me that will explain that," it said. "Well enough; you'll tell me at Fleet, after we're both finished debriefing."

Kirk nodded. "Set aside a good big chunk of time. Some of the debriefing I have to do requires a friend and not the Admiralty."

"All right. We'll meet for drinks, and I think I can find you a friend around here somewhere."

"Fine. But Katha—no cards."

Katha'sat made a long-faced grimace of hestv resignation. "The problem with you, Jim," it said, "is that you're incapable of taking risks."

"Noted and logged, Commodore. I'll see you in San Francisco. Kirk out."

"Anything else, sir?" Sulu's voice said from the Bridge, as the view of ships and stars came back.

"No. See that this goes out on crew access, though. They did this—they should enjoy it."

"Aye, sir. With all due respects—you enjoy it too."

"I will. Out."

Jim gazed out at the ships globed about *Enterprise,* a little galaxy of fires around the ship whose screens sang rainbows. One screen Jim noticed particularly, as they rode in toward Mars's orbit together: an actinic white deflector screen bright with the fire of the faraway

Klingon homestar. *Manhattan* wore that screen, holding the place-at-honors till the day the Klingons should join the Federation. There in his cabin, where no one could see, Jim drew himself slowly straight and sketched a little salute at the colors of the ships that had followed him with such terrible blind bravery to their deaths. Then he grimaced at the uselessness of waste, and sat down.

He leaned back in his chair again, watching the halo of glories around the *Enterprise* as she coasted in past Mars, still slowing. Jim glanced down at the little thing he held—spiky and glittering, knitting the dim light into itself—and smiled slowly, feeling the sorrow transform to sober joy once again. *You would have liked to see this, this splendor—even though it marked your failure. Your lesser failure. On the great level, you succeeded. And on the lesser one, some day—some day—*

The screen whistled again, not the Bridge this time. It was the different note his department heads used to let him know they were calling. "Yes?"

The starry night full of ships blanked out, replaced instantly by Scotty's face. Jim sat up straight, almost alarmed by the change in it—for his chief engineer was alive again, and smiling. *"I've got it! Jim, I've got it!"*

"Got what? Are you all right?"

"The equations! The Hamalki physics! Jim, I understand it!! And there was another set of possibilities, K't'lk never saw them, the poor lassie!—a whole new range of options! Another intergalactic drive, maybe, one that won't breach space! But in any case, access to a whole new kind of power—"

There was no use telling Scotty to calm down—and on second thought, Jim wasn't sure he wanted to. "How soon will you know?"

"Ach, a few days. A week perhaps. I'll write you a report, though I doubt it'll make any more sense to you

than it did to me earlier. Every physicist on Earth is going to want to lynch me. But we'll ha' a bonny time fightin' before they settle down—!"

"Well, don't just stand there natterin', Scotty," Jim said, tolerant and amused. "Go write me a report."

"Aye, sir! Out—"

The stars came back. Kirk sat back again, shaking his head. *I might have known you would leave a legacy,* he said to the empty air—

In his hand, something twitched, hard. Jim looked down in shock. The glassy construct—it moved again. A hard shudder, and another. On first impulse he leapt to his feet and almost flung it across the room like some venomous insect—then stifled the urge, but too late; the shocked movement made him fumble the delicate thing. It fell to the table and shattered.

His heart seized irrationally, as if he were a child about to be scolded. *I broke it!* he thought, sad and annoyed—and only had time enough to complete the thought before the scattered pieces suddenly and terribly began to *move,* scrabbling toward one another. Spikes and fragments clustered, huddled, jumped and jumbled about on the table as if looking for proper places, a puzzle assembling itself—into a shape Jim knew. Round body no more than an inch in diameter, little delicate glass-needle legs, iridescent fur finer than human hairs, glittering; and last of all, the empty eye-vessels that filled with blue-hot fire, swirling, laughing, living—

"J'm," the tiny voice cried in a hasty music-box chiming, exuberant, triumphant, "there's another answer! *Where's Mt'gm'ry??!"* And K't'lk's daughter-self scuttled down off the table, pausing only long enough to swing merrily once around Jim's leg as if it was a pole put there for her convenience. Then she went bouncing out the door in four or five small but exultant leaps.

Jim stood there, staring after her. Through the

still-open door, he could hear the shouts of surprise and delight and celebration beginning down the hall. For once he didn't bother telling the door to close. Jim just sat down, and started to laugh, and kept on laughing till the tears came. And minutes later, when Spock came in—looking gravely nonplussed as only an amazed Vulcan can—Jim looked up at him sidewise, with a cockeyed expression. "You were saying about death, Mr. Spock?" he said. "That, like everything else, it has its exceptions?"

Still gravely, Spock inclined his head just a fraction, the polite bow of a man in the right for the thousandth time, who asks to be forgiven for it. But was that smile twitching almost unseen at the corners of his mouth one of joy? "We may yet find it so ourselves," he said. "In the meantime, Captain, we will be making rendezvous and docking at San Francisco Orbital Annex very shortly—and we seem to have at least one crewmember aboard whose authorizations are in need of, shall we say, updating. Starfleet does tend to be rather insistent about these things. Perhaps we should head down to Engineering and ascertain that crewmember's status—"

"—and Scotty's? I'll drink to that." And he did, afterwards pausing for just a moment to put down the empty glass with great care. Smiling, Jim Kirk headed out into the hall to see to his crew. "Business as usual, Mr. Spock," he said over his shoulder, as he went out. "A Captain's work is never done."

Spock raised a tolerant eyebrow, and followed his Captain out into their world.

Bibliography

Those "non-causal" sciences are already with us, in their embryonic stages. Those interested in more information about them will find numerous works concerning them in the popular press, probably the best known of these being *The Tao of Physics* by Fritjof Capra. For information about de Sitter space, or details concerning anentropia and its related subjects, curious readers are directed to the following sources:

De Witt, B. S. "Spacetime as a sheaf of geodesics in superspace." In Carmeli et al., *Relativity*. N.Y.: Plenum Press, 1970.

Gott III, J. Richard. "Creation of open universes from de Sitter space." *Nature*, vol. 295, January 28, 1982, pp. 304–307.

Isenson, T. K. "Primary space as a 'solvent'; the evidence for a nonisotropic entropy gradient." *Paraphysical Cosmology*, vol. 15, June 1, 1996, pp. 1052–1058.

McCoy, L. E., MD, FICX. "Somatic, hypersomatic, psychological, and philosophical/eschatological effects of exposure to entropy loss and 'secondary creation syndrome' in Terrans, Sulamids, Vulcans, Sadrao, and Hamalki." *Journal of the Interstellar College of Xenomedicine*, vol. 470, sd 9315.0, pp. 5566–5593.

Spock. "Mathematical implications of nonhomogeneous paratopological convergences between orthogonal unbridged n-spaces; with substantiating field measurements." *Review of Modern Hypercosmology and Cosmogony*, vol. 388, sd 9258.0, pp. 82–97.

T'pask, Sivek, B'tk'r, and K't'lk. "An elective-mass inversion apparatus." *Proceedings of the Vulcan Science Academy*, vol. 7295, sd 8939.0, pp. 665–672.